RIGHTEOUS DAWN

A GIDEON WOLF STORY

ERNEST DEMPSEY

138 PUBLISHING

For my friend, Greg DeCicco.
I can't believe you're gone. And I can't wait to talk with you again.
Until then, the Dude abides.

PREFACE

Whether you choose to believe it or not, the fact remains there is a supernatural war of good and evil going on around us, beyond the veils of human eyes and between dimensions unseen.

1

NASHVILLE, TENNESSEE

The men waiting for me at the bottom of the escalator weren't exactly the welcoming type. They were either there to arrest me, or at the very least take me in for questioning.

Their presence came as no surprise. After all, I'd gone to Mexico with my wife and returned without her.

The authorities, and my wife's family, would want answers.

The four men standing at the escalator's base wore suits and ties —same as one of those drivers holding up a sign with your last name on it that you always see at the airport. But that's where the similarities ended.

These guys held no sign. And there were four of them. I didn't recall ever seeing an entourage of drivers waiting for a single fare.

Then there were the weapons hidden under the men's jackets. Outside of airport security and some TBI agents, I figured they represented most of the firepower in the building.

Of course, we were in Tennessee, so outside the airport was a different story altogether. I smiled at the thought as the escalator carried me closer to the four spooks waiting at the bottom.

When my foot touched solid ground, the man standing slightly ahead of the other three took a step forward. He'd swept his dark brown hair to the left side of his tanned forehead. He either spent a lot of time at the beach or golf course, or in the field on assignment.

Based on the grim frown on his face, I reckoned it was the latter.

"Gideon Wolf?" he said, halting a stride away from me.

"Have you been asking everyone that as they step off the escalator? Or just me? Because I have to say, that would be embarrassing and frustrating to keep asking every single person who gets off this thing if they were—"

"We know who you are, Dr. Wolf," the guy clarified. "I was being—"

"Socially conventional?" It was my turn to interrupt. "So," I mused, inspecting the man first, then his three associates, "which agency are you guys with? I'm guessing not CIA since I seriously doubt I represent a national security threat deemed worthy of the Executive Branch."

"Agent Polson. FBI. And we're also part of the Executive Branch." He nearly suppressed the corner of his mouth from turning up. "You seem to be in a fine mood, Dr. Wolf, for a man whose wife is missing." The corner of a smile stayed. His eyes never left my face. He let the statement hang in the air like stale cigarette smoke.

For a brief second, I felt thankful that airports, like most buildings, were nonsmoking. I smirked—probably the wrong thing to do at the time—at the thought.

"Where is she, Wolf?" He pressed the question like oil through cheesecloth.

"Agent... Polson, was it? I assume you and your buddies here"—I motioned to the other three with a carefree index finger—"are trying to piece together what happened to my wife, Amy, in Mexico."

The agent nodded. "Yes. Sorry if the circumstances surrounding her disappearance seem suspicious, Dr. Wolf." He kept saying my name like I was the devil himself. "But when you alerted the authorities to the incident, no suspects turned up. None that were alive, anyway. When we looked at the life insurance paperwork, we saw that you're the primary beneficiary."

"I already explained, both to the Mexicans and to our guys: she was murdered by Vicente Carrillo."

"Convenient," Polson countered. "Since Carrillo has dropped off the map."

"Has he?" I asked, already knowing the answer.

"Yes. We've been monitoring Carrillo for some time now."

"And done nothing about it," I risked. Catching more than a splinter of anger from the man, I continued. "You knew what he was doing. You knew the threat he posed. And you did nothing."

"Not our call to make, Professor. There are other agencies that deal with cartel problems. We deal with American problems."

Interesting that this man thought a cartel don shipping billions of dollars' worth of heroin into the United States wasn't an American problem. Then again, I also knew there were other agencies responsible for handling narcotics and trafficking.

The agent looked around the airport, then gave me an upward jerk of the head. "Come with us. We will continue this at the office."

"Mind if I see some ID?"

Polson tilted his head to the side and started to fish his identification out of an inner jacket pocket.

"Just kidding," I said. "Just let me get my suitcase at baggage claim."

"One of my men will take care of your bag," Polson countered. "Time to go, Dr. Wolf."

I rolled my eyes.

"We can do this the hard way if you prefer," the agent added.

I huffed at the threat. I knew it wasn't empty. The guy came across as one of those bureau relics from the 1950s with a petulant attitude toward anything fun, and the haircut to match. He didn't look a day over thirty, which meant he must have missed his time by a few decades.

Or maybe he was just a real sack of—

"I prefer the easy way, for all of us, Officer. I mean Agent. Do you have a preference? I'm not sure what to call you." If only the tool had known who he was messing with. Oddly, the red mist that surrounded the wicked was faint with this one. I wasn't sure what that meant. A quick look at the others revealed the same. The crimson fog seemed dim compared to others. I wondered what that could mean, but knew I wasn't going to get an answer from these guys. As far as I knew, I was the only one who could see the mist.

Normally, I went out of my way to be polite and respectful to authority figures. I'd have never been so indignant to a cop. But I wasn't the same person I'd been before... before Mexico. And I felt like these guys were doing nothing but slowing me down.

"You can call me Agent Polson," he responded.

"Fine. But I hope this won't take long, Agent Polson. I need to see my wife's parents. That's not going to be an easy visit."

"No, I imagine it won't be. Seeing as they believe you killed their daughter."

So it *was* true. My suspicions had been that Amy's parents would think I was the reason she'd disappeared. I understood why they might have believed that. They'd never liked me, and blaming me was the easiest, most logical route despite the fact I'd never done anything but right by their daughter. Still, hearing it out loud came as something of a shock. I'd hoped they would give me the benefit of the doubt.

No such luck. That also meant the conversation I was going to have with them would be much more uncomfortable than I initially anticipated.

"Our car is right outside," Polson said.

"Hope security didn't tow it," I joked. "You know how they are about that. They give you like thirty seconds to drop off or pick up your passenger, and then they're all, 'Hey, you gotta move.'"

He didn't think the joke was funny, but I snickered at it anyway. Because it *was* funny.

When we got out to the car, one of the agents opened the back door to a black Chevy Tahoe and held it open for me to get in while the other three guys climbed in.

"Thank you so much," I said, "but if you don't mind, I prefer not to ride in the middle." I eyed the agent getting in the back seat on the other side.

The agent stared at me with a promise of pain in his eyes. "Get in."

I pouted my lips and nodded, pretending to be impressed by his silent threat. *If he only knew.*

"Fine," I surrendered. "But next time I get shotgun."

I pointed two fingers into my eyes and then at Agent Polson, who was climbing into the front passenger seat. "Looking at you, Polson."

He shook his head at me and closed the door as I slid into the middle of the back seat.

I felt the smooth leather and looked around at the interior. "This is a nice ride," I said. "Glad to see my tax dollars are doing some good for the country."

"Do you ever shut up?" the guy to my left asked after he slammed the door shut.

"It's a strange thing," I answered. "I'm not normally so outgoing and talkative to strangers." I threw my hands up in the air and slapped them onto my legs. "I guess I just like you guys."

"Or maybe you're overcompensating for murdering your wife," Polson fired over his shoulder while he buckled the seatbelt.

"That's what you really think happened. Isn't it?" I asked the question sincerely, still thrown off by the reality of it all.

"Doesn't matter what I think. It matters what the evidence says. Right now, the evidence tells us that you and your wife went to Mexico. And then she disappeared. So, if you want to fill us in on what happened, we're all ears."

I wondered if I should call my attorney, but at the moment, I was confident I could get myself out of this mess.

I'd done nothing wrong, and I'd managed to rid the world of an evil man, a drug lord who'd caused no end of pain and suffering to a countless number of people.

That didn't help me right now. It wasn't like I could just tell these guys I'd killed Carrillo. They would never believe me.

"What's the matter, Professor?" Polson asked. Interrupting my thoughts. "Got anything you want to confess? Might make this whole thing a lot easier."

I looked him dead in the eyes, wondering if he could sense the power trickling through me. I was glad the sun still hung in the sky, because I wasn't sure if I could control the spirit of Xolotl that rested within the medallion. With only a fraction of the energy or magic or whatever it was, the beast within wouldn't come out. That was a good thing.

Had this little pickup been at night, there was no telling what might have happened.

I knew I wasn't supposed to kill these guys. Not yet. But that could always change. And the light red mist hanging around them didn't convince me that future wasn't a possibility.

"No," I said. "I didn't kill my wife. Vicente Carrillo did."

"Seems like you know a lot about this Carrillo. Maybe you hired some of his goons to do the job for you."

The driver pulled out into traffic and guided the SUV away from the airport.

All the talk about my wife finally took its toll, and I didn't feel immune to the pain anymore. That numbness had come and gone over the last two days. When it was there, I felt fine, albeit callous.

It caused a pang of guilt at first, but then allowed me to keep going with my life, and my newfound mission.

I had to locate the other six medallions of power before someone else did. With six years of experience in the field, I had a pretty solid network of peers in the historical community, including a few top-tier anthropologists and archaeologists, along with history professors and researchers.

I'd never heard of these medallions, or the bizarre legend surrounding them.

There were a few doors I could knock on, some phones I could ring, but I doubted any of those people would know much about this. There was, however, one person I knew would be all over it.

My friend Jack.

"What's the matter with you, Professor?" Polson interrupted my thoughts. He was good at it, which annoyed me. And him calling me professor in that derogatory tone didn't help things. "Guilt eating you up from the inside?"

"I thought you said we were going to do this at your HQ or whatever," I commented dryly.

"Oh, we are. There are some other folks who have questions for you. But if you want to expedite things, be my guest."

I shook my head. "No. I'm fine waiting. I'd like everything to be on record."

"Fine by me. We get paid either way. But you don't look so good. Maybe getting the truth off your chest would make you feel better."

"I'm fine," I countered, snapping a little more than I intended. I lowered my tone. "Just not feeling myself lately."

If he only knew.

2

———

Those scenes in movies where you see someone sitting in an interrogation room are overdramatized.

There's always a single light bulb hanging from the ceiling or wall, sometimes a fan twisting slowly overhead—probably creaking. And the person answering the questions is typically handcuffed to a metal table while seated in a metal chair.

The room Agent Polson put me in did contain the metal chair and matching table—complete with some scratch marks on the surface I thought might have been from fingernails. But other than that, the interrogation room was well lit by a couple of fluorescent bulbs overhead and painted in a sort of gray-green color that reminded me of public-school bathroom stalls from the 1980s.

And there was no overhead fan.

Fortunately, the air conditioning worked. Too well, actually. I shivered from the cold as I sat there waiting for my inquisitors to return.

I didn't have to wait long. And thankfully, I hadn't been handcuffed to the table. I had no desire to be bound again. My fingers unconsciously rubbed my wrists, recalling the discomfort from the bonds I'd shed in the Mexican jungle.

It had been less than twenty-four hours since I left Mexico. Such a short time, yet it felt a world and a lifetime away. So did Vero.

Veronica had helped me, taking a huge risk in the process.

My thoughts that lingered on her weren't just of gratitude. There was a genuine curiosity about the beautiful woman. While I'd promised to return, and soon, I couldn't guarantee that.

She'd offered to come with me, but the kids in her village of Santa Rojo depended on her. Sure, Myra could have taken over the cantina, but that wasn't a job Vero wanted to put on the older woman.

I felt like she could handle it just fine, but Vero didn't agree with that sentiment. Or if she did, she squelched it.

I found myself missing the tiny village, despite not spending much time there. It was a place where clocks didn't matter, where appointments were vague, and where you could lose yourself in the bottom of a margarita glass, or in the dark brown eyes of the cantina's proprietor.

Two faces appeared in the door window across from me two seconds before it opened.

Polson and one of his other agents stepped into the room. The lead agent held a folder in his hand. It wasn't the same yellow color as most of the folders in this kind of movie scene. Instead, it was navy blue and bore the FBI seal on the cover.

He plopped the file down on the table with a loud clap, then eased into the seat across from me, forcing the other agent to stand there with his arms crossed while wearing a fierce, disturbing scowl.

The guy looked like a kid who was just told candy wasn't real.

"Agent Polson," I said then looked to the one standing. "Other guy." I nodded.

The standing agent only sniffled, but it felt like a threat.

Polson flipped over the file to reveal what I thought to be a pretty thin stack of documents on the inside.

He pulled the top sheet to the side revealing a photo underneath. I felt my heart catch and had to swallow back the dagger of emotions that ran through my chest.

It was a picture of Amy, happy and smiling in an evening gown she wore to an exhibit we attended earlier in the year.

"Beautiful woman," Polson said. "Not sure what she saw in a piece of crap like you."

"You and me both," I agreed, though I didn't appreciate the degradation. My self-esteem was low enough, and I was perfectly adept at putting myself down.

Polson only huffed. "Comes from a wealthy family, too. That must have been nice. Did her parents buy your posh condo in the Gulch? I have to wonder if you ever even paid any of the bills."

I could see what he was doing, and Polson's goading wasn't going to get a rise out of me. The voice in my head whispered for me to keep my calm. I agreed and replied calmly. "I paid my part," I informed. "I've never been one to look for a free ride. Not from anyone."

"Sure," the agent said. "Whatever you say, pal."

"I've worked since I was fifteen," I continued. "I got no problem with an honest day's work. That's more than I can say for some people."

He blinked hard, then lowered his eyebrows. "What's that supposed to mean?"

I shrugged. "Nothing. Just that some folks don't do things honestly."

"You saying I'm a dirty agent?"

That came out of left field.

"Uh, no. But you're abrupt and defensive response might."

He shook his head and thumbed his nose like he had an itch, then dragged the photo of Amy off to his left, my right.

Another photo occupied the space now, one of the two of us. And it was from Mexico.

"Wow, your people work fast," I commented, staring at the picture of me and Amy standing in front of the backdrop on the red carpet. It had been taken just prior to entering the exhibit and the gala—the last place we'd been before she was murdered in the hotel.

"Yes. They do."

"Did you have one of your photographers at that gala? Because that's a little weird."

"No," Polson admitted. "But you should know that there isn't much that gets by us. Even if it's in a foreign country."

I thought that was an odd thing to say. The bureau wasn't an international agency, as far as I knew. Not in the sense that they conducted clandestine operations. Still, the FBI sought good relations with friendly governments for the sake of extradition. When Americans committed major crimes abroad, FBI agents loved being the ones to bring them in and parade them in front of the cameras—they were notorious attention-seekers. But my knowledge on the subject was as thin as Lake Michigan ice at Easter.

So the question was, how did this guy and his squad get these photos so quickly? One explanation was that I was being watched. But that made no sense. I'd been a law-abiding citizen my entire life, with only a couple of traffic violations filed away deep in my past.

There was no reason for the FBI to watch me.

Then again, maybe they didn't have to. There'd been a dozen photographers or more at that gala. Most of Guadalajara's elite had been on hand to witness the grand opening of the exhibit. The guys from the bureau could have easily contacted all the media outlets and requested pictures of the event to see if they could nail down a suspect.

Which brought us to the next photo Polson revealed as he pulled the top one to the side. This one sent a chill through my spine. The image portrayed a profile of me... talking to Vicente Carrillo.

Polson slowly dragged the photos to the side into the new stack. One after the other, he showed me pictures of the handshake with Carrillo, of me looking at the photos he'd procured, and of me smiling uncomfortably at the drug lord as I turned down his offer. Of course, to the FBI that picture looked like I was agreeing to whatever Carrillo had offered.

"You see, Professor," Polson drawled, "we know about your little arrangement with Carrillo."

He was grasping at cheap plastic straws, and I knew it. "Oh? Is that right?"

"Yeah. That's right." His voice deepened, taking on a bucket of gravel in the process. "You see, this evidence right here"—he tapped his finger on the last image—"is pretty damming. Tell me, Dr. Wolf, do you honestly think a jury would look at this and think you *didn't* kill your wife and leave her somewhere in Mexico?"

I took a deep breath, measuring my words to make sure this new snarky side of me didn't somehow break free and really piss the guy off.

"Do you want the honest truth, Agent Polson?"

"Obviously. Ready to confess? That would make things so much easier for all of us."

I leaned forward, folding my hands atop the table. "There was no deal with Carrillo." I stared Polson in the eyes. "The truth, Agent Polson, is that he approached me to help him find something."

"And what was this... something?"

Now I had to lie. If I told him Carrillo wanted me to find the medallion, the very one around my neck, he might start asking too many questions

"An artifact." I gave him the answer with the most nonchalant expression I could find. Even threw one hand up as if the answer should have been obvious.

"What kind of artifact?"

I forced a chuckle to convey just how absurd the notion was. "He thought there was some ancient Aztec jewel hidden in a temple that only appears at sunrise." I mixed enough truth with the lie so the agent wouldn't even consider the amulet around my neck to have been the artifact in question.

For several seconds, Polson didn't say anything. He merely peered back at me from his drab, lifeless blue eyes. I figured the ladies probably thought they were dreamy. But to me, they looked like dirty circles of ice.

He let out a long exhale, and I knew right away he didn't buy it.

"You expect me to believe that one of the most feared cartel bosses in all of the Western Hemisphere, a guy who makes hundreds of millions a year moving heroin into the United States—and who knows where else—and who has killed no telling how many people... that this guy wanted to talk to you about archaeology?"

I nodded, pressing my lips together as I did so.

"You must think I'm an idiot," Polson laughed.

"Your words."

He slammed his fist on the table and reached across with the other hand, grabbing me by the shirt. He pulled but found it more difficult than he'd probably imagined. Resigning himself to leaning forward, he brought his nose within six inches of mine. I could smell his cheap cologne and aftershave, both of which I had already detected in the SUV. I guess some of these new superpowers, like the heightened sense of smell, weren't always advantageous.

"Did you have coffee earlier?" I asked calmly. "Because your breath, man. Jeez." I turned to the other agent. "Can you get him a mint or some gum? Maybe a bottle of Listerine?"

Polson tightened his grip and forced me to face him again.

"We know you killed her. Maybe you did it for the insurance money. Maybe you did it because you were sleeping around. Or maybe you're just a psychopath who killed his wife because it seemed like a good time. I don't care what your motive was. You did it. And we're going to prove it."

I tilted my head to the side. "Good luck with that. The next time you talk to me, you will have to call my attorney." I casually looked over at the stack of pictures and shook my head once. "Because if all you have is a bunch of pictures with me and several hundred other people in Guadalajara, you're going to have a hard time proving anything. And my attorney will make sure you understand that. Okay? Pumpkin?"

He shoved me backward, but I barely moved an inch. I felt like a mountain sitting there, dense and permanent. I was in human form, but I knew the energy radiating through me from the medallion was the cause. It was almost as if it acted on its own on my behalf, like a

sort of ancient artificial intelligence. Based on what the shaman and
Myra had told me, that might not have been too far off.

"In the old days, I would have told them to turn off the cameras
and recorders, asked my partner here"—he jerked his thumb over his
shoulder—"to cover the window, and I would have beaten the ever-
living snot out of you."

"But we're not in the old days, are we, Agent Polson?"

His face burned red. He wanted to pummel me, not that it would
have done him any good. Sure, it would have hurt for a minute or
two, but I would have healed. No matter how many times he punched
or kicked or did whatever he wanted to do, I would bounce back up,
ready to take more punishment.

"Lucky you."

A knock came at the door. Polson twisted his head around and
nodded for his partner to see who was there.

The other agent walked over, looked through the reinforced glass,
and then opened the door. He whispered with two more agents,
though these looked different. They wore matching black suits and
ties and looked suspiciously familiar, though I was certain I'd never
met them.

Something told me I didn't want that introduction.

I focused my new super hearing toward the doorway and overheard one of the new agents say the word classified. Then he issued a
warning.

"You have no idea what you're dealing with, Agent," the man said.
"Call in our credentials if you like. You'll get the same answer."

"How come I've never heard of you and this Division Three?"

Division Three? What's that? I'd never heard of it either.

At first glance, the guys looked like a couple of CIA spooks, but
they'd just explained to the bureau guy that they were from a
different agency. Just because I'd never heard of it didn't mean it
wasn't real, but it definitely caused me to wonder if their division was
one of those redacted line items in the federal budget—one of those
things it was best no one in Congress or the White House knew
about.

One thing I knew about politics was that plausible deniability trumped almost everything. And there were plenty of scapegoats to be found in the pool of ambitious go-getters.

"What is the matter, Flickerstaff?" Polson asked.

I crunched my eyebrows together. "Flickerstaff? That's an unusual name."

The agent named Flickerstaff glanced at me with a flame in his eyes, then returned his attention to Polson. "These guys say they're with something called Division Three. I've never heard of it."

"Me either. What do you two want?"

The first of the two agents, the cleanest-cut guy I'd seen in my life, stepped through the door and into the room. The lights seemed to brighten the second he entered.

It must have been an illusion, probably the glow bouncing off the white button-up shirt in just the right way.

"My name is Special Agent Gabriel Keane. This is my partner, Special Agent Az Miller."

Az? What kind of name was that?

Miller had looser blond hair compared to Keane's short dark haircut. While Keane looked like someone that might have hung out with J. Edgar Hoover, Miller bore the appearance of someone who'd rather be surfing.

Polson stood up.

I didn't feel comfortable with these two new guys in the room. But they didn't have a trace of mist around them. For what it was worth, that made me feel a little better. At least for a few seconds.

"Well, what are you doing, Flickerstaff? Call it in." Polson urged his partner by rolling his hand around in the air.

Flickerstaff took the phone out of his pocket and started pressing the screen, I presumed, to call someone who might have the answer he and his partner sought.

"What is all this about?" Polson demanded of Keane.

To his credit, Agent Keane didn't seem threatened or even the least bit bothered by the rude way Polson spoke to him.

"Your partner will find out shortly."

"Oh, is that so? Well, this is my investigation. You got that? This is a bureau matter."

"I'm not arguing that," Keane agreed, raising his hands out wide. "A murder investigation is certainly in your realm, Agent Polson. I'm not here to interfere with that."

The man's utterly calm disposition threw Polson for a loop. I thought—maybe hoped—his head would pop like the guy in the movie *Scanners*. I quickly dispelled the notion, primarily because I was in the splash zone.

"Then why. Are. You. Here?" Polson questioned, forcing the issue.

"Our investigation has to do with what Carrillo was trying to find." His gaze shifted to me. "The artifact he wanted you to locate, Dr. Wolf."

3

First, the color drained from Polson's face. Then he turned that pale, disbelieving expression toward me, mouth hanging like an old barn door missing a hinge.

The newcomer's statement about the artifact negated Polson's argument that I was lying about my conversation with Carrillo, though it didn't completely exonerate me. Not yet.

Just because knowledge of the artifact wasn't solely mine didn't mean I hadn't killed my wife, or that I'd been working with the king-pin. It was easy to connect the dots from a relationship with Carrillo to having one of his goons off my wife so I could collect life insurance money.

As far as I knew, that little theory didn't hold much water. My wife's policy and all its benefits would fall to her parents if she committed suicide or, as was the case right now, she disappeared.

The only reason I remembered any of that is we discussed it prior to leaving for Mexico. She'd told me the last part with a laugh, obviously thinking disappearing wasn't on the menu for her.

A macabre thought crept into my mind. *Where is my wife's body? What have they done with it?*

A splinter of grief stabbed me again, just like it had every day, every hour, since Amy's murder.

Flickerstaff stood outside in the hall as he spoke to someone on his phone. Fear swept through his eyes, and his face darkened. "I see. Yes, ma'am. I understand. Thank you."

He ended the call and stepped back into the room.

"Well?" Polson insisted.

Flickerstaff nodded, a look of disappointment covering his face. "We have to let them do their thing."

"What? Are you serious?"

"I assure you," Keane interrupted. "We will let you continue your investigation as soon as we have some answers from Dr. Wolf. You can torture him as much as you like."

Polson scowled at the comment, but he missed the wink Keane offered me behind his back.

"I'm going to find out what is going on here," Polson roared. "Whoever you are, I'm going to get answers." He turned to me. "This is not over." He jabbed his right index finger toward my face.

"I certainly hope not, Agent Polson. I so enjoy chatting with you."

His left eye twitched as rage pulsed through his veins, but he knew there was nothing he could do. Not right then.

He spun and stormed out of the room with Flickerstaff in tow, then slammed the door shut behind them.

The two remaining agents looked at each other as if the tantrum amused them, then Keane pulled the seat out from the table where Polson had been sitting. "Mind if I sit here?"

The question carried no malice, no vitriol. He asked sincerely, and in a kind tone as if approaching a frightened animal.

If he only knew about the animal part.

"Did you mean what you said?" I led off.

"About what?" Keane asked.

"About the artifact. Is that really why you're here?"

He looked a little surprised. But only a little. "Of course. Why else would we be here? The FBI is already handling the murder investigation."

"They need to be looking for Carrillo."

"Yes. We heard you mention that. I don't mean to step on the Bureau's fragile toes, but would you mind me asking? What happened to your wife the night she disappeared?"

I didn't mind the question at all. In fact, it was refreshing that someone with a badge wanted to know my side of what happened.

I shrugged, my mind wandering to that fateful night that had spun my entire world on its axis.

"It's okay," Miller encouraged. "You can tell us."

I didn't know exactly why, but I felt like he was being truthful. I trusted these two, even though they dressed like someone I'd seen before. I still couldn't place it."

I drew a long breath and began. "It's like I told the FBI before I came back to the States. Carrillo found us in our hotel room the night of the exhibition. I had just got out of the shower and reentered the room when one of his thugs grabbed me. He..." I faltered for a second, seeing the vivid image of my wife being murdered right before my eyes. There was so much blood. More than I recalled seeing when it happened. "They showed me pictures of her with another man, a guy we both knew. Then Carrillo said he was doing me a favor. In return, he wanted a favor from me."

"To find the artifact," Keane finished.

"Yes," I nodded. "I'd never heard of it before. Seemed like some crazy old legend to me. I get approached now and then with things like that—treasure hunts for lost cities or priceless artifacts that have been missing for hundreds, sometimes thousands, of years. But this was the strangest one I've heard so far."

"You say Carrillo murdered your wife? Is that right?" Keane asked, finally sitting down. I realized I hadn't told him he could. I guess the guy was one of those old-school literal types.

"Yeah." My eyes fell to the table. "One of his bodyguards held me while he showed me pictures of her cheating on me. Then he ordered one of his other men to kill her. The guy... He did it without hesitation. No remorse. He pulled the trigger like he was shooting a bottle on a fence." I shuddered as the memory rocked me.

"That must have been horrible," Keane said. And he meant it. Compassion poured from his eyes. The one named Az offered the same silent condolences.

"Thank you," I managed. My voice quivered. I hadn't felt the emotions so strongly since I was in Mexico. All the travel. The sheer exhaustion. Getting back into the States. And now all the questions were taking their toll. A person could only compartmentalize so much, even if they *were* superhuman.

"Carrillo," Keane started up again, "do you know where he is?"

"No," I answered honestly. "I have no idea. I hope he's dead."

"Yes. That's an understandable sentiment." He turned to Miller, who reached into his jacket and retrieved a manila envelope. It was more like the kind I was accustomed to seeing, at least in movies and television shows.

"More pictures?" I hedged.

Keane snorted a laugh with his nod. "Yes. Satellite images of Carrillo's yacht."

Goose bumps ran across every inch of my skin.

"His yacht?"

"Yes. Here." Keane removed a set of high-resolution black-and-white images from the folder and fanned them out on the table in front of me. "Now this one," he pointed at the image on my far left, "is a couple of days ago outside his mansion on the gulf."

"Okay," I said with a slow nod, trying to pretend I was following along, but all I could think was that they knew. I didn't know how they did, but these guys were on to me.

Still, no mist swirled around them, so I had to assume they weren't a threat.

"This one over here," he shifted his focus to the fourth image on the far right, "is what was left after the two images in between occurred."

"Wow," I said, poring over the pictures. They told a story. A very short, fatal story about a helicopter flying into Carrillo's yacht. The explosion at the end didn't leave room for hope that anyone survived.

Not that anyone would be hoping that. "You guys sure were watching his boat closely."

"We watch a lot of people closely," Miller chimed in.

"He's telling the truth. We do watch a lot of people, Dr. Wolf."

"You been watching me?"

"No. Not until yesterday. Now you have our attention."

"That a good or a bad thing?"

Keane shrugged. His eyebrows mimicked the movement. "That depends on you. We want to know everything that happened the night your wife died."

We were going around in circles now. Or that's how it felt. "I already told you. Carrillo killed her."

"Then what happened?"

"I explained that to the FBI before."

"I want to hear it," Keane insisted. "For myself."

I sighed. "Fine. One of Carrillo's guys drugged me. Maybe he did it. That part is a little fuzzy. You know, because they *drugged* me." I felt angry for having to talk about it again. I just wanted to get out of the room, go take my medicine from Amy's parents, and then get my things before returning to Mexico.

The thought of seeing Vero again was the only thing that seemed to calm me, to warm my soul.

"Try to walk us through it. You need a glass of water or something?"

This guy really was a sweetheart, and I immediately felt bad for lashing out. Still, something told me to reserve my judgment of him. I'd seen enough detective shows to know that there was always one good cop, and one bad cop. For all I knew, this guy worked with the Bureau and Polson's whole spiel from before was nothing more than an act to get me to confide in someone who appeared to be showing me kindness.

I actually was thirsty, but I refused. "Thanks. I'm fine. Anyway, I woke up in a tent, tied up. Didn't know where I was at first. Carrillo came in and confronted me, demanding that I locate this ancient artifact of power. He claimed it was in a temple that only appeared for a few minutes at sunrise. The whole thing sounded nuts to me."

"Does it still sound crazy to you?" Keane asked innocently.

"Obviously," I detoured. "A necklace that gave the wearer super-powers? In a temple that isn't there except at sunrise? Doesn't it sound weird to you?"

"We've heard stranger," Miller confessed.

What was that supposed to mean? And who are these guys—really?

"Then what happened?" Keane redirected.

"They left me alone in that tent. I managed to escape when a jaguar attacked the camp. Killed a couple of their guards, I think. Maimed a few others. I don't know why the big cat didn't come after me."

The two agents looked to one another with a curious expression. It was a look of familiarity—not with each other but with something I said.

"This jaguar, it came into the camp? When?"

"Early morning, I guess. The sun came up not long after that."

"What happened when you escaped?"

I knew that question was coming, and even though I did, I had no believable lie. "I... uh... Well, I found my way into the village of Santa Rojo."

"Santa Rojo?"

I nodded. "Yeah. I stumbled into that village and eventually got a ride back into Guadalajara."

"Where you flew back?"

"Yes," I said, leaving out the part about the narrow escape from the city, and the men I'd killed during the getaway.

"How did you manage to get your things back?" Keane asked. "We've seen no reports of your personal items being held by police."

I nearly choked on the statement. "Yes. That's correct. I had to return to the hotel to get my things. My passport, wallet, all that."

"Returned to the scene of the crime, then?" Miller asked. It didn't sound threatening, but it certainly felt that way.

I could sense these guys corralling me now, steering me toward a confession—or at the very least allowing me to hang myself.

"Yes," I forged ahead, regret lacing my voice. "I went back to the room."

"That was risky."

"I know. There could have been cops there. I didn't even know if the body would still be there." I grimaced at the thought. "It was weird. When I opened the door to my room, Amy was gone. They must have taken her and brought in some cleaners or something to take care of the—" I couldn't go any further. They knew I meant the bloody mess.

Keane nodded, quick shallow nods. "That must have been difficult," he offered.

"It was. And confusing. They'd left my things, although they had rummaged through a few items, probably tried to hack into my laptop. Nothing was missing, though."

"Strange," Miller said. "Don't you think?"

"Yeah, I did think that. I guess I was what they wanted. Not my things. I'm fortunate they weren't stolen. Made coming home easier."

"Until the Bureau picked you up at BNA."

"Yeah," I agreed.

Keane leaned back and folded his hands across his lap. He cocked his head to the left as he spoke. "But you never found the necklace?"

"Necklace? Who said anything about a necklace?"

His eyebrows lifted. "You did."

4

I grasped at a response but found nothing. "What are you talking about? I never—"

"A few minutes ago, you slipped and said the word 'necklace' when referring to the artifact—the artifact that we believe Carrillo wanted you to find."

I blinked rapidly, but answers escaped me.

"I think we should finish this conversation in the car," Keane suggested. "Miller?"

"Agreed, sir."

Keane twisted his head to the side, looking at me with a goofy *you up for it* grin. "Shall we?"

"Do I have a choice?"

"You always have a choice, Dr. Wolf. Everyone has a choice."

"I thought you might say something—"

"Cliché like that?" he finished.

My face flushed with heat. "Yeah."

"Clichés exist because they're so often true." Keane stood up and motioned to the door.

Miller walked over to the exit and rapped on the surface a couple of times. A second later, Flickerstaff opened the door and straightened his spine, as if in a show of power.

"Thank you, Agent Flickerstaff," Keane said.

I walked out between Keane and Miller, the former taking the lead. He stopped in front of Polson, who blocked our way.

"We'll be taking him with us."

"The he—"

"Here's my card if you need to reach me." He palmed a card from his jacket, or I thought it came from his jacket. Where else could it have come from? I thought I saw him make a motion toward his chest, but it was so quick, I missed it.

"You are not taking our only suspect." Polson protested. "I don't care what level clearance you have. This is my murder case."

"I know. And you're doing a terrific job. Don't worry. Your suspect won't leave town. We're taking him to his home. And then he's going to see his late wife's parents."

That last part seemed to give Polson a little consolation. He huffed. "Good luck with that. Better you have to deal with them than me. They might kill you."

"I doubt it," I said. "But I guess you never know. Today might be your lucky day."

"Come along," Keane ordered. "Let's get you back to your place."

Polson shook his head in disbelief, watching as I followed Keane down the corridor. He must have called his superiors while I was being interrogated by these Division Three guys because the look of sheer disbelief on his face was priceless.

After navigating our way through the maze inside the building, we arrived outside to warm, muggy air and a sun that was nearly three-quarters of the way to the horizon.

"You hungry?" Keane asked as we stood on the steps looking down to the busy street.

I knew a dozen places within walking distance. All of them sounded good. I really was famished, but I didn't think it was a good idea for me to be out here on the streets at night without knowing whether or not I could keep the beast under control.

I'd need to test that out first.

"No, thank you," I refused. "I'm not really hungry." I hoped they didn't hear my stomach growl.

"I can understand," Miller said. "That's our ride down there." He pointed to a black GMC Yukon Denali near the corner. From the looks of it, the driver was already behind the wheel.

"There's three of you?" I asked.

Keane laughed and patted me on the back like we were old friends. I found the gesture odd, but not unwelcome. "There are more than three of us, Dr. Wolf. Come on."

He led us down the steps to the vehicle and courteously opened the back door for me. No threat of handcuffs. No barking orders at me. The guy acted genuinely nice. If it weren't for the lack of red mist around them, I would have believed it a ruse. I still wasn't completely sold, though, and kept all my senses on high alert. For all I knew, the second I got into this SUV, they might drug me and take me to some covert underground research facility.

I wondered, for a second, what drugs like the one Carrillo used on me would do to my body now that it was... different.

After only a second's hesitation, I climbed into the back seat and started to slide to the middle, then realized only two of us were getting in the back. Keane closed the door behind me and got in the front while Miller joined me in the rear.

"Cool enough back there?" the driver asked. He was a huge guy, ripped with muscles that nearly tore through his black suit.

"Yeah," I said, disoriented by the contrast between the way these guys treated me, and the way Polson had. "It's good. Thank you."

The driver bobbed his head once and then merged into traffic.

"This is Jasher Stokes," Keane said over his shoulder.

My eyebrows shot up at the name. "Jasher?"

"Yeah. I know. It's a little unusual." Baritone didn't do the depth of this guy's voice justice. It was more like a tuba.

"No, I mean, not many people know about that name. Were your parents religious?" He glanced into the rearview mirror at me for a second. The man looked Middle Eastern, with a light tan accented by black hair and eyebrows.

"You could say that. Why do you ask?"

He returned his eyes to the road and turned right at the next intersection.

"Because not a lot of people know about that name. In the Bible, that name is mentioned twice, referring to the Book of Jasher. Jasher, as I've learned through my studies, was Moses' scribe. He was the one who likely wrote the first five books of the Bible."

"Hmm," Jasher said. "That's interesting."

"Yeah. I always wondered who wrote the books after Moses died. I guess most people just assumed Joshua or one of his assistants might have done it. That or no one bothered to ask the question."

I looked around at the familiar buildings passing by. I'd thought, at least for a moment while captive in the jungle, that returning here and seeing all these buildings would make me feel right. The sight of the familiar can bring a sense of comfort, or so I'd believed. Now, though, this city felt strange, almost foreign.

Jasher turned into the drain clog known as Broadway and stopped immediately behind a black Dodge Challenger. Hundreds of pedestrians lined the sidewalks on both sides of the street, and more packed the concrete up the hill.

The famous signs jutted out from the buildings, hanging over the walkways to tease visitors into checking out their live music, cold beer, smooth whiskey, hot chicken, spicy tacos, and just about anything else you could imagine.

A bridesmaids party strutted by on the right, the bride-to-be waving her hand around in a drunken stupor as she tried to direct the group to their next party spot.

"More bachelorette parties than any other city in America," I muttered.

"Probably in the world," Keane chuckled. "Can't imagine there's a place anywhere else that has so many."

"If there is that spot, remind me not to visit there."

The agents laughed, which seemed way off-brand for a group of guys that belonged to an ultra-covert, probably redacted, operation.

I'd always loathed the bachelorette party scene. There'd been more than a few occasions where I was sipping a drink at a bar only to have my evening ruined by some young women in goofy outfits trying to get me to do tricks for their little games. The other part I detested was how they felt like they owned every place they entered.

It was always funny to see a musician take zero crap from them when they begged to be let up on stage or to be allowed to sing a song in a drunken stupor. That last one was always a win-win. If the singer said no, the subsequent tantrum that followed was a must-see. And if the singer allowed them on stage to sing, well, that material wrote itself as the drunk young woman made an ass of herself in front of hundreds of strangers.

"I don't care for them either," Keane admitted. "But they help the local economy, so what can you do?"

I knew he was right. Even if I didn't care to admit it.

Traffic slowly crawled toward the next turn. After several minutes of sitting still, Agent Stokes turned away from the mayhem to enter another street.

Within a few minutes, we were in the area known as the Gulch. Some people thought it was a posh place to be. In recent years, new buildings seemed to pop up everywhere to offer condominiums or apartments to the massive influx of people coming to the city.

In the old days—less than a decade before—people had moved to Nashville to make it in country music and the emerging hybrid pop industry. Now, though, many fled their home states where crime had become rampant, taxes were too heavy a burden, and the cities unlivable.

I hadn't minded at first, but now the town was getting crowded, and the traffic unbearable.

"Tell me about Division Three," I blurted as we passed a coffee shop I frequented on the weekends.

Keane and Stokes glanced at each other. Miller only smiled as he stared out the window, his chin resting on a thumb.

"Seriously," I insisted. "What is all this about Division Three? I heard you say something about it to the other agents. I've never heard of it."

"Neither has anyone else," Keane responded. "It's a shadow agency. No one knows about it unless they need to know about it."

"But now Polson and his buddy know about it. What's stopping them from running off and telling everyone about it? Or starting a conspiracy blog?"

That produced a laugh. I joined them, uneasily, but I wasn't kidding.

"Division Three has the highest level of clearance the government maintains, Dr. Wolf. And that's all we can tell you about it. Unless you're granted the same clearance."

Granted the same clearance? Why would I be granted that kind of security clearance with a government agency?

I'd never heard of an archaeologist being given that before. Then again, that was probably because I didn't have that kind of clearance to be told about it.

The thought made me grin.

Stokes pulled up to my building on the right and parked along the curb.

"Fine by me, guys," I said. "Keep your secrets."

Keane smiled back at me and got out of the vehicle. I opened my door, and he circled around behind me to open the back.

"We collected your things from the Bureau," he said.

I walked around to meet him, and sure enough, all my stuff was there. "Thanks," I offered. "I feel like I should tip you like a rideshare driver or something."

Keane shook his head. "No. But I have something for you." He produced a white card. It only had his last name on it, and a phone number. "Call me if you need anything."

"Like what?"

He shrugged. "You'll know when it happens."

I puzzled over the mysterious statement.

Keane snorted and closed the back.

"I see they gave you guys the upgraded models. Is that a division thing? The Bureau only gets Tahoes."

He ignored the question and started back toward the front of the SUV.

I stepped up onto the curb and watched as he opened the door and stood there for a second. He looked back at me with a strange expression, one full of mischief. Or was it something else?

"We'll keep our secrets, Dr. Wolf. Make sure you keep yours as well. We'll be in touch. One way or the other."

He climbed into the vehicle before I could stop him. Stokes stepped on the gas, and the SUV roared away down the street. The tires squeaked on the asphalt as the driver whipped the truck around the corner and out of sight.

Keane's words hung in my head, echoing off the inner walls of my skull without end.

The "one way or the other" sounded cryptic. And what did he mean about me keeping mine?

Had he seen the medallion? Even if he had, what difference would it make to some random government spook? He wasn't an archaeologist. Not that I knew of. Maybe he really was. Maybe they all were.

I'd heard of archaeological agencies that did work around the world discovering, recovering, and securing artifacts from all kinds of civilizations and cultures. NUMA and the IAA in Atlanta were two that hung around the top of my mind.

I shook off the distraction and turned to the white building with black doors and windows I called home. At least for the near future. Something told me I wasn't going to be staying here in Nashville very long. And not just because I was on a mission.

I needed a home base somewhere, but it was starting to feel like the United States might not be it. Partly because of the encounter with the FBI earlier. The guys from Division Three didn't seem to shake me as much, but the jury was still out on that one.

With a last glance down the sidewalk toward the corner where the SUV vanished, I stepped toward the door and held out my electronic key card.

"If they know about my secret," I muttered, "I wonder what else they know. And who are they really working for."

5

After taking a long shower to purge myself of travel grime, I slipped into some jeans and a Soulcrush T-shirt and wandered into my living room.

The place felt so empty, completely devoid of life. Before, when I was here alone, I'd just thought it quiet—with the exception of the sounds of the street twelve stories below.

I stood by the balcony and looked out at the downtown skyline, along with all the busy people scurrying around as evening approached.

I sighed, noticing the red mist swirling around so many.

It physically hurt me to see it.

"How can the world be so full of wickedness?" I murmured. Then I turned away and fell into the couch.

Gravity felt like it was working double. Exhaustion gripped me and tugged me toward the darkness and a promise of sleep.

I couldn't knock off just yet.

Coffee would wake me up. And in a few short minutes, I knew that the coming of night would give me more than enough fuel.

I picked up the remote from the black leather armrest on the couch and pressed the power button.

The speakers blasted a man's voice, and I squinted while I turned the volume down. One of those television pastors was preaching something about Judgment Day and how only the righteous would see the dawn.

I snorted at that part, seeing how dawn and dusk now played so prominently in my life. And the part about the righteous seeing the morning—for a second, I wondered if that was some sort of sign.

A blue banner hung behind him with the words "Reverend Vernon Wells | Harvest Church Head Pastor."

I shook it off and changed the channel the second he started talking about Hell.

I'd never believed in a permanent state of hell. In my opinion, I thought it strange that a Creator who loved their creations would also think up and create a place for eternal torture. Didn't make a lot of sense to me.

I did believe in the afterlife, though I wasn't really sure how it worked. Once, a friend explained resurrection to me in terms of computer hardware.

"You see," he'd said, "when an old computer stops working properly, or the battery can't hold a charge anymore, you go get a new one. Then you take the memory from the old one and put it in the new hardware. With all your stuff saved in the cloud or on an external drive, it's like resurrecting everything from the old. Surely, a higher power can figure out how to do that with organic material."

I snorted an appreciative laugh at the memory. Jack Morrow was the friend who offered that theory, and I couldn't refute it. The logic was sound even though the science of it was out of reach—for now, anyway.

The thought of Jack reminded me that I needed to call him.

His bookstore would still be open at that hour. I had questions, and Jack was one of the few people I could trust.

I took out my phone and called his number. Jack picked up within two rings, just like he always did.

"Hey," I said, a bit nervous for the first time I could remember when talking to my friend.

"Gideon. Are you okay? I heard bad things, man."

He spoke fast, which was unusual for a guy from the South. Usually, we took our time to say what we needed to say.

"I'm... managing."

"I'm just glad you're alive. Where are you?"

"I'm back home now. I came by to take a shower and change clothes before I go see Amy's parents."

There was a pause—a long one. "Uh, I don't think that's such a good idea, bro."

I frowned. "I know. They think I killed Amy."

"Did you?"

The bluntness of the question was what I'd come to expect from Jack, but this time it caught me off guard.

"I mean, you don't have to answer that," he added.

"No, Jack. I didn't kill my wife. And if there are any FBI goons listening in on this conversation, you can document that."

"FBI? Gideon, what happened?"

"I'll tell you all about it. You mind keeping the bookstore open a little late tonight?"

"Never a problem for my best friend."

"I appreciate it. I'm going to swing over to the in-laws, and then I'll head your way."

Jack sucked in a long, audible breath. "You sure you want to do that? They've said some pretty horrible things to the media about you."

"The media?"

I hadn't thought too much about that facet of all this. As a student of history and ancient cultures, I didn't pay attention to current events the way most people did. I preferred to do my job, essentially keeping my head in the sand.

I had a few social media accounts to keep up with friends or to share pictures from places around the world, but I didn't use them all that often. I'd always kept my life fairly private.

Now, apparently, the media was roasting me, and I felt certain the fuel for that fire came from my in-laws.

"What are they saying?" I asked, uncertain I wanted the answer.

"Well, her dad said that he'd always had a bad feeling about you, like you were hiding something. He said he could never put his finger on it, but that he worried someday you would snap and do something to hurt his little girl."

"That's how he said it?" I clarified.

"Yeah. And that's not all."

"You know what, Jack? I think I'm good. I don't need to hear any more." I scoffed at the notion that Amy's father had worried I would hurt her. And she was far from a little girl. Amy had been a grown woman. She had done what she wanted. With whomever she wanted.

The spiteful part of me wondered how her father would react to the photos Carrillo had shown me, but I knew those pictures were long gone. Probably burned up in the explosion in the gulf.

I decided then that I wouldn't be paying her parents a visit. If her father was going to say those kinds of vile things about me, maybe he didn't deserve an explanation as to what really happened.

I had no intention of dragging my wife through the mud with her indiscretions. That wasn't how I rolled.

"I close up in thirty minutes," Jack said, interrupting the endless string of thoughts rumbling in my mind. "Come on over. Use the back entrance."

"Okay," I said. "Sounds good." I paused and exhaled, feeling a tiny sliver of relief. At least Jack was someone I could trust. "And Jack?"

"Yeah, bud?"

"Thanks."

"No problem. I'll see you in a few."

I ended the call and set the phone down on the counter. The sun's rays disappeared to the west, casting hues of pale purple, orange, and pink across the sky to the east as darkness encroached.

The words of the preacher still reverberated through the room. I shook my head, trying to rid it of the sound.

Another noise interrupted.

Someone knocked on my door. It was a heavy, rapid knock that sounded much like it would have if the cops were there.

Why would the cops be here? I just got dropped off by what was apparently the highest-level agency in the land.

No harsh voice announced "Police, open up!" That gave me confidence that it wasn't the police; not that I'd have been surprised.

I ambled over to the doorway and stopped a foot short, then leaned forward to look through the peephole.

To my surprise, Amy's father stood just outside. His face showed heavy fatigue on top of a body sculpted by leisure and poor dietary choices. The man was twenty pounds overweight, which wasn't so bad compared to many Americans. He stood an inch shorter than me. A thin wisp of gray hair circled his bald head.

He looked angry and nervous, a combination I was in no mood to deal with. But now that the sun was down, I felt power radiating through me, dousing the exhaustion in what seemed like a fire hose of caffeine. For a brief second, I wondered if that was what cocaine felt like.

With that thought, I pulled the door open wide and threw on the best fake smile I could muster.

"Hello, Jerry," I said. It took enormous effort to speak to the man without malice in my voice. I wasn't sure I pulled it off.

"Hello, Gideon." His response was diplomatic, like a presidential candidate meeting his opponent unexpectedly at a bar. He straightened his spine and raised his chin. "May I?"

He motioned to the door, requesting entry.

If I'd been a more honest person, I'd have told him where to go, and where to shove his accusations. But I chose the nicer path, the path of forgiveness—the high road.

Funny thing about regrets, we always have them when it's too late to change anything.

"Sure," I said. "Come on in."

He walked by me with his khakis swooshing against his inner thighs. He wore a blue vest over a white polo. He smelled like beer, and lots of it.

"What did you shoot today?" I asked, closing the door behind him.

He stopped by the counter, looking around at the kitchen, his eyes lingering on the photos of Amy. I'd tried not to look at them, but she was unavoidable. For the moment, I was glad I hadn't taken them down. I'd considered doing that, but I wasn't quite ready.

If Jerry had shown up and seen all the pictures missing, that definitely would have looked suspicious. Not that it mattered. He hated me. Always had. Always would.

I stopped on the other side of the counter and crossed my arms, waiting to hear his answer to my golf question.

Another question circulated in my head, one that Jerry couldn't answer. *Why is the red mist following him?*

I knew the answer, but I didn't want to face it.

I didn't like Jerry; that much was evident for all to see. But I'd never considered him evil. A jerk? Absolutely. Blind to his daughter's flaws? No question. But wicked?

"Interesting choice of words," Jerry said, his back still to me as he pored over the pictures of his dead daughter.

"I'm sorry?"

"Where is she, Gideon? Where is Amy? Where is my daughter?"

There it was. The anger. The betrayal. The utter grief. He may not have been a good man, but even bad people could feel pain of loss.

"I don't know, Jerry. That's the truth. I saw them kill her. Then—"

"Don't lie to me, boy!" He spun around with a gun in his hand, leveled at me from the hip.

My eyes fell to the 9mm pistol.

It didn't worry me as far as death was concerned. But man, those bullets hurt.

"What did you do to her? Where is my daughter?" Tears welled in his red eyes. His fleshy cheeks jiggled and burned, hot with righteous fury.

"Jerry. Please, put the gun down. I didn't do anything to Amy. If you want to talk, I'll tell you everything."

He shook his head. "No. I don't want to talk to you."

Then why did you come?

"I know you killed her. You murdered my little girl and left her somewhere in Mexico with those... animals!"

For a second, I didn't know if he was talking about the cartels or the Mexican people, because if it was the latter that might have been the most offensive thing I'd ever heard him say. Or nearly anyone for that matter.

"Jerry, I didn't kill Amy. Vicente Carrillo's men did. They wanted us to help them find some artifact, some mythical item that would give them power."

His eye's twitched at the explanation, and I knew it wasn't going well in the convincing department.

"Artifact? You expect me to believe that?" He huffed derisively, then with his free hand pulled out a folded card. He pried it open with his thumb and forefinger and held it up for me to see. "Doesn't look like you turned him down."

It was one of the FBI pictures.

I started to ask how, but my uninvited guest cut me off.

"Oh, I have connections, Gideon. I have connections all the way to the DA's office. You see, while they believe in due process and innocent until proven otherwise, I like to take a more proactive approach."

"Taking matters into your own hands."

"Precisely. See, I could let due process take its course, let the courts figure out whether you did it or not. But it could take years to collect the evidence, if there is any. Smart guy like you probably destroyed what little there was. But I know the truth. I know what you did to my daughter. And now it's your turn."

I shook my head. "You're making a mistake, Jerry. I didn't hurt Amy. I loved her." For the briefest of seconds, I considered mentioning the infidelity, but that would have been below the belt. And I didn't play that kind of game. "You don't want to do this." I held out my hands, as if that would convince him.

"Oh, I assure you, son, I really do. When I came in here, you asked me what I shot today. And I said that was a funny choice of words."

I saw where this was going, and I didn't like it.

He raised the pistol, setting the sights squarely on my forehead. He shrugged. "Didn't play great. But I did have a hole in one."

The suppressor on the end of the pistol puffed a short cloud of smoke with the sound of a click.

6

I played dead. Like a good doggy.

But it was a battle to suppress the beast from coming out and ripping Jerry into a hundred pieces.

Killing Amy's father wasn't what I wanted. Well, not officially. There'd been times when I'd joked with buddies about that, but I never actually meant it.

It took enormous focus to keep from wincing at the pain of the bullet lodged in my head. The part where it drilled through my skull was the worst. Then there was the nauseating feeling of the round slowly expelling itself from my prefrontal cortex.

All of that was bad, but not blinking with Jerry looking down at me in disgust was probably the most difficult to manage.

With every passing second my eyes felt like a dust storm was slapping them over and over again.

Jerry held the gun by his hip, staring at me with loathing. "It should have been you," he muttered, adding in an expletive he tied onto "you piece of..." He shook his head. "It was supposed to be you."

What was that supposed to mean?

I understood it when he said, "It should have been you." But when he changed the context to "supposed to be," that caught my attention.

Thankfully, he turned away and I was able to blink about fifty times to lubricate my drought-stricken eyes.

He walked over to the door, and for a few heartbeats I thought he was going to leave my body there on the floor.

But when he opened the door, he nodded toward me, and two men entered.

Two Latino men with tattoos that looked frighteningly similar to the ones worn by those in Carrillo's organization.

They didn't dress like guys Jerry would associate with—he in his golf attire and they in their baggy black jeans. One donned a white T-shirt with YOLO in black letters on the front. The other's black shirt looked like it couldn't make up its mind what design needed to be on the front, so there was a silver dragon surrounded by barbed wire and a cross standing behind all of it.

I stopped blinking as the men approached.

"Get him out of here," Jerry said. "Is it ready?"

One of the goons nodded without looking back. He bent down and grabbed my wrists while the other took my ankles.

"Not as much blood as I would have thought," the guy with my wrists said.

A small pool collected on the floor, and I let my head fall to the side as the men picked me up.

I would have gone ahead and changed right then, shifting into the Chupacabra to lay waste to these two and then get some answers out of Jerry, but I wasn't ready to play that hand yet.

Instead, I wanted to know what these idiots had in store for me.

A third guy entered the room dragging a black plastic bag. I felt relieved that they were going to wrap me up. Breathing would suck, but I could manage that. The blinking thing, however, was driving me crazy.

The guy with the black bag slid it underneath me, then the other two lowered my body down into it. They wriggled me around until my feet and head were inside, then they zipped it shut, plunging me into an airtight darkness.

"Get that cleaned up," Jerry said.

I assumed he meant the blood on the hardwood floor.

I wondered what he was going to do next, and how these thugs were going to try to dispose of the body.

Jerry's odd choice of words still rang in my head. "It was supposed to be you," he'd said.

The men picked me up again. My weight swung the bag back and forth as they carried me out of my condo and into the hall. No light pierced my shroud as the men grunted, hurrying down the corridor.

From the momentum and direction, I knew they were going to the maintenance elevator at the other end of the building. It was a farther walk, but that elevator—unlike the main one—went down to the lower parking garage.

There was a dumpster down there with a hydraulic compressor that compacted the building's trash.

Ugh.

That's when it hit me. Their plan was to dump me into the trash compactor and crush the evidence with all the other refuse. No one would ever find the body.

It was old-school. Just like I'd seen on mob movies at least a dozen times. But if it worked, why do anything else?

They reached the end of the hallway, and I heard one of them press a button. Ten seconds later the lift dinged, and the doors opened. The men set me down on the floor and pushed the button for what I assumed was the basement.

When we arrived at the bottom, the doors opened, and the men picked me up. They'd said nothing on the ride down, which didn't surprise me. Neither of them looked like the talkative type. They were the kind of guys that did as they were told, never questioning orders.

Stone-cold killers. Or in this case, the cleaners.

They carried me out through what I knew were black metal doors

—having taken several large trash items out that way before—and out into the cavernous underbelly of our condominium complex.

My body bounced along in the bag as the men descended the first of two staircases. They turned to the right and wound their way down a ramp. At the second set of steps, the one in front lost his grip and dropped me.

I hit the ground with a hard thud, smacking the back of my skull against the concrete. My vision would have blurred if I hadn't been surrounded by total darkness. I grimaced at the throbbing in my head, but that passed within seconds.

I had to admit it: this rapid healing thing didn't suck.

One of the men said something in Spanish, ordering the other to open the hatch.

We were there.

Now it was just a matter of how I wanted to play this.

7

The hinges on the compactor creaked so loud the sound reached to the other end of the building.

I lay there on the cool concrete pad next to the dumpster that was to be my temporary coffin.

I closed my eyes and summoned the power from the medallion. In less than two breaths, I began the transformation.

I felt the men grab the ends of the bag, but they were unable to lift me off the ground.

"What did you put in here?" one of them said. It must have been the guy who opened the hatch.

"Nothing," the other defended.

"Then why is it so heavy now?"

"I was wondering the same thing."

I growled. And I let them hear me growl.

It was a deep, horrifying sound, like that of a timber wolf in the northern forests.

"What was that?" the first asked.

They both let go of their ends. I assumed they stepped back.

"It sounded like a dog."

"No," I said in Spanish. "I am the Chupacabra."

I tore through the bag as my body lengthened, ripping the plastic at the seams.

Bright fluorescent light rained down on me from the high ceilings.

The men panicked and drew their weapons. They opened fire without thinking, peppering my body with a dozen rounds from point-blank range.

The killers winced at the deafening sounds of the firearms in the enclosed parking garage.

If they weren't going to be dead soon, they would have had one serious case of tinnitus.

I lay still, dropping my monstrous head to the concrete once more. It was the second time in ten minutes I'd played dead.

The men inched closer; their pistols extended downward in case they needed to shoot again. Not that it mattered, but both of their magazines were empty.

One, the guy with the white T-shirt, stretched out the tip of his boot and nudged me in the ribs. He did it again, making sure I was dead.

"What is that?" the other one asked.

White T-shirt shook his head, a look of disgust and curiosity painted on his face. "El Diablo."

"No. Chupacabra," I said, twisting my head up to face him.

He squeezed the trigger in a panic, but no rounds flew from the muzzle.

The guy in black tried to fire, too, but his weapon only clicked once, then did nothing.

Before he could stop me, I bounced to my feet and grabbed the throat of the one in white. I squeezed hard until his eyes nearly popped out of his head. Then I threw him into the long, green trash compactor. He hit his head on the bottom of the opening as he flew in. The blow might have killed him. It for sure knocked him out.

"One for one," I said as if shooting free throws in the driveway. I looked to the other guy, but he'd taken off up the stairs, fumbling with a spare magazine along the way.

"Now, wait a minute," I toyed. "Don't you want to play? You acted like you wanted to play before."

"*Dios mío*," he said, finally able to shove the full magazine into the gun's grip.

"No. That's not going to help you. He's on my side," I snarled at him as I stalked toward the stairs.

He took a shabby aim and started shooting again. Some of the rounds pinged off the compactor behind me. Others ricocheted off the concrete, spraying debris on my fur. Red mist swirled around him, pulsing with bright light.

The fog sensed the kill.

And I obliged it.

A bullet struck my gut. Another hit my shoulder. But I kept going, undeterred.

"No!" He shouted the protest. "This isn't possible."

He ran out of ammo again, and in a panic, threw the pistol at me.

The gun sailed by my head, and I stopped. I frowned at him, then leaped thirty feet up the steps in a flash. Before he could offer the simplest reaction, I landed on him with all four paws and pinned him to the ground.

He stared up at me in terror. A glaze in his eyes told me he'd hit his head pretty hard when I landed on top of him.

I lowered my nose until it nearly touched his. "What are you doing working for Jerry?"

His head lolled to the side.

"Oh no. You're not getting off that easy. Why are you working for him?"

The guy returned his vapid gaze to me and grinned a smug, crap-eating grin. Then he told me what to do with myself.

The word didn't offend me. I'd used it from time to time. But right now was the wrong time to use it.

I rolled off him and in one move grabbed the killer by the neck and raised him high. He kicked and grunted, trying to wriggle free. He was going nowhere.

"Why are you working for Jerry? I've seen these tattoos before. In Mexico. Are you one of Carrillo's guys?"

He looked down at me and tried to kick me in the face. I tilted my head to the side, easily dodging the attack.

Red fog twisted around his legs like a serpent.

"If you're not going to talk, then you're of no use to me. You do know that, right?"

Out of the corner of my eye, I caught sudden movement. I turned and saw another guy with similar tattoos running toward a black BMW sedan in the corner. It wasn't Jerry, which meant it was either the other goon who'd stayed behind to clean up my condo, or he was a random resident whose night was about to get very scary.

"Fine by me," I said to the one I still held in the air. "I'll try him."

I twisted my body like an Olympic hammer thrower and flung the gang member through the air a good sixty to seventy feet.

He flew through the opening in the giant trash compactor, hitting the interior with a thud. I thought I heard some glass break, too.

The BMW revved its engine, and the driver steered it around the corner out of sight.

I knew where he was going. The dumpster sat close to the street so garbage trucks could come empty it every week. There was an open area next to it that served as a loading dock for moving vans.

Just beyond that was the street. And there was only one way in or out.

"I was gonna take out the trash anyway," I said, and leaped high in the air, flying over the first set of stairs and landing next to the second.

I descended the steps two at a time and slammed the green button on the control panel to start the hydraulics.

"No! No wait!" I heard a voice echoing off the metal interior of the dumpster.

As I hurried by, I slammed the door shut and slid the locking bar across it and through two holes.

The cries for help muted to almost nothing, overwhelmed by the sound of the machine groaning to life.

I jumped down from the platform and onto the loading area just as headlights curved around the wall of the next building across from me.

I waited next to the wall, and when I heard the engine gunned, I sprinted from my hiding spot, lowered my shoulder, and rammed into the driver's side.

The door caved with the sound of crunching metal and breaking glass. Tires screeched. I kept my legs moving, driving the heavy vehicle at an angle until it crashed into the other building.

The airbag deployed inside, and something started dinging.

I didn't have much time. Here in the city, out in the open for way too many witnesses, it was only a matter of seconds before some random pedestrian or driver saw me.

Then my cover would be blown.

I punched through the cracked glass and grabbed the dazed driver by the collar. In a quick move, I jerked him through the window and rushed back across the street, dragging him with me like a burlap sack of coffee beans.

He kicked a little, but the blow I'd delivered to his car knocked him a tad senseless. I sped up the steps to the trash compactor as it completed its cycle. I stopped next to the panel and waited, holding the guy by the back of the shirt, sitting him on the ground.

When the light on the panel turned green, I pulled my hostage over to the door and opened it. Then I hauled him up to the edge and forced him to look inside.

Bloody streaks stained the empty bottom. Farther back in the container, I wondered if the bodies were visible. Part of me hoped they were, but I wasn't going to check.

"Now," I said in Spanish, "I want to know why you're working with Jerry. Tell me everything that's going on."

The mist wrapped around him, swirling and dancing, pulsing with red light as if anticipating the next soul.

"I'm just the cleaner," the man managed, his voice distant and tired.

"Right. So you just get called in whenever someone needs to disappear? That about it?"

"Yes. But—"

"How many times have you done this for him?"

"What?" He looked at me with genuine confusion.

"I said... how many times have you been called to take care of a body?"

"I don't know."

That was a dark answer as far as I was concerned. Jerry had killed other people? But why? What was he up to?

"How did he get mixed up with Carrillo?" I decided to press my luck with this guy since he seemed to be in a talkative mood.

The guy breathed harder. "I don't know."

I shoved the guy's head farther into the opening. "You sure? Because if that's all you got, I might as well throw you in there with the other two. They *are* dead, right?"

"I swear. I don't know anything else. We're just the muscle, man. Jerry needed some guys. Carrillo sent us to him."

Hit men? What did Jerry need them for?

"I'm going to ask you another question. And it's really important that you answer me honestly. Okay?"

The man said nothing.

"I'm going to take that as a yes." I held his collar firm. "Men like Jerry Hanlon don't just make friends with someone like Carrillo out of thin air. What's Jerry doing?"

The prisoner snorted in derision. "Seriously? You don't know? The man is your father-in-law, and you don't realize he's working with one of the biggest heroin dealers in the South?"

I frowned. "Biggest heroin dealers? Who is that?"

"A man of God."

"What? You'd better start making sense quick, or it's squishy-squishy time for you."

"You think Carrillo is bad? Wait until you meet the preacher." The goon shook his head in warning. "He's more powerful than anyone you know. Money. Fame. And he moves more heroin than anyone in this half of the country."

"Who is it?" I asked.

He smiled a wicked grin, and I knew the guy was done talking.

"You'll have to figure that out on your own, Chupacabra."

I guess he wasn't done talking. Although I figured he was after that.

"Really? You're going to give me all that and leave me hanging?"

He offered an obscenity, the same one the other guy'd spat at me.

I shook my head. "Suit yourself."

With a grunt, I slung him through the opening. He screamed on his way through until he hit the other side where the compacted trash was mashed into a tight wall. Then he slid down to the floor.

"No! Please!"

"Wow. That was a quick change of heart," I offered.

Then I noticed a billboard on top of the building across the street. It showed a man, probably in his mid-fifties, a gold necklace bearing a cross around his neck. His brown hair looked like it had been added with Photoshop, and his white teeth gleamed brighter than a nuclear blast.

He wore a white button-up shirt that had a black undercollar with the top two buttons undone and a bright blue blazer over it.

"I'll tell you everything you want to know!" The cleaner tried to run across the bottom of the dumpster but slipped in the muck and hit the deck with a dull thud.

"You know what?" I said, an idea bubbling in my head. "I think I know where to start."

"No! Wait!"

He reached up, looking at me with desperation on his face—illuminated by the red, churning fog that surrounded him.

I slowly closed the lid, muting his screams for mercy, then slid the bar across to lock it. Then I turned to the panel and mashed the green button.

I stood there for a second as the machine groaned to life once more. The thug inside the container yelled for help. But it wasn't loud enough to hear. And soon his voice would be silenced forever.

Looking back up at the billboard, I noted the text in the upper left and lower right corners.

Harvest Church.

With Reverend Vernon Wells.

The unexpected attack from Jerry had altered my plans. I touched the medallion against my chest and closed my eyes—calming the energy that raced through me.

I opened my eyes and turned to run, then realized that I'd changed back to my human form. The garment around me had as well, back to its normal size.

Had I just shape-shifted on command?

I'd come close when changing into the Chupacabra. But never back to the real me. Maybe I was making progress.

A car drove by a second later, and I instinctively ducked down. I needed to get out of here in case someone happened to come by the dumpster and look inside.

I retreated back up the stairs and into the building.

I doubted Jerry would still be at the scene of the crime, unless he was taking a long moment to reminisce about his daughter, who now seemed to be part of a much bigger scheme.

I'd pay the preacher a visit, but not before I went by my friend's bookstore first. Jack knew more about weird myths and legends than anyone—obscure stuff that very few others ever bothered to research.

After this crazy night, Jack was going to need to pour me a double.

8

Jack Morrow's bookstore, known as Morrow's Folly, sat on a quiet street corner in one of the less visited areas of downtown.

It was one of the last places that hadn't been renovated and rebuilt like so many other areas in Nashville.

The city's renaissance had changed the landscape, and old brick buildings like this one either became hip new honky-tonks or were leveled and replaced by towering apartment buildings or condos of glass and steel and gleaming-paneled façades. All of them came with swanky rooftop bars or patios that offered sweeping views of the city and the latest in cocktails and music.

Sounded cool. But it was the new Nashville.

Not that there was anything wrong with that. Progress happens. Things change. Hopefully, for the better. But there was something fake about the new city, or parts of it. I should know. I had a condo in one of those spiffy, modern buildings.

But the old town still felt cooler to me.

The brick buildings there had seen some of the greats of country music pass through their doors to perform in their halls. Their voices had climbed to the weathered rooftops, joining the long chorus of legends that set this city apart in American culture.

Ghosts of great performers still lingered here, hanging out at dive bars after a show, sipping beers and whiskey and living like tomorrow might never come. For many it didn't.

I walked around to the back of the bookstore, a wide and dark alley that stretched for a block to another street at the end.

I stopped by the red metal door and waited for a second. I looked both directions, suddenly concerned that someone was watching me. I didn't hear anything unusual other than the normal sounds of a city.

Somewhat satisfied I wasn't being followed, I knocked on the door three times and stepped back.

A minute later the lock creaked painfully, and then the door opened.

Inside stood Jack Morrow, illuminated by a vintage light bulb directly over his head. He scratched his scruffy blond hair and nodded at me. "Been a minute, stranger," he said, blue eyes full of good times from years gone by. It was a look that wondered what trouble we might be getting into next.

"Let's get inside," I suggested. "I'll tell you everything."

I followed him down the short hall, the walls covered in pictures of superheroes, gods from fallen kingdoms, and spaceships from science fiction. A few movie posters in black frames hung with the artwork.

"Still love the smell of this place," I said, inhaling the scent of paper, hardcovers, and whatever type of material comic books were printed on. I knew it was paper, but not the usual kind you'd find it books.

There I went again on another thought tangent.

"Yeah, doesn't get old," Jack said.

He turned the corner into a large room that stretched sixty feet in both directions. Bookshelves filled with tomes lined the walls. Shorter ones occupied floorspace throughout the room, separated by old brick columns.

A brown leather couch sat in the front corner by huge windows. Two more chairs, vintage like so many other things, sat at either end. Their dark velvet upholstery looked like it had come from the White House Green Room.

He led the way to a bar in the back corner, where another collection of club chairs surrounded a round coffee table. The bar had an excellent assortment of whiskeys, tequilas, and rum, with a few vodkas for people who were into that scene.

Mostly, though, Jack kept the bar there for his personal use. The majority of the patrons that came here usually drank coffee. If they wanted to get hammered somewhere, there were only a few million bars within a five-minute walk from here.

Jack walked around the reclaimed wooden façade of the counter and grabbed a bottle of Colonel Taylor bourbon, single barrel.

"The colonel okay with you?" he asked, setting out a couple of tumblers.

"Always," I said, suddenly excited at the prospect of drinking one of my favorites. "Been a while since I had that stuff."

"Sometimes it's easy to find. Sometimes it isn't."

He poured three fingers into each glass, corked the bottle, and set it to the side. Then we raised our drinks.

We recited our old toast we'd used since college. "To friends and heroes, and all the zeros. May we always, all of us, be blessed."

I couldn't remember which one of us came up with it, but I felt like it was Jack. He'd always been the poet.

I tipped the glass and took a sip. The caramel and vanilla washed over my tongue. Only a slight burn tickled my throat as I drank.

I looked at the glass appreciatively, admiring the amber liquid within. It shimmered and danced in the yellow light from the bulbs over the bar.

"Man, that's good," I said.

"I know. I love this stuff."

Jack walked around the counter and motioned to the chairs in the corner. "Have a seat. Tell me what's going on. You sounded... different on the phone. And a little urgent?"

"Maybe," I admitted. I found a seat across from him and eased into it. The clock on the wall said it was already 11:15. I had no idea why Jack kept his bookstore open that late. Then again, he didn't do it for the money. He'd made a small fortune as an app developer. One nice exit, and he was set for life. Along with generations of Morrows after him.

He loved books, though, and stories of all kinds. Including film.

"So," he said, "what gives?"

I passed him a grin I knew he'd catch and perceive as cryptic.

"What?" he insisted.

"I have questions."

He nodded. "About the grieving process?"

"No," I said, a little too much like his suggestion was absurd. I corrected quickly. "Amy was murdered in front of me. I was right there when it happened."

"Ugh, jeez. So, she's not just missing like some reports suggested."

"No," I shook my head. "Carrillo." I exhaled. "He wanted me to find something for him. An ancient medallion of power. I told him he was crazy. I guess they broke into the room while I was in the shower. They killed her and drugged me."

I relayed the rest of the story about my escape and gauged his reaction.

He listened without judgment, nodding now and then. The part about the jaguar seemed to pique his interest more than the rest.

"So," Jack said when I finished talking at the point of the story where I entered Santa Rojo. "How did you get back here?"

I left out the part about the shaman. Even though Jack was a trusted friend, my most trusted, I didn't know how he would react to the segment of the story where I found the medallion and turned into a powerful shape-shifter.

I shrugged and raised the whiskey to my lips. "I flew," I offered coyly.

He snorted. "You know what I mean, wise guy. How did you get back to the city and then fly here? You must have had questions from the Mexican authorities."

"Not really. That came after I arrived back home. The FBI took me in for questioning."

"What was that like?" He asked the question with curious fascination, like seeing an exotic animal for the first time.

"Uncomfortable," was all I could come up with. It hadn't been frightening. I supposed if I'd been interrogated that way in my previous life, I would have felt nervous or scared.

"You can do better than that," Jack coaxed.

"No. That about sums it up."

My host eyed me for a second, as if by doing so he could pry into my mind and read my thoughts.

"You said you had questions," Jack segued.

Apparently, he was okay with the story I'd given him.

"Yes. And you have to keep in mind, I know what I'm about to ask is a little out there."

He smirked. "You're a little out there, my friend." He raised the glass. "But ask away. I have a question for you, too, when you're done."

"Fair enough." I set the glass down on the table and leaned back. "What do you know about a legend involving seven ancient guardians?"

I fired the question at him in the middle of his sip. He froze, the amber liquid still touching his lips. He blinked slowly, then finished his pull and set the drink down.

"Seven ancient guardians? Who wants to know?" He raised his eyebrows and crossed his arms.

"Come on, Jack. I want to know. Have you heard of it?"

Jack looked around as if afraid the walls might hear his response. "Yeah, I've heard of it. I'd wager to say most people haven't. Including some of the top historians in the world. How did you find out about it?"

"Well—"

"Unless," he interrupted. Jack held up a finger to keep me silent. "Unless you... This is the part where I ask you my question."

"You haven't answered mine yet," I protested.

His grin widened. "I will." His eyes fell to my chest, and I felt the medallion pulsing warmth through my skin. "But I want to know. Did you find it?"

"Find it?" I played off the inquiry. "Find what?"

He shook his head slowly at me. "Don't lie to your best friend, Gideon. You know what I'm talking about. Did you find the medallion Carrillo wanted? Or didn't you?"

I held his gaze for several seconds, trying to decide if it was okay to tell him. If I couldn't trust Jack, there was no one else I could trust —except my parents. But they wouldn't be helpful with a situation like this.

The voice inside my head offered no counsel, which I took to mean it was okay.

I nodded and lifted my T-shirt so Jack could see the amulet with the dog's head.

His eyes widened. Disbelief drained the color from his face.

"Are you serious?" He asked the question like he'd just found out Santa was real. "You actually found it?"

He stood up and walked over to me, then bent down and reached out as if about to touch the amulet.

I shrank back. "I wouldn't do that if I were you."

His eyes narrowed to slits. "Why not?"

I lowered my T-shirt. "Because the legend is real."

9

_____

For a minute, Jack simply stood there staring at me like I had fireworks erupting from my ears.

"You're serious, aren't you?"

"Yeah."

He nodded, as if finally understanding a great truth. "Come with me."

I puzzled over the sudden request and watched him walk by the bar into an alcove, stopping at a closed door.

I stood up and watched him take the key necklace from around his neck and insert it into the keyhole. The doorknob looked like it was original, from when the building was built. Come to think of it, so did the key. It was brass, and shaped like a skeleton key, but didn't appear as old as the doorknob, though since my friend wore it, he may well have kept it polished.

Who polishes a key?

I shook off the thought and joined him in the alcove as he twisted the key and unlocked the door.

A dark room lay just beyond the threshold.

Jack reached in and flipped on the lights.

Three vintage bulbs like the ones in the rest of the shop hung from the ceiling via black rods.

A single bookshelf ran the length of the room and reached to the eight-foot ceiling overhead.

These tomes looked different than most of the ones in the bookstore. They appeared older. The lettering on some had been worn down over time so it was nearly impossible to read the title and author.

"What is all this?" I asked, following my friend into the little room.

"This," he said with pride, "is my secret stash. Sure, I sell some first editions out there in the shop, but in here is my personal collection. These are the things I like to study when the store closes and I need something inspiring to read."

"Inspiring?"

"Legends, myths, folklore, ancient treasures, conspiracies, secret societies. You'll find all that stuff in this room. Anything you can imagine. From the Seven Wonders of the Ancient World to possible locations of Alexander the Great's tomb to stories about Atlantis, it's all in here."

I stepped past my friend, scouring the volumes with a careful eye.

"I knew you were into stuff like this," I confessed. "Which is one of the big reasons I needed to see you tonight." I rounded and faced him. "When you saw this necklace, you recognized it. I could see it in your eyes. You've heard of this."

I pulled it out from my shirt and let it hang over the collar.

"Yes," he said. "Well, sort of."

He leaned close to the shelf and ran his finger along one of the levels, examining the titles until he came to a book with a gray hardcover. There was no title on the spine, and the top of it was frayed.

"Here it is," he said.

I didn't bother asking how he knew it was the right one without anything visibly written on the side.

He pulled it out by the top of the spine and cradled it with both hands. The words *Guardians and Myths of the Ancient World* adorned the cover in gold lettering.

The first word of the title sent a shock through my body. It was all I could do not to gasp.

"Where did you get this?" I asked.

It wasn't just the title that struck a chord with me. Surrounding the words were seven circles, each with an animal head represented within. The one on the top looked exactly like the medallion around my neck.

"I've had it a long time," Jack said. "Honestly, I don't remember where I got it. Seems like I bought it when I was traveling. Europe maybe? I can't be positive, but I think Copenhagen. There's a bookstore on the Strøget close to an Irish pub and the Kongens Nytorv—the square, or whatever it's called.

I'd not heard of the place, but I had only visited Copenhagen once, and it was for a conference.

Jack had probably visited a million places like the one he just described. When he traveled abroad, he hit two types of spots more than any others: pubs and bookstores. If there was a third, it would be cathedrals—in part due to his penchant for finding correlations between lost or forgotten mythologies and modern religions.

"You can't remember where you found this?" I asked him, meeting his eyes to make sure I'd heard correctly.

He merely offered a shrug before saying, "I mean, I think probably Copenhagen. Look, I may not remember all the places I got these things, but I've read this one several times."

"You've read it?"

Jack nodded. "Yeah. I've read everything in this room multiple times." He pointed at the book, shaking it with the hand that held it. "But this one? It's special."

"Yeah?" I felt my heart beating hard in my chest. And the medallion seemed to be beating, too. "Why's that?"

"It's fascinating," he said, then opened the cover.

When he did, I thought I felt a burst of air blow through the room.

Jack looked around, sensing it too.

"It's never done that before when I opened it." His eyes fixed on my chest. "What's that thing doing?"

I lowered my view to the medallion and saw it pulsing red at the same pace as my heart.

"I don't know," I admitted. "But when you opened the book, it's like the amulet reacted."

"Yeah," Jack said, mystified. "Let's go back out here."

I followed him back into the shop and over to the bar, where he carefully laid the tome down on the counter.

The title page reflected what I'd read on the cover. *Guardians and Myths of the Ancient World.*

Jack turned the first page and began giving me the CliffsNotes.

"This book talks about seven ancient families, clans that came from all over the world—the seven continents that formed after Pangea. Each of the clans was bestowed with a special power. The people who used these powers were considered above humans—gods to some. Which makes sense if you think about it. And it accounts for all the different myths we get from ancient cultures and religions. Well, not all. But several."

I nodded. I'd heard this part before.

"I have to ask," Jack said, unable to take his eyes away from the amulet. "The one you're wearing looks a lot like this one." He pointed to the emblem over the first page. "Where did you say you got that?"

"I didn't," I hedged. But I had already decided I'd give my friend as much info as I felt necessary. "The cartel boss known as Vicente Carrillo wanted me to find this. This is the artifact he was seeking and the reason he killed Amy. He wanted me to lead him to it because it possesses power."

Jack suddenly looked excited. "I knew it!" he exclaimed. "I knew that was one of the medallions of power. At first, I wasn't sure if it was just something you picked up at a novelty store that lights up."

"I wish," I said.

"Where did you find it?" He stopped himself. "No, wait." He looked into my eyes to make sure I understood he wasn't entirely ignorant on the subject. "Did you find the hidden temple? The one that only appears at sunrise?"

Jack really did know his stuff. "I'm impressed. And yes, I found the temple, though it wasn't due to any of my skills as a riddle solver. It also required no study or archaeological skills. I was running from Carrillo and his men, and probably the jaguar, too. I just needed to escape."

I thought back to that fateful night and could smell the trees, the leaves, the flowers, the dirt, the moisture in the air. "I was running as fast as I could. Then all of a sudden, the ground fell away from under me."

The gleam in Jack's eyes was exactly like when Ralphie opened his surprise gift at Christmas and realized it was his coveted Red Rider BB gun.

"You found the hidden temple," he said with reverence.

"Yeah."

"What was it like? Were there any monsters?"

"You could say that," I teased, keeping it vague for the moment. I still wasn't positive he was ready for this.

"No way!" He nearly jumped to the ceiling. "That is awesome. You're not messing with me, right? Because if you are, I don't think we can be friends anymore."

I didn't share his excitement. Holding up both hands to temper his enthusiasm, I glanced out the front window. A red sports car drove by. From the sound of it, the thing packed a V-12, but I didn't catch the make and model. Those European high-end vehicles all looked the same to me.

"What happened?" Jack persisted. "You fell into the temple, then what?"

I proceeded to tell him about the mysterious torches that lit on their own, and the voices talking to me, which felt a little insane to say out loud.

Then I relayed how I'd discovered the amulet and how the voice told me to put it on.

He simply shook his head, absorbing the tale. "I knew it." He raised a finger. "I knew these things were real." He pointed his attention back to the book.

"You never mentioned any of this before," I countered.

He chuffed. "Seriously? Do you have any idea how crazy everything you just told me sounds? You'd better keep that to yourself."

It was my turn to laugh. "Yeah, you only know the half of it now."

"I kept it to myself because most people think it's make-believe, that all of this stuff falls into the fiction category." His grin widened. "Please. Please tell me you have some kind of superpowers."

I swallowed, trying to figure out the best way to let out my secret. Jack sincerely believed me, and in all this. He was probably the only person on the planet who did.

His eyes widened at the sight of my mischievous smirk.

"You do, don't you?" he said, his voice intense with the possibility.

I drew a breath and crossed my arms. "I have to ask you, Jack. Have you ever heard of the Chupacabra?"

10

———

"**T**his is the coolest thing that's ever happened to me! You know that, right?" Jack peered at me with the intensity of the brightest star in the heavens.

He wasn't joking.

"Yeah, well," I turned and picked up my drink, "I paid a heavy price."

"To become the Chupacabra? Like a blood sacrifice, or no, you sold your soul?"

I chuckled. "No. Nothing like that."

I explained to Jack how the medallion worked, how the only way I could die was losing my head, or total annihilation. I told him everything—including the super strength, the rapid healing, the heightened senses, and even the red mist that surrounds the wicked.

"Wait," he said, suddenly worried. Jack held a drink close to his lips, a hint of fear tingling his eyes. "I don't have any of that mist around me, do I?"

I took a step back and looked him over, then opened my eyes wide. My breathing quickened, and the trickle of fear on my friend's face opened into a river.

"Yes," I said. "You do. And that's why I'm here."

He stared at me, confused and uncertain. "Really?"

I waited for three seconds before I said, "No. Not really. You're fine. Which is good because I would have to kill you."

"Seriously?"

I paused again, once more letting the suspense in his mind build. "No, man. I don't have to walk around killing everyone with that mist. That would be like half the global population."

"Good point," Jack said. "But that is part of what being a guardian is, a vigilante against the forces of evil."

"Is that what your book told you?" I asked, nodding to the volume on the counter.

"Yep. It talks about the roles of guardians, and how they arise during times of need." His voice dropped off, and I could tell he was considering the implications.

"Makes you wonder why now, doesn't it?" I asked.

"Does that thing give you the power to read minds too?" Jack asked, full of wonder once more.

"Yes, Jack. I can read your mind now. Sicko."

"No way!"

"I'm kidding, Jack. No, I can't read minds." I could tell he was a little relieved to get to keep his inner thoughts secret. "I came here because I need your help."

"You do?" He looked surprised.

"Jack, all of this is new to me. I've never heard about any of these legends before. Not this one, anyway. I'm not sure about the others." I took a deep breath. "The voice, it's like a feeling in my head that guides me."

Jack listened without judgment.

"I think there's a reason the medallion chose me. Or the power of it, anyway."

He nodded. "The power of Xolotl."

"That's right." I paced over to the wall and stared at a Pearl Jam poster from a concert in 2018 at Wrigley Field. "I remember that show," I said, veering off topic. "Probably the best I've ever been to."

"It was a fun couple of days, man." Jack didn't stop me from getting distracted. He'd always been good like that, allowing me to process things in my own way.

"Simpler times," I said, nostalgia climbing over my skin and into my brain. I rounded on my friend. "The shaman... He told me some of the stuff I just explained to you. But he also told me that the wolf would be the one to resurrect the other guardians. He said I'm the wolf."

"Well, it *is* your last name."

I shot him a look. "Thanks, Captain Obvious. But I got to thinking. Maybe I'm the first one because I'm an archaeologist, a student of history and cultures; civilizations. The voice confirmed it, Jack. I have to find the other medallions. And the other guardians. I don't know why, but I feel like something big is coming."

"Because it's the end of the age," Jack explained, as though everyone on earth knew that.

"I'm sorry. What?"

"Just hear me out, okay," he said, putting his hands up as if I might turn and walk out. "I know this sounds like kooky stuff to you, but you are aware of the cycles, right?"

"You mean like the five-thousand-year cycles with the Mayan calendar and all that?"

"Sort of, yes. Lots of civilizations had those cycles built into their cultural beliefs. The most common is with astrological signs in relation to the position of Earth's axis. It's called the Precession of the Equinoxes, which a twenty-six-thousand-year cycle, or "age," when our axis moves through, and out of, a particular zodiac sign and into "the house" of the next one. Usually, at the end of an age, as our axis moves into another part of the sky ruled by the next sign of the zodiac, life here on our planet goes through a big transition."

"Let me guess. It's some kind of apocalyptic transition."

He bobbed his head side to side, as if weighing whether or not that was the correct answer. "That depends."

"Depends?"

"Yeah. Sometimes, it's a cataclysm. Sometimes, not so much. It all depends."

"On what?"

"Hard to say, really. The Hopi people have an old prophecy that shows two outcomes. Both are related to the choices of humanity as a whole. In other words, whatever people choose also determines the outcome of the age's end. If we are moving forward, getting to a place where we feel more peaceful, more appreciative, happier, loving, then the outcome is a good one. The turn of the age will come with prosperity and peace."

"Doesn't seem like that's the direction humanity is headed. People hate each other more than ever now. And they're all just out to see what they can get for themselves."

"Right," Jack agreed with a raised finger. "Which brings us to the other outcome. Devastation. Destruction. Sickness. Death."

"How am I supposed to stop all that? I'm just one guy." It sounded like a cliché thing to say, but it was valid. I couldn't stop a flood or an asteroid or the poles shifting as a result of twelve thousand years of the planet getting hotter. All of that was out of my control.

"Perhaps," Jack hypothesized, "you begin by making an impact on a smaller scale. Help those in need. Those who can't defend themselves against evil."

It was like he took the words straight from the shaman. "That's what I was told."

He grinned. "Well, it's also in that book. The guardians aren't always there just for the big jobs, like defending the entire human race. It's also about individuals. Seems like a good place to start."

I grew quiet, melancholy, for a minute as I pondered my friend's words.

He chuckled. "I can't believe this. All this time I hoped there were aliens or monsters or that magic was real. And now I'm getting something totally unexpected." I could see an idea popped into his head from the light bulb switching on in his eyes. "Wait. You said the power of the Chupacabra. What does that mean? I think I know what it means."

"What do you think?"

His smile widened. "The book says that guardians are humans that walk among us, but they can change shapes when necessary."

"Yes," I confirmed. "At night, I can shape-shift into the Chupacabra."

"Like a werewolf?" He sounded giddy.

"Sort of, yeah. But not a werewolf. More like a huge dog."

"Sounds like a wolf to me, and that *is* your last name." Now he just looked goofy.

"Stop with the look, okay," I said with a laugh. "And yes, we've established my last name. I'm strongest when I'm in the dog form. But I still have some of the powers during the day. Like the near immortality thing, the healing, all that. And I'm slightly stronger but not nearly like when I'm the... creature."

Jack shook his head, still trying to grasp it all. "This is so cool. I hope you realize that."

"I guess," I said with a shrug. "There are better people for something like this. I'm not a hero, Jack."

"That's exactly what a hero would say," he argued.

I knew he was right in the context he was using the words, but they didn't feel right with me. I wasn't a savior and never had any designs on becoming one. Now here I was, supposed to do that exact job: saving people from evil.

"Please don't use the great power and great responsibility line," I begged.

He laughed. "I would never. That's not how I roll."

My eyes focused on the wall behind him. "That's not what your Spider-Man poster says." I pointed at the wall, and he looked over this shoulder.

A guilty look washed over him. "Fair enough. But it's still true."

"Didn't need mind powers to know you were going to say that. Anyway," I steered us back on track, "I need to know more about these other medallions. This book can help?"

He nodded. "Oh yeah. Anything you need to know about those things and the guardian history, it's all in there."

I stared at the first page with a tiny bit of dread. Then I sighed.

"Looks like it's going to be a long night of reading." Based on the thickness of the book, it was probably more like several nights."

"I can give you the highlights on each one," Jack said.

"Let's start with that then."

I sat down on a barstool, and he pulled one up next to me, taking a seat with his spine straight, excitement coursing through his veins.

"Are you going to visit Amy's parents tomorrow?" Jack asked.

The question came out of the blue and caught me off guard. It was my turn to exhale slowly. It pained me what her father had done, the things he'd said, the accusations in his eyes. But that torment faded when I remembered the cartel thugs he had working with him.

That part still didn't make sense. And I wasn't ready to talk about that facet just yet.

"No," I said plainly.

He stared at me for ten seconds, waiting to see if I was serious.

"They're going to want to see you," he insisted. "Good, bad, or otherwise."

"Yeah." I took a drink and set the glass down with a clank. "I'm aware."

"You can't just run from that one forever, Gideon."

I shook my head. "I'm not. Jerry already paid me a visit earlier."

Concern immediately filled Jack's eyes. "Oh. How did that go?"

"He shot me."

Jack's eyebrows shot up. "Whoa! What? Wait a second. Where did he shoot you?" He started looking over me, trying to find bullet holes. "What's that hoodie you have under your T-shirt?"

"Oh yeah. Almost forgot. It's a guardian outfit, I guess. That's what this old woman in Mexico told me. She gave it to me."

"A crafter?" Jack asked.

"What?"

"Crafters. You know? Like in video games or movies, television shows?"

"Like a blacksmith?" I figured.

"Sort of. And some crafters do that sort of thing. But they take elements, sometimes mystical ones, and combine them to make something more powerful or more useful." He reached out to touch the fabric of my undershirt, and I pulled away.

"Hey, weirdo. It feels like Dry Fit. Okay?"

Jack laughed at me. "Sorry. Anyway, the book talks about crafters and how they help guardians, often serving as their quartermasters in some regards."

Fascinating.

He kept looking at me, his eyes searching me from head to toe.

"You're still trying to find the bullet hole. Aren't you?"

He bit his lower lip. Guilty. "Yeah. I am."

I snorted. "He shot me in the forehead. Right here." I pointed a few inches above my nose.

Jack leaned in closer, his stare so intense he might have been able to see through me. "I can't tell. Are you sure he shot you in the head?"

I laughed. "Pretty sure, pal. And by the way, it hurts. Just because it doesn't kill me doesn't mean it feels like tickles and pillow fights."

Jack looked down at the book, but his eyes were somewhere else, distant. "I can't believe your father-in-law tried to kill you."

"I know," I said. "And that's not all." I felt ready to tell him everything. "He had some guys with him. They were going to dump my body in the compactor at our apartment building."

"What happened?"

I told him how I'd killed the assassins and gotten intel about a preacher I believed might be Vernon Wells. It was that, or I had to accept coincidences were a real thing—and I didn't believe that for a second.

"I didn't see Jerry after I took out his goons. Who, by the way, are Mexican cartel guys?"

"You sure?"

I tilted my head to the side, begging him to connect that dot for himself.

"Oh right," he said. "You've dealt with those types... this week."

"Carrillo is dead," I said. "I wiped out his entire operation, except maybe a few stragglers that managed to escape. But I know he's gone.

I don't know if Jerry knows yet, or what their relationship was, but I need to find out."

My eyes drifted to the book once more. "And I need to know where to start searching for the second medallion. I have to find it before someone else does. That's my mission, Jack."

He rolled his shoulders and pulled up his sleeves. "Let's get to work then, buddy."

I nodded. "There's one more thing, Jack." I waited a second. "Amy's dad... He had the red mist swirling around him."

Jack understood the gravity of the statement. He knew what it meant, and I saw the conflict in his eyes.

"You can cross that bridge again when you reach it, Gideon," he said. "For now, let's focus on finding the next medallion. Like you said, we don't want it falling into the wrong hands."

"Okay," I agreed. "Show me."

Jack turned the pages until he came to the next chapter with a medallion at the top. "You, apparently, come from the House of Claw and Fang," he said. "This one"—he pointed at the medallion with a bear's head in the center—"is the House of Winter's Dawn." The animal looked fierce and determined—alive.

"Winter's Dawn?" I questioned.

"This medallion contains the power of Artemis. Of course there are other cultures that are attached to this one. Celtic, Hungarian, Finnish... All have legends that tell of a powerful bear goddess who defended forests and wildlife and could heal people with her magic."

"Wasn't Artemis also associated with a deer?" I recalled the fact I'd learned while studying Greek mythology.

"Yes, but some consider that her secondary... animal... thing. Whatever. The point is the bear was also Artemis."

"Okay. Where do we start?"

He ran his finger along the first page and then onto the second. "Trying to remember what it said." He flipped the page again and stopped. "Yes, here." He read the lines out loud. "Where lions guard the gates of the temple unseen, the House of Winter's Dawn dwells in the spirit of Artemis."

"Lions guard the gates?" I puzzled over the riddle.

"And it sounds like another invisible temple," Jack added.

"You think?" I joked. "I was lucky to find the last one, and I was basically right on top of it. How in the world am I supposed to find one I'm looking for based on nothing but an obscure clue?"

"It's not that obscure," Jack argued. "We just have to find the right combination of answers."

I suddenly realized that even with all the history I had studied, I'd never considered the potential for hidden secrets. Sure, the movies did stuff like that, but how much of that was real? In my experience, none of it... until recently. But that's exactly what this was: an ancient clue surrounding a mysterious, invisible temple, and a priceless artifact waiting at the finish line.

This was going to take some work on my part.

"What else does it say about this temple?" I asked. I stood from the stool and took my drink with me, pacing over to the first row of bookshelves that filled the floor space in neatly arranged aisles. I looked at the spine of an archaeological thriller I'd read before—*The Coelho Medallion*. "Lot of medallion stuff going around," I muttered.

Apparently, Jack didn't hear me and went on to answer my question. "It says the temple will reveal itself only at dawn, just like the one you found in Mexico."

"At least that's consistent."

"But there really isn't much more about the location. There's a map here at the end of the chapter. Looks like the Cyclades."

"So it's in Greece?" I realized. "That should make it easier to narrow down."

"You do realize how many islands there are in that archipelago, don't you?"

I actually didn't remember the exact number, but I knew it was a lot. "More than we have time to search," I answered.

"Yeah. It would take forever. Unless you got lucky."

"Which means we're going to have to narrow our search field." I felt like I was repeating myself. "At least we have a general area to begin our search."

"For sure," Jack agreed. He'd always been a glass-half-full kind of guy, and that was coming through.

I caught movement through the front window. This time, it wasn't a random car or some pedestrian passing by on the sidewalk. It was quick, shadowy.

"Get down," I ordered.

"What?"

Before Jack could react or protest further, I slid over to him and shoved him down on the floor.

A bullet zipped through the shop's front window and punctured the wall directly behind where Jack had been standing only a second before.

"What the—" He started to ask the question, but I cut him off.

"Stay down!" I barked. "Someone found me."

"Found you? Who was looking for you? More of Jerry's guys?"

I didn't know the answer. And I didn't have time to figure it out. We were under attack, and Jack didn't have the immortality advantage I did.

I felt the power of the dog pulsing through me as my skin mutated into the creature of legend.

Bullets ripped through the bookstore, most missing the volumes stacked on the shelves. Some, however, tore through spines and pages, sending the shreds to the floor like confetti.

A bullet struck me in the chest, which only made me angrier.

Red dots danced on my figure. A few strays wandered onto the bar behind me.

Outside the window, red fog illuminated the assassins. They weren't the guys Jerry employed, at least not that I could tell. Their faces were covered in black masks and head coverings. They wore matching tactical outfits, too, with black cargo pants, shirts, and vests.

The streetlights helped reveal their presence, and combined with the red mist, I had no trouble spotting them.

They must have closed off the street on both ends because I hadn't seen a car go by in a few minutes, now that I thought about it.

There was no way an assault team or anything related to a SWAT-type group would do something like this without setting up containment.

Did that mean this was local cops? Feds? Or a private group?

A bullet grazed my shoulder, stinging my nerves. I winced at the pain and shook my head. It didn't matter who they were. Red mist plus trying to kill me and my friend equaled one angry Chupacabra.

11

I ran through the center aisle of the store in a flash of fur and gray fabric.

At the door, I leaped forward, crashing through the glass— diving headfirst into the night.

I landed on the sidewalk and rolled to a stop, bumping into a Jeep Wrangler with my back.

The blow didn't hurt, but the bullets popping out of my skin did. Fortunately, that pain only lasted a few seconds as my body healed.

I crouched next to the vehicle and waited, though not for long.

Down either end of the sidewalk, men in matching assault gear approached, one from each direction. They aimed their submachine guns at me with laser sights stuck to me like magnets on a fridge.

A furry fridge.

I dropped to the ground and rolled under the Jeep just as the men started firing. Rounds ricocheted off the sidewalk and curb, sending sparks and pieces of the concrete curb into the air. A few chunks hit me in the face as I rolled to the other side of the vehicle.

I'd only avoided the onslaught for a moment since the brunt of the enemy's forces were amassed on the street.

With only a split second to count them, I quickly saw there were ten men surrounding the bookstore in a semicircle. They took cover behind other vehicles, a park bench, a real estate magazine dispenser, whatever they could find.

Their collective aim settled on me, which was where I wanted it. They'd done enough damage to Jack's store. I hoped he hadn't been hit in the gunfire.

If he stayed down like I said, he should be fine.

I smelled the bitter scent of gun smoke in the air. It hung thick in the air like the aftermath of Fourth of July.

For a brief second, I wondered if the men were going to tell me to get down on the ground with my hands over my head, or on my knees, or whatever happens when you're being arrested. I'd never done a second in the back of a squad car.

Looking down the ends of both streets, I saw there were black Ford Explorers blocking the road in each direction.

The absence of government plates told me everything I needed to know.

These guys were hitters, mercenaries sent to kill.

The only question was, who sent them?

I overheard the order from one of the assassins. It was a guy straight across the street from me behind a silver minivan. He looked down the sights of his weapon and spoke into a radio, telling the others to open fire.

Thanks to my enhanced hearing, I was able to pinpoint exactly where the order came from.

The men fired, their guns erupting in a serious of loud clicks that sounded like a typing class from yesteryear on exam day.

Their suppressors coughed rounds at me, but I'd already made my move.

I jumped high into the air, soaring above the street toward the assault group's commander.

The man looked up and tried to take aim as I descended toward him, but his reaction was too slow. He managed one shot that missed my head by four inches a second before I crashed into him, my knee crushing his face into the concrete.

He died instantly.

Men on either side of him reacted, both turning and whipping their weapons around to take me out in the middle. The pulled their triggers as I dove forward. Bullets riddled their bodies, putting their Kevlar vests to the test, though a few of the rounds strayed and struck weak spots in the body armor. The neck was particularly vulnerable, and it happened that both men took each other out with multiple shots to that soft spot.

They fell next to their comrade as they desperately grasped at their throats to stem the wounds.

I chose to take out the left flank first, and another gunman crouching behind a park bench.

I lifted the dying man at my feet and held him in front of me as I charged the next enemy.

The gunman fired over and over, dumping more bullets into the body I held in my clutches. The human shield absorbed them until I was only ten feet away. Then I hurled the man at the shooter as more guys behind him rushed to his aid.

The body hit the gunman and knocked him to the ground.

He pushed the corpse off of him and tried to roll up onto his feet. Spinning around to fire again, he was met by a fisted paw. I struck him so hard, his head hit the top of the park bench with a disturbing crack of bone.

The hit man fell behind the bench and lay there unmoving.

Two more approached, one from the sidewalk to my left and one from across the street—the one who'd tried to corral me right in front of the entrance to Jack's shop.

I ripped a trash can lid from a bin next to me and held it in front of my chest as the gunman on the sidewalk opened fire first. More hit men approached from the rear, rallying to help their comrades in what was turning into a bloodbath.

Bullets pinged off the heavy lid in my hand, only producing dents on the side where I gripped the handle.

The shooter lowered his aim in an attempt to take me out at the legs, but I darted left and right, zigzagging until I reached him.

He emptied the last three rounds of his magazine into my gut when I was only three feet away.

I grimaced, howling in pain.

I made him pay for shooting me by whipping the lid around and crushing his jaw. The bone cracked audibly from the blow.

Another gunman approached as his teammate fell to the ground, unconscious from the strike.

A bullet hit me in the back, burning my muscles and skin. I turned like an Olympic discus thrower and flung the lid at the shooter. The object struck him right between the eyes with such force that he flipped up into the air and onto his back, landing with a thud on the asphalt.

The last four approached with knees bent and weapons held tight against their shoulders as they closed in, surrounding me on all sides except behind me, where an old fabric shop stood.

Red vortices of mist swirled around their legs, the light from the ethereal matter pulsing brightly.

The men continued pushing forward, using cover where possible. The two to my left shot first.

Bullets struck my back and side. Then the others opened fire. More rounds sank into my body, stinging tissue and muscle. I howled in fury, then leaped up onto the roof of the shop behind me.

I hit the surface and rolled to a stop. Closing my eyes, I willed my body to heal itself. Within seconds, the pain from the gunshot wounds had evaporated.

With the ancient power flowing through me, I listened closely and heard one of the men below issuing orders.

I was no tactical expert, but it seemed to me like these guys should have been using some hand signals or some other form of silent communication as opposed to speaking through the radios.

I twisted around and looked to the back of the building. An old metal ladder connected to the lip of the roof. Soon, the hit squad would find their way up here and resume their attack.

And I was in no mood to get shot again.

I prowled on all four paws over to the roof's edge and looked down. One of the gunmen crept toward the rear of the building through the adjacent alley. Another was ahead of him by ten steps.

A predatory grin crossed my face, and I felt my fangs hanging down over my lips. It was a strange feeling, but it also felt familiar in an equally weird way.

I waited until the first of the two gunmen disappeared around the back. Then I dropped down on top of the second, smashing him and his weapon into the ground before he could get off a shot.

I bit into his neck until I felt the gush and the familiar metallic taste. His body twitched as I stood and leaped back up to the roof a second before his partner returned to see what had caused the noise.

I watched him hurry back to check on his fallen comrade. He quickly surmised that the other guy was dead and must have figured I'd retreated back to the main street.

My grin intensified with anticipation of the next kill. And the second he reached the sidewalk, I hung down over the edge of the roof and dropped down.

12

I landed silently despite my bulk, and the gunman continued around the corner in the front of the defunct shop.

I stalked toward the street, the pads of my paws completely silent on the asphalt. The assassin was creeping toward the other side of the building, hoping to get the drop on me.

Narrowing the distance between us, I silently followed him until I was only a step away. The man froze inexplicably. Then I realized it wasn't so inexplicable. I saw him in the reflection of the only store window that didn't have a board over it, and he saw me.

The gunman tried to turn in a desperate effort to defend himself. I grabbed him by the ankles and yanked him off his feet. His head hit the ground hard, and I felt the body get heavier.

Taking no chances, I kept holding on to the ankles and spun around in a circle, whirling around as the center point of centrifugal force. Then I stepped to one side and slammed the would-be killer into the shop's brick corner with a devastating crack.

The body went completely limp a second after his skull caved against the brickwork, and I dropped him to the ground to let the mist do its thing.

I started toward the corner when another of the gunmen emerged around it and quickly aimed his gun at me.

I dove to the right as he opened fire. Rounds bounced off the concrete, smashed into car windows and doors, and some danced across the street to hit other random façades.

A quick roll to the right, then a boost from my hind legs—that was so weird to even think—and I surged forward, twisting my body in the air to avoid the bullet storm flying at me.

I crashed into the gunman, and my momentum carried him into the wall. Grabbing him by the collar, I beat him against the bricks over and over again until the body grew heavy. Looking into his vacant, glazed eyes, I knew he was gone, and let him drop to the ground.

"One to go," I said, and ducked around the corner.

The guy wasn't there. I listened intently and heard the sound of something tapping on metal. The deliberate rhythm told me exactly what I needed to know. The gunman was climbing the ladder in the back.

I hurried down the side of the building and stopped at the back corner. A peek around the shop revealed the man's boot as he climbed over the lip at the top. I grinned with a sick kind of glee and padded over to the ladder.

Climbing it quickly, silently, I moved with incredible speed until I was at the top.

I saw the gunman moving toward an industrial HVAC unit in the middle of the rooftop. The way he approached the thing, I knew he figured I was hiding behind it.

I finished climbing over the top and prowled across the roof toward the killer's back. He reached the side of the HVAC and paused. Sensing he was about to check his rear, I shifted behind a ventilation shaft and waited. Sure enough, the guy spun around to check his six before going forward.

This was my chance.

I stalked him across the rooftop until I was mere feet behind him. I could smell his sweat, but more than that I sensed his fear. His heart pounded hard in his chest, and his jerky movements betrayed his true inner turmoil.

That didn't keep the red mist from giving me my orders.

The guy stopped at the edge of the HVAC and snapped his weapon around the edge, pointing it down to the rooftop. If he'd expected me to be sitting there waiting for him to show up, he was sadly mistaken.

Panic gripped him, and he whirled around—unknowingly—to face me.

"Looking for me?" I asked.

He managed one shot from his submachine gun. The round tore through my trapezius muscle over my left shoulder. I grabbed the gun with my right paw and started to slowly turn the barrel toward his face.

"Ouch," I said, grabbing his shoulder with my left paw as the pain started dissipating within seconds.

To his credit, the gunman did his best to fight it. He was strong, probably 215 pounds, a few inches short of six feet tall, and his outfit bulged around swollen muscles. Even all those hundreds of hours in the gym couldn't save him against my superior, superhuman strength.

I continued turning the weapon on the man, slowly, as if his resistance were slowing me down. It wasn't.

I could have broken the guy in half like a twig, and I might have—except that I needed answers.

When the muzzle was nearly under his chin, I stopped and let him keep progress at a stalemate.

"Who do you work for?" I asked.

He shook his head. "I'll never tell you."

I nodded, then jabbed the claw at the end of my left thumb through his trapezius. He howled in agony.

"That's a little like what it felt like when you shot me in the same place. Doesn't feel good, does it?" I twisted the nail and produced more screams.

He took his free hand and tried to remove my paw, but it was no use.

"Who do you work for?" I asked.

He offered an obscenity in response.

"I don't know that person," I said and eased the muzzle a little closer to his chin. "I wonder if your gun knows that person. Why don't we ask it?"

He shook his head. "No. Please."

"You're not a cop," I said. "And you don't look like a fed. You're workin' for someone. I want to know who. Tell me, and I'll let you go."

"I can't tell you."

"Yes. Yes you can. You have to. Or I'm going to make this the most painful experience of your entire life."

I saw my glowing red eyes reflected in his. Deeper in his eyes I saw fear, uncertainty, panic.

He swallowed. "I can't," he persisted.

I moved the gun a little more.

"You don't understand. He'll kill me."

"I. Will. Kill. You. Or maybe you don't understand that concept. See, I'm the one holding you right now with a gun under your chin. Your employer, whoever he is, can't save you. So, you can take your chances with him. Or you can take your chances with me, a very real and present threat to your well-being."

He contemplated the offer, and I could see the conflict going on in his head. Who was it that this guy was so loyal to? Mercenaries didn't have any allegiances except to cash.

"Why are you protecting him?" I asked, taking a different tack. "You're nothing but a hired gun, a killer. Mercenaries are loyal to no one."

He looked me in the eyes, the fear replaced by something else— righteous indignation maybe. I wasn't sure.

"I'm not just a mercenary," he said. "I'm a believer."

"What?"

The killer grinned. It was a sickly, evil expression. "Oh, you don't have to wait long. He's coming for you. And that medallion around your neck."

This guy knew about the medallion, and apparently, so did his boss. If they knew about it, how many others did as well?

I threw a Hail Mary with the next question. "How much did Jerry pay you? Where is he getting his money? Carrillo?"

The goon frowned at the question. It was an honest, body-language response that he couldn't fake. Not with me.

Then his expression changed to a scalding, derisive look. It was the kind of smug expression I'd seen on the faces of people who thought they were holding something over me, like I was the guy on the outside of an inside joke.

"I don't know who those people are," he said.

There wasn't a lie in his words, which didn't help me with my investigation.

"If it isn't them, then who?" I insisted, nudging the barrel so close it pressed against his throat while the muzzle brushed the underside of his chin.

"I already told you; I can't say."

"You do realize if you don't tell me, I'm going to kill you."

He snorted. "You were going to anyway."

He had me there, but I wasn't going to let him know that.

"There are fates, Dr. Wolf, much worse than death." His eyes narrowed as he uttered the cryptic words.

"I assure you, I'm well aware."

He smiled, and I sensed his forearm tighten. "No."

It was too late. His finger pulled the trigger as I jerked it to the right.

The gun erupted with a quiet cough.

He grimaced in frustration as the bullet sailed into the night, just past his ear.

"Who do you work for?" I pressed. "All I need is a name. Then you can die if you want."

"My place in the kingdom is assured, Dr. Wolf."

How did this guy know my name?

"Fine," I said. "So is your pain."

I lowered the gun against his resistance and pointed it at his right knee. "Have you ever been shot in the knee? I assure you," I didn't wait for a response, "it is one of the most excruciating things a human can experience."

"Now," I said when the muzzle was aligned with his kneecap. "Pull that trigger again."

He shook his head. "No. I don't want to."

"I don't care." I shifted my grip on the gun and put a claw on the trigger. "Last chance. Who sent you?"

He swallowed but didn't answer.

"Fine," I tensed my claw on the trigger. "All those bone fragments from your knee are going to cause the nerves around it to scream in pain, probably for several days. But hey, at least your place in some kingdom is assured."

I let him see my claw trigger.

"No. Wait. Please. I'll tell you. He sent us."

"He? Who's he?"

The man said nothing after his whimpering explanation. But his gaze told me everything I needed to know. I followed his line of sight across the street to another one of those billboards I'd seen with the face of Reverend Vernon Wells on it.

"The pastor?"

I knew some of those megachurch pastors had some seedy things going on in their lives, but this was next level for someone whose brand was being a man of God.

The gunman neither confirmed nor denied.

"Well. I guess I'm going to have to pay him a visit."

The goon shook his head. "He'll kill you before you get to him."

"Oh? What makes you think that? That fact he sent ten of you guys after me, and every single one of you died?"

He questioned the last part of my statement with a confused frown. "You said you were going to let me go if I told you."

"I know," I said. "And I always keep my promises."

I lowered him back to the ground, then in a quick burst, gripped his hips and tossed him sixty feet into the air.

He screamed in terror as he flew into the night, over the edge of the roof, and back down toward the sidewalk. I jumped down to the ground and made my way to the front of Jack's bookstore.

I didn't look back as the body smacked into the ground twenty feet behind me, instantly cutting off the screams.

Red mist consumed the bodies on the sidewalk and in the street, filtering into their nostrils and ears until the corpses pulsed red.

So much death, I thought.

And so gruesome, the voice in my head added.

Across the street, I stopped at the entrance and looked inside. "Jack?" I shouted into the bookstore. Windows were shattered all along the front façade. "You okay in there?"

"Gideon?" the familiar voice answered.

"Yeah. It's me. You can come out. They're gone."

"Gone?" I saw my friend stand up in the back of the shop. He was still near the bar. As far as I could tell, he wasn't hurt. "Like dead gone?"

I nodded. "Worse," I said and walked in through the tattered door.

"Worse?"

"Yeah." I met him halfway down the aisle. Most of the bookstore and its inventory were intact. Only a small percentage of the books had been damaged in the gunfire.

Light fixtures and walls on the other hand hadn't been so fortunate.

"What's worse?"

I drew a breath and calmed down, allowing my heartbeat to return to its normal, docile rhythm.

"The mist causes the bodies to disappear," I said, pointing to the nearest one out on the sidewalk."

Jack looked through the broken glass at one of the hit men. As I'd described, the crimson fog disintegrated the husk, leaving nothing but a bloodstain on the concrete.

"Whoa," Jack said. "That's so messed up." He turned to me. "Um. Would you mind... changing back? It's really awkward talking to you when you're... a dog."

I snickered at the request and nodded. "I think so."

As my mind continued to calm, I felt the change happening again.

"That's better," Jack said, relieved. "Those clothes you have on—they just grow and shrink depending on your form?"

"Yeah. It's weird. I know."

"Better than you being naked."

I laughed. "True." I looked down the street at traffic redirecting itself. "We should probably get out of here," I suggested.

"Yeah," Jack agreed, looking back into his shop. The forlorn expression on his face said it all.

"Sorry about your shop," I offered.

He nodded. "Insurance should cover it. I hope."

"Well, if not, I can help you pay for repairs."

"I saw what you did to the door. You can definitely pay for that."

We shared a quick laugh and then walked back into the bookstore, glass crunching underfoot.

"Who were those guys, Gideon?" Jack asked once we were back in the bar. Miraculously, our drinks remained unmolested.

I drew a long breath and picked up my glass to finish the drink. "I don't know, but I know who they work for."

"Who?"

"Vernon Wells."

"The pastor of Harvest Church? He's a preacher." Jack made the argument as he picked up his glass. Then downed it.

"Plenty of good ones and bad ones alike," I said. "The last one I killed coughed up the goods. Now I need to find out what the Good Reverend wants, and why he wants me dead."

"I didn't even realize you two knew each other," Jack said, setting his glass down with a satisfied exhale.

I chuffed a laugh and followed him to the hall leading into the back. "We don't."

"Sounds like he knows who *you* are."

"Yeah, well, I don't know him. But it sounds like he and I are going to have a come-to-Jesus meeting."

I followed my friend out the back door to his red four-door pickup truck. "Not gonna lock the back?" I asked.

He looked back over at the building and the rear door. "Nope. I'm gonna call the cops once we're out of here. Then I'll come back and do all the paperwork, take care of getting insurance claims filed, all that."

"Ugh," I breathed. "I'm so sorry, Jack. I had no idea."

"It's all good. Am I pissed they wrecked my store? Yep, but it looks like only the common books were damaged. The first editions and other rare ones seem fine."

"You got all that just from a quick pass through?"

He lifted his shoulders as he unlocked the truck with the key fob. I walked around to the other side. "No. I'm being hopeful. Honestly, I don't want to look. But we need to get you out of here. If someone was following you, and trying to kill you, then they are probably connected. Best if you're not around when the cops show up."

"We going to your place?" I wondered, opening the passenger-side door.

"No," Jack said. "If they connect you to me, that'll be the next place these people look. They knew you were here. That means they'll figure we'll hang together."

I didn't say anything, but I was surprised at how much of this Jack already had figured out, and I wondered how many brushes with danger he'd had.

"Okay," I conceded. "Where we going?"

"I know a place. No one will find us with her."

"Her? Girlfriend?"

He snorted and climbed in the truck, easing into the plush, brown leather seats. "I wish. No, she's just a friend. But she's cool. And no one will know."

"What does she do?"

I closed the door, and he started the engine.

"Um, she's... an entrepreneur?"

I didn't like the way he made a question out of his answer.

"Okay..."

Jack shifted the truck into reverse and backed out of his spot.

"You'll like her. Trust me. I'll drop you off there and then come back to the shop to deal with the fallout."

"All right, man. I trust you. Whatever you think we need to do."

He sighed, looking over at my strange clothes. "I think we need to get you some new duds. That whole druid-looking thing you got going on isn't going to work here in NashVegas."

I smiled at the local reference. "Yeah, I know, but all my other stuff rips to shreds when I... you know, shift."

He nodded. "My friend may have a solution for you. After all, she's a crafter."

13

J ack pulled the truck into the driveway and killed the engine. I stared through the windshield at a mid-century modern house with white painted brick walls and black window frames and front door.

No lights were on inside.

"Is she home?" I asked, opening the door as Jack climbed out.

"Yeah," he said, slamming the door shut. "She's usually out back in the pool house."

"She has a pool house?" I looked around the property. Pine and oak trees dotted the side yard. A white oak stood in the center of the main yard that the driveway encircled.

I'd never been to this part of Nashville before, to the northeast of the city. It was quieter here that downtown.

The neighborhood looked like it had been constructed in the 1950s, when homes were built solid and made to last. I was always so impressed by the older things—especially when it came to construction. We had all the technology and innovation of the last century at our fingertips, but we couldn't build houses as well as they did sixty or eighty years ago. Maybe even longer.

I recalled talking to an engineer once who was overseeing some big expansion at the locks on the dam in Chattanooga. He said the project was half the work of original construction but would take them twice as long to complete.

"They just did it better back then," my friend had said.

Jack led the way up the driveway where it forked and led to a two-car garage and, I assumed, a basement. A black wrought-iron gate blocked the asphalt path to the back yard, where a rectangular pool sat in the center of a deck covered in tiles that looked like gray wood.

He opened the gate, much to the protest of the creaking hinges, and entered the back with nary a care.

"Did you tell your friend we're coming?" I asked.

"Nah. She doesn't care."

"So, she's not one of those shoot-first, ask-questions-later types?"

Jack looked over at me as we proceeded to the edge of the pool deck. "No. Why would she be?"

"I don't know. Some people are afraid of trespassers."

He chuckled. "Not Jess. She's not afraid of anyone. But she is armed, so don't do anything stupid. Okay?"

I laughed uneasily, and at the lack of his laughter, I stopped and put on a somber face. "Understood."

We continued by the pool toward the one-story pool house. It looked like a decent place to live, not just a luxury item attached at the back.

"This place is nice," I said. "What did you say she does again?"

"I didn't," Jack said, still being coy.

I noticed there was a light on in what appeared to be a kitchen, and a huge television flashed brightly in the dark.

We stopped at a sliding door, and Jack rapped on the glass.

A silhouette inside popped up from the couch. I saw long hair shift around the head from the movement, and then the woman stood up.

She walked over to the door. A floodlight glowed in the corner above the door—the light only touching her face when she stopped and smiled through the glass at Jack.

She slid the door open a crack and stopped before Jack could enter, despite his meager effort.

"What the—"

"Hey there, Jess," Jack said, cutting her off.

She turned toward him. Her long black hair hung in multiple braids, some jumping off the top of her head and diving down toward her shoulders. She wore a black hoodie and gray scrubs. From the looks of her, she was in for the night, and I didn't necessarily want to interrupt.

I also detected an odd smell—familiar, but in a far-off-memory kind of way.

"So, do you mind if we come in?" Jack blurted, clapping his hands together.

He sounded and looked very nervous all of a sudden.

"Yeah, sure, Jack. Of course. You okay? And who's this guy?"

She curled her thick, red lower lip as she studied my strange clothes. "Nice threads," she said, then bit that lower lip.

"Uh," I looked down at my unusual clothes, "thanks."

"We were hoping you might have something he could change into?" Jack explained.

"You came here. To my home. Me. A woman. To see if I had something this guy could change into?" She didn't look like she believed the story.

"Yeah. I mean, we ran into some trouble earlier, and he—"

"Trouble, Jack?" She interrupted him with the casual playfulness of siblings.

Yep, she definitely didn't know about his feelings for her. And that didn't surprise me. Stand-offish was my first impression of her. That might have been unfair, but first impressions often are.

She crossed her arms over her hoodie and kicked her right hip out to the side the same way an angry mother would to a lying child. "What kind of trouble? You aren't bringing trouble to *my* doorstep, are you?"

Her Southern accent was deep, and when she said the word "kind," it sounded more like *canned*.

"It's not the cops, if that's what you're saying," Jack defended.

"Then what? Mob? Gangs? There's no telling what kind of sick crap you're into."

I snickered.

"What's so funny, dude in the druid costume?"

I nodded at the solid burn. "Yeah, it's weird, isn't it."

"See?" Jack reemphasized, "he really does need some clothes. Do you have any?"

She rolled her eyes and opened the door wider, stepping to the side to let us in.

I felt her brush the fabric of my tunic as I walked by. She tried to do it subtly, but I noticed.

"Where did you get that?" she asked, suddenly very interested in my weird-looking garment.

"A friend," I answered honestly.

"What friend?"

That was a strange one to add on top. "A lady in Mexico. She gave it to me."

"Where did she get it?" Jesse closed the door behind us, and as Jack continued into the living room where the gas fireplace crackled under the television, she focused on my clothes—eyes poring over them.

"Um, I don't know?" I offered. I felt like that answer would only make her angry.

I could see in her eyes that she didn't believe me, almost as if she knew I was lying. I admit, I'd never been a good liar. I believed in the old saying from Mark Twain: "If you always tell the truth, you never have to remember anything."

"Seriously?" she asked.

"She's a quirky lady," I added quickly.

"The cops aren't after us if that's what you're thinking," Jack said, diverting the conversation back to the original topic.

"I know who they're working for," I corrected.

Jack turned to me. I couldn't tell if he wanted me to say it or not. So, I waited.

"They tried to kill you?" Jesse asked with modest concern. "That's messed up. Who did you piss off?"

"It would seem," I said, swerving my eyes to my friend, "the Reverend Vernon Wells is behind it."

"What?" she laughed. "Vernon Wells?"

"Yeah, I thought it was weird, too, but I got a hint from one of his goons earlier. And confirmation from another guy before we came here."

"Confirmation? What did you do, torture them for information?" She arched her left eyebrow.

I sighed.

"Whoa. Did you really?"

"Why do you sound excited about that?" Jack asked.

Jesse glanced at him. "It's kind of cool."

"Cool? My bookstore was just destroyed."

I frowned at him. "Destroyed? I thought you said most of the books were fine."

"Wait. Destroyed? Vernon Wells destroyed your bookstore?"

"No," I corrected. "He sent a hit squad to take me out. Some of the books got damaged."

"Along with all the windows and the front door. No telling how many rounds we'll have to pull out of the drywall. I'll be closed for a month."

He sounded hurt, but we both knew he didn't need the money from book revenue.

"Speaking of," I interrupted, "shouldn't you be getting a call from the cops right about now?"

On cue, the phone in his pocket started vibrating, accompanied by the theme song from *The Mandalorian*.

"How did you... Is that one of your powers, too?" Jack asked.

Jesse's eyes studied me intently. They were deep, mysterious blue glaciers staring into my soul. "Powers?"

"Good one, Jack," I said. "You gonna answer that or keep making things more awkward with your friend?"

He sighed. "I guess I have to take this." He looked at Jesse. "You okay if I leave him here while I handle the reports and paperwork crap?"

"A total stranger wearing some kind of weird druid-looking outfit who you just said has some kind of powers?" She raised both eyebrows then grinned fiendishly. "Absolutely. I'll be fine."

"You sure?"

"I'm a big girl, Jack. Answer your phone before it goes to voice mail. You'll never get ahold of them if you have to call back."

He put the phone to his ear as he walked back out to the pool deck, closing the door behind him. "This is Jack Morrow."

His voice faded the farther away he got until Jesse couldn't hear him anymore. Her focus, however, had remained on me. And for a second, I thought she might devour me.

"So, our mutual acquaintance is bad at introductions. I never caught your name." She tilted her head to the side. "Or are you just going to stay a stranger."

It sounded flirty, but I didn't take it that way.

"My name is Gideon Wolf. You're Jesse."

"Jesse Marsh. He's mentioned you once or twice. You're the archaeologist, right?"

I nodded. "Yeah."

She nodded and casually spun around, walked over to the kitchen counter, and pulled a bottle of bourbon out of the corner. "Drink?"

I didn't think it was a good idea, but I also felt the sweet numbing of alcohol calling my name.

Every second, it seemed, had been a trial by fire the last week. *How long had it been? How many days since Amy was murdered?*

It all felt like nothing more than minutes or seconds to me.

"Yeah, I'll have one."

"I drink it neat. That okay for you, or are you one of those people that needs it mixed with something and on the rocks?"

I liked her immediately.

"Neat is perfect. If the whiskey is good."

She held up a bottle of Angel's Envy, one of my favorites.

"This good enough for you, cowboy?" she asked.

The moniker immediately caused me to think of Vero back in Mexico. She'd called me that several times, and when Jesse did it, I was thrown off.

"Yeah," I said, collecting myself so I didn't look or sound creepy. "I love Angel's Envy. You have good taste."

"You're a man who knows his bourbon. I like that."

I felt warmth rush over me, and realized I was blushing. Both from the awkwardness of being flirted with and from the fact that my mind kept returning to Vero. On top of that, I knew Jack liked this girl. I wasn't about to even attempt to mess that up for him.

I responded with a shrug. "Yeah, I mean, I like the good ones."

She finished pouring the drinks and then brought them back over to where I stood. She handed me the drink and raised hers. We clinked them together, and I nodded at her.

"What are we drinking to?" I asked.

"To new friends and old whiskey," she said without hesitation.

"I like that." I took a sip of the bourbon and let it melt over my tongue. "So good."

"It is," she agreed.

"Have a seat on the couch. You play video games?" She walked around the sofa and eased into the soft leather. Firelight flickered off her pale cheeks and danced in her ocean-blue eyes.

I sat down at the other end of the couch and nodded unconvincingly. "I like to play. Just don't get enough time. Always working."

"You out there in the dirt digging for fossils and stuff at nighttime?" She took another sip.

I laughed at the insinuation, and at the subsequent visual it thrust into my head. "No. But there's paperwork and other research, project planning, that sort of thing."

I wondered how much of that I would be doing in the future, especially with Amy gone. We'd always worked together. Well, almost always. Apparently, she'd been working with other men on separate projects.

"Yeah, you need to unwind. Relax a little. All work and no play make Gideon... You know the rest."

"I do," I laughed. "Usually, I enjoy the work."

"That's good. It's important to enjoy what you do."

"Definitely. Nothing worse than spending a full third of your life working in a job you hate." I took another drink then asked, "Speaking of. What do you do?"

"Jack didn't tell you?"

I shook my head.

"Well, I shouldn't be surprised. He's a coy one. I get the feeling he's into me, but he won't make a move." She turned her attention to the flames in the hearth, watching them twist and rise, lapping at the air with orange tongues.

"What would you do if he did?" I had to ask, now feeling like one of those life coaches who was poking their nose a little too far into others' business.

"I guess he'll have to find out," she said.

It was her turn to be coy, and she plainly saw through my ruse.

"You were about to tell me what you do?" I said, detouring back to the topic.

"I grow pot," she said matter-of-factly.

I was in the middle of taking a sip when the words came out of her mouth. I nearly did a spit-take, but managed to keep it together without wasting a single drop of the amber gold.

I pressed my free hand to my mouth to make sure I didn't dribble on my chin, then looked over at her.

She turned her head slowly toward me and smiled. "What? You got a problem with that?"

"Not at all," I said, and meant it. "I think it's great." Now I sounded like I was overcompensating even though I truly felt that way. "It's just that's not a typical job. Especially here in Tennessee."

At the moment, the legal situation for marijuana in the state of Tennessee was still up in the air. It was illegal, yes, but things were in the works to change all that.

"You worried about the cops or the DEA?" I wondered.

"Nah," she said. "There are over four thousand licensed hemp farmers in this state now growing the legal stuff for CBD. That's a lot of plants for the inspectors to check. On top of that, the authorities are more concerned with the more dangerous drugs. Cocaine, heroin, all the pills people are getting from Big Pharma. They're not worried about a small operation like mine. And my stuff isn't hurting anyone."

"Sounds like you have it all figured out."

"Not all of it. The second you start thinking that, is the second you get sloppy. But it helps that I know a few cops. They've told me they don't care about it, that they have bigger things to take care of."

I let that topic die since I didn't have a problem with what she was doing. Instead, I took a drink and stared into the fire.

"So, you going to tell me about the power thing your buddy mentioned or not?" She didn't look at me while asking the question. Her eyes remained fixed on the flames.

"Yeah. If you don't mind hearing something that is completely insane."

"I'm always down for some insanity."

She was cool. I could see why Jack liked her. And she wasn't hard on the eyes, either.

"Not sure if you want this kind," I countered.

Jesse shrugged. "He said power. So either you're some kind of ambitious political type who wants to control the world, or maybe just a small county. Or what he meant was you've got some kind of superpowers."

I huffed. "That's a pretty big leap."

"Is leaping one of your powers?"

I tried to diffuse the question with another laugh, but it did nothing.

"Yeah," I sighed. My voice lacked any confidence, almost as if I regretted saying the word.

"Seriously?" She sat up a little straighter, and her eyes lit with excitement as she faced me, crossing her legs one over the other atop the couch cushion. "What else?"

I frowned at her, confused. "Um. I just told you that leaping is one of my superpowers. Me. A total stranger. In your home. Telling you that I have the ability to leap—"

"Tall buildings in a single—"

"No. Not that high. But maybe a few stories. Three stories? I haven't tested it out, to be perfectly honest."

Her eyes widened, and I could see what she was thinking.

"No. No way. I don't think that's a good idea." Fortunately, I didn't see the red mist around her. That put me at ease, relatively speaking.

"Oh yeah," she said, nodding dramatically. "I want to see what you can do."

It was like she hadn't just heard me tell her the incredibly ludicrous truth. "You're just ready to accept it? And you don't think I'm crazy? You must believe in this stuff."

She nodded slowly. "Yes, Gideon. I do."

14

"Wait. What?"

I set my drink down on the end table next to me and turned to face her.

"Yeah," Jesse said. "I do."

"You believe in supernatural stuff like that?"

She bobbed her head, and her shoulders mirrored the movement. "Yeah, I mean, I don't know how much of it I believe, but think about it. Do you really believe that people thousands and thousands of years ago were able to imagine wars in space like the ones in the Vedas? What about incredible monsters that litter ancient mythologies and literature?"

"Maybe they were using psychedelics," I offered.

Jesse chuckled. "Yeah. Well, there's probably some truth to that, too. I read a book about that recently. It was good."

"I think I heard about that on one of the podcasts I listen to. Sounds interesting."

"It is. And my point is, using hallucinogens aside, how else can we explain all of the spectacular things in the legends and histories? We can't. Yes, early fiction writers used their imaginations to a certain degree, but imagining those kinds of things must have come from somewhere. The cyclops? Medusa? The hydra? All of those were pretty out there."

"Maybe they just took things around them and imagined they were different." I wasn't trying to kill her steam, but I wanted to make sure she knew what she was really getting into.

Jesse wasn't stupid.

"You seem to be going out of your way to persuade me that there aren't supernatural things that happen in this world, meanwhile you're telling me that you have the ability to jump really high, and your best friend let it slip that you have powers. So, you can quit the act. You don't have to vet me. I'm in. So, tell me." She crossed her arms after setting her cup down.

I took in a long breath, ran my fingers through my hair, and exhaled, blowing the air through my lips in a low whistle. "Okay. So, like I said, I'm an archaeologist. That's what I've always done, what I wanted to be when I grew up."

"That's cute." She said it like she didn't mean it, but I sensed sincerity in her expression—soft eyes that portrayed kindness instead of sarcasm.

"Anyway, I was in Mexico with my wife—"

"Where's your wife?" Jesse asked. "At home? Good thing you didn't take her to the bookstore. Sounds like that was a mess."

"She's dead," I blurted before I could stop myself and ease her into that part of the story.

"Oh. I'm—"

"Don't. It's okay. I mean, it's not okay. It just happened a few days ago. We were in Guadalajara. The cartel killed her to force me to find this."

I raised the medallion, tired of telling the story for the umpteenth time. "Vicente Carrillo wanted this. It's a medallion of power."

I explained how I'd never heard of it, and how I thought it was ridiculous to spend any amount of time or resources on something that hadn't been verified. Sure, the letters, the maps, all the clues that Carrillo possessed looked like the genuine articles, but only extensive testing could prove that to be true or not.

For her part, Jesse was really good about listening to the story and not judging any of it as the ramblings of a crazy person. She looked like she truly believed everything I said. While her expression was blank, I took that as open-mindedness—something that seemed in short supply in society.

When I finished—including the ending at the bookstore—she nodded, picked up her drink, and swallowed a long gulp to finish it off.

She let out a satisfied "Ah" then looked at me with the slyest grin I'd ever seen. "That is the most fascinating story I've ever heard."

"I know," I agreed. "And I also know how outlandish it sounds. So, if you want to kick me out of the house now, I understand."

Her head retreated an inch to emphasize how ridiculous my statement sounded. "Are you serious? Kick you out? I want to see what you can do, Dr. Wolf."

"Please, just call me Gideon."

I felt myself blushing. Or maybe it was the heat radiating from the medallion.

"Fine. Gideon. But listen, I've never met one of your kind before."

That was a weird way of saying it, but as a person who was almost never offended by anything, I let it slide.

"I've always hoped," she continued, "that I could meet someone with superhuman powers. And I've searched. Believe me, I have searched."

"And I just sort of fell into it. Literally, as it were."

The comment caught her, and she laughed, connecting the joke to my story about falling into the temple.

"On top of that," I added, "I've never believed in anything like this. It was all fantasy, fiction. Children's make-believe."

"Yet here you are, Mr. Chupacabra." She scooted closer, staring at the amulet. "How does it work? Can you change on command?"

Everyone wants to know that. I gave what was quickly becoming the standard answer. "I'm working on it."

"Well," she said, standing up with her glass in hand. "I think this is exciting. You have the power to help people, Gideon. You could be a real-life superhero if you wanted. And since you shape-shift, you won't even need the mask or the costume." She stopped herself and stared at my outfit. "Although we could probably do better with that. Looks like the crafter you met before doesn't know how to do cloaking."

"So, it's true," I said. "You're a crafter."

She shrugged like it was no big deal. "I guess you could say that."

"And how many guardians or supernaturals have you helped?"

"None," she answered with a pleasant grin. "You're the first one I've met. Remember?"

"Right." I said the word like a stretched-out piece of taffy. "You did mention that."

Jesse snorted. "You sound suspicious."

"Well, you said you're a crafter, but you've never met someone like me. So..."

"How do you know I'm a crafter? Or how do I know I'm one?"

I smiled awkwardly. "Yeah."

She strode over to the kitchen counter and picked up the bottle, this time bringing it over to the sofa. She refilled my glass, then her own. When the tumblers were half full, she set the bottle on the wooden coffee table and sat down again.

"I have been told about supernaturals since I was a kid," she began. "I grew up in a religious home. I read the Bible a lot as a child, and my mother made me memorize verses that she deemed important."

"Did that cause you to have resentment against religion?"

"Not at all. Quite the contrary." Jesse grinned and snickered. "I know I don't look like the typical, proper church-going lady. I don't own any of those Kentucky Derby dresses like I've seen some women wear to church. I don't really go anymore. Not because I don't believe, but because I always knew there was more to it."

"How did you know?" I asked, leaning forward to pick up my refilled drink.

She sipped hers and shrugged. "My mother."

"Your mother?"

"Mm-hmm. The same woman taught me about other religions and cultures, beliefs from all over the world and throughout history. She wanted me to have a well-rounded view of things. It was only later in her life I realized the real reason why."

"Which was?" Before she could answer, my eyes lit up. It was a pretty big leap to reach the conclusion, but something inside told me it was right. "Because she was a crafter?"

My hostess shook her head with a laugh. "No. I'm not a crafter. Although I can be kind of crafty at times." She laughed at herself. "She was simply a believer in the unknown, and in the supernatural. The things that people thought were crazy or outlandish were the things she sought to understand the most. My mother waited her entire life to meet a guardian. As did her mother."

"I don't understand. How did she know about the guardians and all the legends that surround them?"

"I wondered about that," she confessed. "She always used to talk about the gods from the ancient world, demigods, heroes of incredible powers. For a long time I figured it was nothing more than bedtime stories. Unconventional ones. When my mother died, I was left with so many questions. Then, when I was going through her things to take care of the end-of-life stuff, I found something that took away all my doubts."

"What?" I asked.

"I think it would be easier for me to show you than tell you."

She stood up and motioned to the hallway beyond the hearth at the back of the little house. "This way." She nodded with her head and started down the corridor.

I didn't have much choice. At least it didn't seem that way. So, I followed her down the hall to a closed door in the back right of the house.

She opened it and looked at me with a serious expression. "I would warn you that what you're about to see is pretty out there, but then again, you're a shape-shifter. So..."

Dim yellow light glowed inside the room.

A long wooden table stood against the back wall. A book sat on top of it. The tome looked like it was old, probably a first edition.

What's with all the book collecting? I started wondering if maybe I should start a collection just so I wouldn't be left out.

I preferred to be somewhat minimalist. And besides, my favorite collections were in museums, featuring priceless artifacts I'd helped recover.

"It's a book," I said, stating the obvious.

"Very astute, Gideon."

I could almost feel her eyes roll.

I moved deeper into the room, drawing closer to the book on the table. I stared at the green hardback; the color faded into a dark olive. On the cover, seven golden emblems stood out, raised above the book's surface.

The familiar symbols represented the seven great houses of the guardians. *How many of these books are out there?*

Then I started wondering how it was that two people who knew each other ended up with one of these. While this volume looked different than the one Jack had in his shop, I couldn't imagine what the odds were that two people who knew each other, like Jack and Jesse, ended up with what added up to two pieces from the same pie.

"Did you and Jack come up with this?" I asked.

"Come up with what?" Her reply was sincere, and I realized I wasn't being punked.

"The book. Where did you say your mother got that?" I hoped my question wasn't insensitive.

"I didn't. Because she didn't. I never knew where Mom got this. But I can tell from your reaction that you recognize it."

I sighed and shook my head. "I don't recognize the book. The seals on the cover look mighty familiar, though. I asked where your mother found this because Jack has a book with some very similar symbols, although his is slightly different."

"Ah. That *is* interesting," she agreed. "What are the odds?"

My sentiments exactly.

"That's what I was thinking." I made no effort to conceal my suspicions.

"I don't know what you're insinuating, but I assure you: I didn't know Jack had a book like this."

I eased closer to the volume and tilted my head to read the cover. "*Relics of Power*." I read the title with interest. "His has a different title. But it looks similar."

"I'm sure there are many copies of these around the world. Perhaps thousands or tens of thousands. Initially, I thought it was simply entertaining to read."

I shook my head. "No, I don't think there are thousands of them. These books are rare. And very old." I turned to her, prying my eyes from the book for a moment. "Was your mother looking for the medallions?"

The direct question caught Jesse off guard, and for a few seconds she looked like a deer in headlights.

"I'm sorry," I said. "I don't mean to be insensitive. You know, about your mom."

"No," she said quickly. "You're not. You're fine. I just... It's still hard to think about. My parents died within eight months of each other. When my dad passed, my mom stopped trying to live. It happens a lot that way."

I knew she was right. I'd seen it or read about it a hundred times. One of my neighbors in my old subdivision lost his wife. He was gone a year later.

It made me sad to think about, but I wasn't here to help Jesse process old hurt.

"My mother left this book in her desk. There was a note inside it written in her handwriting. When I found it and opened it, I read the message she left for me. My mother believed there was a sliver of truth to all the old legends and religious beliefs, as I alluded to before. This book talks about the ones that were true."

I looked over at the book, then back to her. "It's a companion book to the one Jack has."

"I guess. Sure, maybe." She shrugged as if she didn't care, but I could tell there was more to it than just her trying to be cool.

"I wonder, Jesse," I said, "if your mother wanted you to be one of the guardians."

Jesse huffed. "Oh, I'm sure she did. Mom used to make me train when I was a kid. I learned how to use firearms at a very early age. Knives came later."

I almost took a step back out of instinct. Without my powers, I suddenly felt like this woman might kick my tail in.

Fortunately, I did have my powers, so even if she was feeling froggy, she wasn't going to hop. At least not far.

"Sounds like you had an... interesting childhood."

"Mom wanted me to be prepared, both in case I ever found a medallion and in case I was ever attacked by someone. It's more important than ever for girls to be able to defend themselves. That's what she used to say."

"I don't disagree. If I had a daughter, she'd learn to defend herself early on."

"You would have gotten along great with her." Jesse's voice grew distant, and the words trailed off like wisps of fog in a morning breeze.

"You can take a look at the book if you like. We'll probably have some time before Jack returns. I'm sure he's knee deep in filing reports with insurance companies, talking to cops, all the fun things you want to do on a weekend."

I laughed at the last part. "Yeah, I bet he's miserable. And if you don't mind, yes, I would love to take a closer look at that book. Maybe there's something in it that can help me with my search."

"Search?"

I nodded. "Yes. My search to locate the other six medallions and get them to their guardians before someone else steals them."

"Steals them? Who would try to—"

"I don't know yet. But I aim to find out. If you see anything unusual—my shape-shifting into the Chupacabra notwithstanding—you have to let me know."

She stared into my eyes. "Of course."

"Cool," I said, turning my head to stare at the book once more. "Maybe it has more answers."

15

I spent an hour skimming through the old book, exercising the same caution I always did when studying ancient texts. Most people don't realize how utterly fragile those things can be.

But the ancient paper never ripped, and somehow felt stronger than it should have been for something its age. Then again, I had no idea how old it could be.

It was a book, so I doubted it was thousands of years old. Scrolls and tablets were the choice of scribes from that era all the way to the earliest forms of writing—the ones on cave walls.

Jesse was patient, and spent most of the hour playing a first-person shooter on her next-generation console.

It was midnight before I heard a knock at the door. Jesse had taken a break from her game to get another drink when the rapping came from the entrance.

She looked over at me where I sat at a little breakfast table studying.

Jesse walked over to the door and looked out through a side window. "It's Jack," she said, relieved.

She opened the door, and an exhausted Jack stepped into the little house. It was a strange moment for me to wonder why we were hanging out in the pool house and not in the main house, but I kept that question to myself. I figured this was where she spent most of her time. Then again, I hadn't seen any of her growing area yet, so it was possible she used the main house for that.

"You okay?" I asked, seeing the utter fatigue on my friend's face. His shoulders slumped forward, and his arms hung impotently at his sides.

"Yeah," he said, "considering my bookstore was shot up by mysterious assassins and I spent the last couple of hours dealing with the cops and the insurance adjusters."

"It's covered, I hope."

Both Jesse and I waited for the response. He stared down at the floor, as if he didn't want to tell us, which made me feel all the more guilty for the destruction of his shop.

"Yeah," he said with a grin. "I'll actually get more than the place is worth. So, I'll be able to make some much-needed upgrades with the repairs."

"Oh, that's good news," Jesse said, her tough exterior melting with a warm, sincere tone.

Jack closed the door and walked over to the counter in the kitchen. He helped himself to a bottle of bourbon and took a glass from the cabinet.

"Mind if I have one?" he asked, holding up the bottle to our gracious host.

"I insist, actually," Jesse corrected.

"Thanks, Jesse. I really appreciate you helping us out."

She passed me a knowing glance. "It's been my pleasure," she said.

He frowned, then looked at me with jealousy in his eyes. "What?"

"How long have you known he's a guardian?"

Jack was in mid-pour when she asked the question. He nearly missed the glass and spilled the good bourbon onto the counter, but quickly recovered and finished filling the tumbler halfway to the top.

"Thirsty?" I joked.

He raised the glass to his lips and held it there, taking in the biggest swig humanly safe for whiskey.

Then he swallowed it and exhaled.

"Yeah. You could say that." He took another drink, this one smaller than the first. "My nerves are just a little fried, that's all."

"You two planning on staying here all night? Or do you have somewhere else to go? Doesn't seem like a good idea to go back to your place, Jack."

"No," he agreed. "Not a good call to go there."

"I concur," I added, not that the conversation needed my opinion. "Whoever sent those men will think that's the next place we go."

"Unless they're following you," Jesse argued.

"Followed?" Jack asked, suddenly worried. "You think we were followed?"

"We weren't followed," I interjected. "I made sure to watch behind us the whole way here. No cars tailed us."

"Yeah, but I don't want to cause Jess any trouble, Gideon," Jack said. "Maybe we should find somewhere else to lay low for the night."

"No," she declined. "Stay here. You two can sleep in the main house. I'll stay out here in the studio."

I liked how she called it a studio. I guess she did so because she used it for streaming her games online.

"Are you sure?" Jack asked. "I don't want to cause any—"

"Trouble. I know," she cut him off. "And that's very chivalrous of you. But I'll be fine. I sleep out here most of the time anyway. There are two guest rooms in the house. Both beds are made. No one's slept in them in forever since I don't usually have guests."

She struck me as a loner, so that statement didn't surprise.

"What's that?" Jack said, motioning vaguely at the book on the table. His eyelids narrowed, and he took a step toward me. "Is that—"

"It's hers," I said, before he got any ideas. "And yes, it looks like the one you have. In fact, I'd say the same people who wrote this also wrote yours. This one is focused more on the medallions and their powers, their histories, and the Houses who wore them."

"Wait. What? Where did you…?"

"My mother gave it to me. She left it for me when she died."

Jack looked over at Jesse, then back to the book. "Your mother had a book like the one I have? That's—"

"Unlikely," I interrupted. "But not impossible. Sooner or later, Jack, you're going to learn there is no such thing as coincidence. You and your friend here"—I motioned with a nod to Jesse—"seem to have been brought together for a higher purpose."

The two looked at each other, sharing a long stare full of questions and curiosity.

"But the odds..." he stammered.

"Are long, sure. Yet here we are. Two of what may be the rarest books in the world, both in the possession of close friends who happen to live in the same town."

An idea flickered in my head. It was outlandish, silly even. But what if it was possible?

"What?" Jack asked, seeing my expression change. "I know that look."

"It's nothing," I said. "Just a silly idea."

"Gideon," Jesse said, "you're a shape-shifter—so you say—and you found a medallion of power that the book in your hands documents. And you discovered it in a magical, hidden temple in the Mexican jungle. I'd say we're beyond silly at this point."

"True." I bobbed my head absently.

"So, what are you thinking?"

"I don't want to get off track," I said. "We need to find out who sent that death squad to kill us tonight."

"A given," he said, taking another drink.

"And I need to know what Vernon Wells has to do with all this."

"Amen."

"Last and not least, why did Amy's dad try to kill me, and what is his relationship with Vicente Carrillo's cartel?"

The other two eyed each other.

"Sounds like you have a full plate," Jesse observed.

She wasn't wrong.

"What was the other thing?" Jack asked.

I looked down at the book. I'd left it on the page about Artemis. There were other details from Greek mythology, highlighting the goddess Athena.

"It's just that... Well, this book and yours, Jack, talk a lot about the ancient mythologies from many cultures. This suggests that many of these deities were really people who used relics of power to gain their supernatural abilities. Then later on, they were called gods."

"Correct," Jack confirmed.

"Yeah, so I mean, we're hunting for seven amulets of power. But there were more than just seven gods out there."

Jack laughed. "Yep. In almost every religion known to man. And on every continent. Well, except Antarctica. Not sure if they had a belief structure down there."

"Okay, but that would mean—"

"There are potentially dozens more relics out there," Jesse finished. "If you read a little further, you'll see the information about them."

"Why did you say it like that?" I couldn't miss the way she made it sound like there was more to know.

She only smiled mischievously in response.

I flipped the pages and discovered more information beyond the seven medallions of the guardians.

I scanned some of the text and found all sorts of different artifacts, each with its own unique power.

How I'd never heard of any of this as a fervent student of history was shocking. Sure, I'd heard the theories before about the ancient gods being men and women of might, extraordinary people that the commoners could only see as higher powers. Religions, of course, took that ball and ran with it.

"What were you going to mention earlier?" Jack asked.

I sighed. "I don't know. I just think it's interesting. You two are here, both with these extremely rare books, both containing information that I would have called fiction one week ago. And you're both here, in the city of Nashville."

"So?" they both said in tandem.

"So, isn't it also interesting that we're here in the very city where a scale replica of the Parthenon was built?"

The other two looked at each other with wide eyes as the realization set in.

"Dude," Jack said. "I never even considered that."

"Yeah, but that was built in 1897 for the centennial exposition," Jesse pointed out.

"Sure," I agreed. "And I know it was to honor what was considered to be the height of classical architecture. That doesn't change the fact that it seems a little strange they would go to such lengths and to give so much detail. I mean, have you been there?"

They both nodded.

"The plaster sculptures were done from the originals. And the forty-foot-high statue of the goddess Athena? Why was that necessary?"

"They were trying to replicate what it might have looked like in its prime," Jack explained.

"Fine. But that's a lot of detail, and a ton of expense. I know it's been there for over a hundred years and is a museum, not to mention a centerpiece of the park. But it all seems overdone."

"What are you getting at, Gideon?"

I looked at one, then the other. "What if that temple isn't a replica at all? What if it was designed to hold something powerful?'

"Like one of those relics?" Jesse asked.

"Sure. Or another book. Who knows?"

I could see the hypothesis had crawled into their brains and wasn't coming out anytime soon.

"I think you just blew my mind," Jack admitted. "But if it really is a vault for some of these relics of power, how do we find them?"

"Not sure," I allowed. "But it's at the very least something worth looking into. Right?"

They glanced at each other, then nodded together.

"Yeah, I mean, at this point I would say everything is on the table," Jesse joked. "What do you think we should do first?"

I looked at the clock on the wall and realized how late it was getting. "We should get some rest. It's been a long day. I know you two must be tired."

"I'm usually up pretty late, so this is kind of my normal time," Jesse said.

I could tell it wasn't Jack's typical hours. "I don't want to rope you into something here, Jesse. Seriously, if you don't want to have anything to—"

"Um, you're looking at my book of relics," she interrupted. "I've been waiting for this my entire life.'

"Yeah, but this could get really dangerous."

"He's right," Jack agreed. "Those guys shooting up my shop earlier were no joke."

"You seemed to handle them just fine," she argued.

"The beast handled them," I countered. "Not sure I could have taken them out in human form. Which I don't have when it's daylight."

"Oh, so like a vampire," she offered. "Except the daylight doesn't hurt you, does it?"

"No. And I don't need blood to survive." I didn't think telling her about how the blood of the wicked making me more powerful was a good idea at the time.

"Well, you boys get some rest. I'll make breakfast in the morning, and we can figure out what to do first. I have another stream to do until one-thirty before I hit the sack."

"Okay," I said.

"I'll show you to the bedrooms in the house. Make yourselves at home."

Home. The thought of my home in the Gulch seemed like an unfamiliar place now. My things were there. I had some memories there, mostly with Amy. But it didn't feel like home anymore. Rather, it seemed like a place I'd spent several nights and nothing more. Gone was the sense of belonging or pride that I'd once attached to it.

I didn't need that home. I could live anywhere. Go anywhere. Be anyone. Little did I know that was going to be more necessary than I could have anticipated.

16

S leeping with these new powers had become something of a chore. Not that I'd ever really gotten a ton of sleep. Anxiety kept me up until late in the night, and then the insomnia kicked in.

Tonight was different in that I was simply worn out. So, when I lay down in the bed after getting a quick shower, I managed to fall asleep quicker than I had in recent memory.

That didn't stop me from waking up at the sound of voices in radios at three o'clock in the morning.

At first, I thought I'd imagined it. I had a friend in Chattanooga who said he heard voices at night, but only in his bedroom while sitting in his bed or lying down before going to sleep. He'd explained that the voices weren't in his head—so it was just me, then—and that they sounded like several people having a casual conversation as they would in a bar or at a restaurant.

I always thought he was crazy until his wife confirmed she'd heard the same thing.

Neither one of them believed in ghosts, but we couldn't come up with a hypothesis that made sense.

In my case, tonight, the voices most certainly weren't the ones in my head. Not the ones I was getting used to, anyway.

The voice of Xolotl still nagged at me now and then but typically seemed to leave me alone most of the time.

These voices, the ones I heard with a slight crackle, were definitely real. And they sounded like they were coming from outside the house.

My first thought was to make sure Jesse was safe. But she was in the pool house about fifty yards away from the basement door.

"Stay right where you are," a voice said. "Wait until they try to leave the house."

"Are you sure, sir?" The second voice sounded clearer.

I rolled out of the bed and landed on my tiptoes, suddenly aware that someone was outside.

"Did you hear what they did down in the city earlier tonight?"

"Yes, sir. I—"

"Then keep your butts right there and wait until they try to leave. Is that clear?"

"Yes, sir."

"Good."

My super-hearing made the conversation almost easy to hear, except for the little issue that there was apparently another hit squad sitting outside in the driveway waiting to take us out.

"The second they emerge from the house, take them down," the leader said.

I sighed. "Great. Now I've brought Jesse into this."

I padded to the door and eased it open, as if the creaking hinges could signal the men outside that I was awake.

At the bookstore, I'd had no choice in the battle that took place. The men surrounding the shop opened fire. We were lucky Jack escaped unscathed, even if his inventory didn't. Now, however, Jesse could be thrown into the line of fire. I didn't need additional guilt piling up.

We needed to get out of there.

I made my way down the hall to the next bedroom, where Jack slept, and pushed open the door.

To my surprise, he popped up immediately and brandished a 9mm Springfield pistol.

"Whoa," I said, keeping my voice down. "Light sleeper?"

"Gideon?" he asked in the darkness, his silhouette illuminated by the streetlights outside filtering through gray curtains over the headboard.

"Yeah. It's me."

"You scared the crap out of me."

"Do you always sleep with that thing?" I asked.

"Not usually," he admitted. "But I figured with what happened earlier tonight, better safe than sorry."

"You get any sleep at all, or you just been sitting there cuddling your gun?"

He laughed and set the weapon on the nightstand. "Yeah, I slept some. Off and on. Kind of rattled after everything that happened. You know?"

I nodded. Man, did I.

"Well, I'm glad you're up. Because we have company."

He frowned and grabbed the gun again.

"Relax," I said, putting my hands out as if to settle him down. "I have a plan."

"Where's Jess?"

"Still in the pool house, I assume. But I think they have the place surrounded. At least the way to the street."

"How do you know?" He slung his legs over the bedside and planted his feet on the floor.

"Because I heard them talking through their radios. They're going to wait for us to try to leave in the morning. Then they'll attack."

"Attack? Here? In a subdivision like this? That's a lot of eyeballs to see a bunch of SWAT-looking guys opening fire on a house. No way it wouldn't make the news."

He made a good point. But that didn't change anything. "I know what I heard," I insisted. "I don't know why they aren't coming in the house."

"Maybe because they don't have a warrant or probable cause?"

He looked at me with more questions than answers in his eyes.

"Do you even know how those things work, or are you just going by what you've seen on television?"

It was a serious question.

"Maybe both?"

I shook my head. "Doesn't matter. We need to get you and Jesse out of here."

"Okay, but how are we going to do that? And I want to stay with you." He tried to give me a look that said he wouldn't budge on this issue, but I also knew I had the final say.

"You have to stay with Jesse. I need you to get her out of here. Take her somewhere safe."

"I thought this was somewhere safe. Looks like I was wrong." Jack hung his head.

"Don't sweat it, pal. We'll get you guys out of here."

"What about you?"

I didn't know what was going to happen after we split up. I liked to have a plan, and right now the plan didn't have a defined end point.

"I'll call you when I lose them," I said.

"You sure?"

"Yep. But I'm going to need your keys."

A pained expression cascaded over his face. "Aw, man. Not my truck."

"I'm going to leave in your truck and make it look like we're trying to get away. Once I'm gone, you two take one of Jesse's cars and get out of here."

"Which way should we go?"

"Head southwest."

"Any directions other than that?"

"No. I was just going to let you figure it out on your own." After the sarcastic response, I gave him the rest of the instructions on how to find the only place I could think of that might offer a little safety.

My friend Mike owned a farm in the foothills. It was a spectacular spot, and he'd offered the chance for me to build a cabin there close to his if I wanted. He was never there anymore, and leased the thirty acres to a local farmer who grew cotton. While it wasn't as prominent in Tennessee as in other Southern states, cotton was a hardy crop that always turned a profit.

"Will Mike be there?" Jack asked.

"I doubt it. And if he is, tell him I sent you. He'll be fine. And if he isn't there, you'll find a key under a rock in the back next to steps leading up to the deck."

"You sure about this?" He sighed and fished the keys out of his jeans as he slipped them on.

"It's the only way, Jack. Also, thanks for putting on some pants," I snipped.

He shook his head. "You're an idiot."

I smiled back at him, and he reflected the sentiment, then tossed the keys to me.

"Try not to scratch it."

"I make no promises, my friend. But I'll do my best. Keep your phone on. I'll be in touch."

He flapped his lips and followed me down the hall. I spotted Jesse's car keys hanging on the wall by the stairs and took them. "Here," I said, handing him her keys.

He took them and nodded.

We descended the stairs into the basement. When we reached the bottom, Jack walked over to Jesse's Toyota 4Runner and climbed in.

There were no goodbyes. No other words.

Instead, I eased the door open and snuck outside. I froze and listened in the cool stillness of the early morning. I heard a litany of sounds but nothing that clued me into the assassins' positions.

I clutched the keys in my hand and kept low as I skirted the perimeter of the house, keeping close to the wall and the shadows.

At the corner, I stopped and looked around. No sign of them yet.

Wait. I spotted one of the men across a side lawn crouching behind a pine tree. I turned my head and saw three more huddled behind a cluster of large azaleas. Without the red mist wrapping around them, seeing them would have been more difficult.

Well, so much for hoping I was just hearing things.

I took a breath then sprinted to the pickup truck.

I heard the men shouting orders, and immediately, red dots appeared on the wall to my right as I circled the front of the truck and reached for the door handle.

The first bullet struck me in the right shoulder as I climbed in. I growled at the pain but kept my composure and willed myself not to mutate into the beast. I did not want to try driving my buddy's truck in the form of the Chupacabra. I didn't even know if I would be able to fit in the cab if the transformation happened.

I ignored the round in my shoulder and let my body take care of purging it. I shoved the key into the ignition and started the engine. More bullets came now, without the usual loud sounds that accompanied gunfire.

These guys had suppressors, just like the others I'd run into. The neighbors wouldn't hear a thing thanks to those silencers, but I heard them. The clicks had become an all-too-familiar sound thanks to my new hearing.

More bullets sprayed at the truck, and I heard them striking the tailgate as I shifted into reverse and stepped on the gas.

The vehicle surged backward.

I slung my shoulder over the headrest and looked backward, guiding the truck toward one of the silhouettes I saw by the pine tree.

The gunman stepped out from his cover and continued firing. A round pierced the back window and exited through the front with a crack. Another bullet snapped right by my face, but I didn't slow down.

The shooter waited until the last second before attempting to dive to his right. I knew he would go one way or the other, and guessed it would be in that direction.

I jerked the wheel as he leaped.

A muted scream was cut off when the back tire hit the man's body with a thud. The truck bounced over him a second time with the front left tire, and I cut the steering wheel to the right, sliding the truck around to face the road.

Then I shifted into gear and accelerated away from the house.

The gunmen continued firing wildly at me. A few of the rounds pinged off the tailgate again. Thankfully, none of them hit the tires. Or me.

I'd always wondered about that—bullets hitting car tires and how accurately that was portrayed in movies.

I had no idea, but if these guys were aiming for them, they were either inaccurate or ineffective.

As I reached the street, I saw the black GMC Yukons parked on the other side of the asphalt and knew this was far from over.

In the rearview mirror, I glimpsed the gunmen who surrounded the house sprint to their vehicles, while headlights in one of the SUVs switched on.

At least one of the men, probably more inside some of the vehicles, had stayed back just in case something like this happened.

"At least they're prepared," I muttered, annoyed, and steered the truck away from the house and away from the city. I didn't like the idea of taking this onto country back roads, but I'd much rather do that and prevent collateral damage to innocent bystanders or people's homes.

The SUV with the lights on spun around in a U-turn and followed, and after a few moments the other men hurried to their trucks.

I took one last glance back toward the pool house, knowing my friend was going to give Jesse a rude awakening, but an awakening that might save her life.

Then the house disappeared as I drove over a small rise in the road.

I tightened my grip on the wheel, steeling my nerves both against the threat behind me and the one within.

17

The truck engine groaned.

I accelerated up and over the next hill in the seemingly never-ending line of rolling ups and downs.

Every time one of the SUVs behind me went up over a crest, their headlight beams flashed into the night and then dove back toward the asphalt.

I had a slight head start, but they had faster vehicles than Jack's truck. She wasn't much to look at, but she still had it where it counted in that the motor still worked, and it could go fast enough to keep the pursuers at bay until we reached the plains in the countryside. Sooner or later, we'd reach farmlands where the roads were flatter and had fewer curves. When that happened—in a matter of minutes —the lumbering SUVs would be able to speed up, and there was nothing I could do to stop them from catching up.

Avoiding them altogether wasn't my main objective anyway. I was just the diversion, a way to get Jack and Jesse out of the house safely and down to Mikey's farm.

With every driveway I saw coming up ahead, I looked closely for a turnoff—anywhere I could get off the road and maybe lose these guys in a field or something.

No such luck.

The driveways got fewer and farther between, and none of them were vacant. I didn't want to pull into someone's home with a bunch of gun-toting psychopaths chasing me. That was the opposite of what I wanted to do, and what I was meant to do.

The thought flashed the ambush through my head. The four men I'd seen were all surrounded with mist, and from what I could tell, there weren't any others left at the house once I was gone. I hoped that was the case, but there was no way to know for certain.

After zooming over another hill, the road in front of me straightened out into a long, flat stretch. I knew another town was ten miles ahead, but I might not make it there. I'd need to lose these guys before I got there, or I would have to come up with another plan.

Just as I suspected, the SUVs started closing in even though my foot had the pedal jammed against the floor.

The speedometer climbed slowly. The engine roared, and I sensed it was maxing out around ninety. Somewhere near the rear of her old chassis, the truck started to shimmy ever so slightly—on a straightaway. A bad sign of what was to come.

That wasn't going to be fast enough.

I looked back in the mirror and saw the enemy SUVs closing in with every second.

I was running out of time, but my objective had been a success. I hoped.

The SUV in the lead behind me narrowed the gap to a hundred yards.

There was nothing I could do. Or was there?

I looked around the cab of the truck, knowing my friend wasn't going to like what I was about to do.

"Sorry, old girl," I said. "This is going to hurt you more than it hurts me."

I patted the steering wheel, braced myself, then feathered the brakes.

The truck decelerated rapidly, throwing my head forward with the momentum. Once I was outside the risk of losing control, I slammed on the brakes and screeched the truck to a stop right there in the middle of the lane.

The SUVs screamed toward me now. I saw a flash from a muzzle and shifted into reverse, then stepped on the gas again.

A car crash, while painful, wouldn't kill me unless somehow one of the other vehicles happened to take my head off.

While that wasn't outside the realm of possibility, it seemed unlikely.

I guided the truck right at the first SUV, which closed in on me fast.

The gunman propped in the passenger's side window fired over and over again, but at that range and speed, accuracy was at a premium.

The driver in the lead vehicle swerved at the last second, losing the game of chicken as he veered hard to the left. He lost control of the SUV and tried to overcorrect, which sent the truck fishtailing back and forth until the tires caught and flipped it into the air. The SUV tumbled down ahead of me, but I kept my eyes backward, steering deliberately toward the next of three more SUVs.

The driver of the second slowed down and narrowly avoided hitting me. The third did as well, deftly swinging their truck onto the side of the road to turn around.

But the fourth wasn't so lucky.

One of the gunmen popped out of the side window and started shooting. To my surprise, one of the rounds punctured the back window, finishing the job all the other bullets had started.

The glass crumbled and fell into the truck bed or into the back seat.

Wind blew through the cab, ruffling my hair and forcing me to narrow my eyelids to see clearly.

But I could see, and I steered directly toward the last SUV.

The gunman emptied his magazine as the oncoming pickup truck barreled toward them. The driver ducked to the left, then the right, but I managed to control my aim, even though doing it backward was much harder.

The guy leaning out of the window ducked back in at the last second, but it wouldn't save him.

I opened the door and dove out just before the pickup rammed into the SUV's grill with terrible force. The sounds of metal and glass crunching filled my ears as I rolled on the ground. It only hurt for a second where the asphalt ripped away layers of my skin.

Then an explosion rocked the night, filling the darkness with bright orange light.

The SUV erupted along with Jack's truck, engulfing both vehicles in a fiery ball. The assassins must have hit the gas tank when they collided with the pickup.

I heard the other vehicles turning around down the road. I grinned and allowed the transformation to take place.

By the time the two remaining SUVs arrived at the burning wreckage, it was a roaring barbecue, dumping black smoke into the dark night.

The drivers parked their trucks in the middle of the road, and one of the men in the back noticed me the second he got out.

I lay there, pretending to be dead, fully planning on their curiosity being their undoing.

"Hey!" the guys shouted at the others. "Over here. What is that?"

He pointed a flashlight on me.

One of the other guys noticed my strange figure. "It looks like some kind of dog-man."

"It's just roadkill," another said.

"I don't think so. Get over here and check it out."

I figured the first guy speaking must have been the one in charge of their little hit squad.

Eight men approached me with their guns held low, every one of them pointing right at me.

"It's some kind of dog," one of them offered.

"I ain't never seen a dog like that before," the second argued.

"And yet here we are."

They surrounded me, each with their weapons aimed at my head and body.

"Is it dead?" one of them asked.

The leader stepped closer, then nodded to the third speaker. "Check it out."

"What? Why me? He looks dead."

The guy's protests did nothing to change the leader's mind.

"Just check it already. Hurry up."

"Okay. Fine."

The goon took a step forward and poked me in the ribs with the tip of his boot. He did it a second time and received the same reaction from me—none.

The gunman lowered his weapon and looked back to the leader. "Whatever it is. It's dead."

The others relaxed, each lowering their guns, too.

The one who'd poked me looked back down and froze as if noticing something he hadn't seen before.

He bent closer, leaning in until I could almost smell the fear wafting from his nostrils.

"What the—"

Then I blinked. And I let him see it.

"Oh sh—"

The killer never got a chance to finish his exclamation. I thrust my clawed paw up and through his neck.

He turned, just as he fired his weapon, and the bullet found its way through one of his partner's eyes.

That was fortunate, I thought.

Then I sprang to my feet to finish off the other six.

I spun and lunged for the next guard who tried to back away while taking two shots. The first one inexplicably missed. The other barely caught my shoulder, which only made me angrier.

I grabbed the gun and twisted it around, breaking the shooter's hand in the process. He yelled out in pain. I slipped behind him with a quick slide motion, then aimed the weapon at his friends.

"Guys?" the hostage said, suddenly aware that his five teammates were pointing their guns right at him.

"Whether they kill you or I do," I growled so only he could hear, "I'd make my peace with God right now."

His whimper was the last sound he made before I pulled the trigger. The first shot took out a gunman to the left, drilling a hole through the center of his chest. I turned to fire at the next, but the remaining assassins opened fire, pouring hot rounds into my hostage and obliterating his vital organs.

The body shook and gyrated with every bullet that bored into his flesh. I returned fire, taking out another gunman with a shot to the gut, and then turned to the next. The bloody body in my arms grew abruptly heavy, and the sudden sinking movement caused my next shot to miss, but only slightly. The round struck my target in the pelvis. The man howled in agony and dropped to one knee, then fell over on his side.

The men beside him ran out of ammo. That fact made me smile. It must have been a terrifying thing to behold.

I threw the body at the first guy to the right, then leaped at the one on the far left. My jaws snapped, sinking fangs into his neck before he could so much as whimper. I dropped him to the ground to let the mist have its fare, then moved to the next. This one tried to draw a knife on me.

To his credit, the blade looked like a miniature sword. The thing had to be eight or nine inches long and a few inches wide.

He lunged toward me in a heroic and ultimately foolish attack. I merely watched him with rapt curiosity as he plunged the knife into my abdomen.

I winced at the pain, but I allowed it without defense. He held the handle tight and twisted it, probably thinking he had just finished the job.

I sighed and shook my head. He looked into my eyes, his full of terror. Then I ripped the blade from my gut, grabbed him by the back of the skull, and shoved the knife up through his chin.

The second the metal cut into brain matter, his body instantly went limp, and I let him fall.

One of the two men left finished loading his pistol and raised it to fire. I jerked the knife from the dead man on the ground and whirled on the next gunman, flinging the blade through the air.

It struck him in the neck and protruded out the back.

The remaining assassin I'd hit with the bloody body of his comrade had managed to scramble to his feet and took off toward his SUV.

I watched him run, letting the guy have a head start. It was only sporting, I figured.

When he was halfway to his ride, about thirty yards away, I took off at a sprint. I moved in a blur through the darkness and circled around to the driver's side of the vehicle before the gunman could even notice.

He kept looking back toward where all his men lay dead on the side of the road.

When he rounded the front of the truck, the shock on his face was priceless.

"That's impossible," he uttered, raising his weapon.

"I used to think that way, too," I growled. "Not anymore." I took a menacing step toward him.

He continued to brandish the pistol, which I found adorable.

"You realize that thing isn't going to do much to me, right? I mean, if I had a peso for every time I'd been shot in the last week, I could buy a hotel in Cancun."

The killer breathed hard from the run. Probably a little from staring into the eyes of a monster he'd just seen take out his entire team like they were rag dolls.

"Your bullets won't kill me, son," I said. "Unless you want to end up like your pals over there"—I nodded sideways in the general direction of the bodies—"I suggest you tell me what I want to know."

He continued breathing hard, but I could see the conflict in his eyes.

"What do you want to know?"

"That's better." I tried to look nonthreatening, but I knew that had a snowball's chance in Hades. "Tell me who hired you."

He inclined his head, and I knew he was going to resist.

"Don't do that," I cautioned. "Don't think about it. Just tell me."

"You'll let me live?"

"I'll consider it."

"I need your word."

"I can't do that." I lowered my head, keeping my eyes locked with his.

"I don't want to die," he whined, shaking his head dramatically.

"Well, you're going to. Eventually." I paused between words to make him sweat a little more. Instead, I think he might have pissed himself a little.

He kept shaking his head. "I have a girlfriend," he said. "She's pregnant. I didn't even want this mission. I'm done in three days. I thought maybe I might get off easy, but then I got the call for... this."

Something strange happened as he offered his confession. The red mist swirling around him began to fade, as if swept away on the breeze. Within seconds, it was gone entirely.

"What the—?" I blurted unintentionally.

"What?" he asked, confused.

"Nothing." In my head, the voice didn't tell me what was going on. *Anytime you want to help me out with this one, Xolotl, I'm all ears.* Still, no answer came.

I could only take it for what I saw.

I inhaled a deep breath and then exhaled as I spoke. "Tell me who you work for, and I will let you live."

"Thank y—"

"Only if you answer another question first. You said you took the call for this mission. What mission? Is this some kind of government agency?"

He faltered, still holding the gun. Though his grip had weakened and his hand shook.

Bewilderment drained the color from his face, what little there was left.

The conflict in his expression drew his jaws downward. Gravity pulled on his cheeks and eyes, and I knew that whatever he was about to tell me could get him killed just as easily as me killing him for not saying a thing.

"I work for the Sector," he said, and left it at that.

"Am I supposed to know what that is?"

"No." He cussed. "I can't believe I'm talking to a real-life monster."

I closed my eyes for a second and allowed my form to change back to human. He watched, simply mesmerized by the act.

"Is that better?"

"Yeah," he said. "That's weird how your clothes change like that."

I looked down at the garments. "Yeah, I'm still trying to figure out how to make it work with a T-shirt and jeans."

He responded with a careful laugh.

"You're not supposed to know what the Sector is. They work in secret, out of sight from the government."

"Privately funded?" This was getting interesting.

"I don't know. Honest. I just got the call. I'm a Marine. Spent a few years overseas in the Middle East, then came back home and got a call from the Sector. They made me an offer I couldn't refuse."

"Lot of money, huh?"

"Life changing," was all he said in agreement.

Interesting. We're dealing with a privately owned clandestine organization with death squads on its payroll.

"Can you tell me how to find them?" I ventured.

He snorted in derision, shaking his head while he looked down at the pavement. "No. They don't have a headquarters like Langley."

"No headquarters?"

"Not that I ever heard. They move around. One week, HQ might be in New York City. The next, it could be in Charlotte. You never know. Least, that's what the other guys said. I've never actually seen the ones in charge. Only heard the rumors."

Fascinating. And scary.

I still had a couple of questions, and I couldn't let this treasure trove of information go before I had answers.

"So, there's no way to find them, the people running the Sector?"

"If I knew, I would tell you. Okay? I just want to go home to my girlfriend. We're getting married next week." Tears brimmed in his eyes, and I felt my heart being pulled by invisible strings.

It spoke volumes that this hardened warrior—a Marine at that— was showing such vulnerability.

"You can't find them," he continued. "But they'll find you. No one can hide from the Sector."

"I'm not trying to hide," I said. "But they sure are."

"I guess they're afraid the government would shut them down if they found out where the board of directors are," he hypothesized. "The things we've done, I believed they were just. You know?"

I nodded. Up until this week, I might have agreed, but I wouldn't have really known. Not like I did right then, talking to a guy who'd been trying to kill me just minutes before.

He shook his head. "Every order I ever followed... I believed it was for the greater good. Now, I don't know anymore."

The next question had been beating my brain in like a hammer since I saw the red mist disappear around this guy. I had to ask.

"Did you have a change of heart?" I asked.

"What?"

I twisted my head at an angle, feigning irritation. "That's a strange answer. It's a yes-or-no question." That didn't clear up anything, so I repeated. "Did you have a change of heart. You came here to kill me and my friends. Now, you seem different. So, did you have a change of heart, or not?"

He looked lost, but in his eyes, I saw the truth. "I don't know," he said honestly. "Maybe. You mean about the military?"

"No," I corrected. "Tonight. Just now." He still looked puzzled, so I elaborated. "You are the only one who's seen the monster and survived. So, I'm going to trust you with this." I met his gaze and held it tight. "I have been sent to kill the wicked. I know who is wicked because a red fog forms around them. It's sort of a mark."

"Red fog?"

I nodded while he looked around at his feet and hands.

"No one else can see it. Only me. You had the mist around you earlier. But when I ambushed you here, at the car, it disappeared. So,

I want to know what you thought the moment I was about to kill you."

He wrinkled his brow, lowering his head to think. Then he raised his eyes and met my stare. "All I could think of was being there for my future wife, my future kid. I don't even know if it's a boy or a girl yet, but I thought about how much I want to be there for them. I don't want them to go through life without me in it."

I tilted my head back, assessing him. Then I slowly nodded. "That's an unselfish kind of love. The greatest form of it, actually, aside from laying down your life to save another."

I got the feeling he might have done that when he was in the Corps.

"You may go," I said, bowing my head. "Go back to your life. If the Sector will allow it."

He didn't look like he believed me. "So, you're just going to let me go?"

"You no longer have the red mist," I said. "I am not permitted to kill you. Nor do I want to." I took a step closer and allowed the power within me to focus in my eyes. I didn't have to see the reflection in his to know that they were burning red. "But know this: If you return to evil, and the mist finds you again—so will I."

The look of relief and terror on his face was priceless.

"Now, go." I motioned down the road toward the city. The lights of downtown Nashville radiated into the night sky, blotting out some of the dimmer stars.

"On foot?" he asked.

"I don't recommend taking one of the company cars," I said. "Better if you tell your supervisors you escaped on foot and barely made it out with your life."

He nodded, resigned to the long hike back into town. He could get a ride there, and a young, fit guy like him would have no trouble making the journey. He'd run farther than that with a heavy pack on his back in the Corps.

The guy turned and started down the road, then he stopped and turned around. "My name is Gareth," he said. "Gareth Tiller."

"Good to know the name of a new ally," I said.

He understood immediately. By sparing his life, I'd made a friend. And right now, friends were in short supply.

"Thank you, Gideon," he said. Then turned and walked into the night.

I watched him until the headlight beams no longer sprayed across his back. Then I climbed into the SUV and closed the door.

He knew my name, which didn't surprise me. I was the target. What I didn't know was how his Sector group knew who I was, and potentially *what* I was.

18

I slowed down when I saw Mike's driveway up ahead. The gravel road ran between a wooden fence that stretched all the way up over the next rise in the road and another two hundred yards in the other direction until the property ran into a creek.

Mike's white farmhouse stood at the top of a knoll in the dead center of the thirty-acre property. The cotton fields were behind a tree line, keeping them separate from grass fields with maple, oak, hemlock, and spruce trees dotting the hillside.

I turned into the winding driveway and drove slowly up the hill. Relief sucked anxiety out of my chest at the sight of Jesse's truck outside the guest house.

"They made it," I said.

At the top of the hill, I parked next to the truck and climbed out into the cool early morning air.

I imagined my friends would be asleep. I should have been tired. Way more than I felt.

Too many things kept running through my head. Memories, theories, and where we needed to go next were battling it out in my brain, and I couldn't lock it down on just one.

I looked at the farmhouse and sighed. I didn't need to bring them into this. Jack, Jesse, Mikey... They hadn't asked for this.

A light switched on in the farmhouse, and a second later the front door opened. A bright glow spilled into the night, silhouetted by the hulking figure that was my friend Mike.

I walked toward him. He stood there waiting until I was near the steps before speaking.

"You know they say nothing good ever happens after one in the morning." He glared at me in disapproval.

I frowned and blew it off. "Okay, Dad," I replied.

He remained stoic for another few seconds before the tough exterior broke with a smile. "What are you doing out so late, man? Jack was pretty sketchy on the details." He walked down the steps to meet me on the ground. "And what is with your outfit?" He grabbed my sleeve and pulled on it. "Really lightweight."

"Yeah, I need to get some normal clothes on."

"These were normal. About five or six hundred years ago, I guess." He laughed at his joke.

I couldn't help it. I did too.

"They asleep in the bunkhouse?" I asked. It was hardly a bunkhouse. The place was more like a carriage home in an upscale neighborhood. It had two stories, a two-car garage, and eight hundred square feet of living space. The building looked like a miniature replica of the farmhouse, with white exterior panels and black roofing, windows, and doors.

"Yeah. Jack is sleeping on the sofa bed. His friend took the main bed upstairs." He looked at the house and huffed. "She's a bit of a firecracker, that one."

My head bobbed. "Yeah, you got that right. I pity Jack."

"They together?" He looked surprised when he asked the question.

"Jack wishes."

"Hmm. Well, maybe it'll work out for him. She might be a little different, but she seems cool."

"Indeed." I felt my eyes locking on the door and pulled them back to focus on my friend.

"Come on in, I have a bed ready for you in the guest room."

Mike's farmhouse was a large two-story structure that looked out over his acreage and two neighboring ones across the road. He'd made a bunch of money with a startup in Nashville, and when he sold, had decided to buy a farm and live the quiet life.

He wasn't a real farmer. And Mike knew that. Agriculture was about as far from his expertise as the sun from Pluto.

But he was learning. Mike believed in developing Old World skills, like woodworking, growing food, and learning how to be self-sustained. Based on the way things were going in much of society—with everyone seemingly at each other's throats politically and socially—I couldn't say he was foolish for doing all that.

In fact, I felt like he might have been ahead of the curve.

"I'm not staying the night, Mike," I informed.

"What?" He looked down the hill at the road. "Where you gonna go at this time?"

I knew going back to my place was a bad idea, but I figured if the Sector was watching it, or the Division Three guys I'd met before, maybe me showing up early in the morning might draw them out.

"Home," I said.

"You sure that's a good idea? Jack didn't say much, but he told me that some people were after you. Said you led them away as a diversion so he and Jesse could escape. That's mighty brave of you."

I lowered my head, embarrassed. "Not so brave as you might think."

He tried to pry the truth from me with a chiseled stare but couldn't get it.

"I can't tell you all the details right now, Mike. But I will. Promise. You're a good friend. And I appreciate you taking care of Jack and Jesse." I said the words like Mike was twenty years older. He was the same age as me and Jack. Just more responsible, at least in appearance and demeanor.

He exhaled through his nose. A stern look on his face continued to show disapproval. "Sounds like you got yourself into some kind of trouble."

"I guess," I said with a half laugh.

"You need some help? An attorney?"

"Maybe," I conceded. "But right now, I don't need that kind of help."

"What then?" he pushed.

"Amy was killed by the cartel in Mexico," I blurted. The words came faster than intended, but it seemed like I had to personally inform everyone of what happened, and it was getting old. I wanted to fast-forward to the part of my life where I didn't have to tell anyone anymore.

That day seemed far away.

"I'm sorry." And he meant it. "I didn't know, Gideon. I've been out of the loop lately. That's awful."

"Yeah. It was." I looked out into the sky and the moon looming over the hills to the west. "I don't care to rehash it all right now if that's okay. Amy's parents blame me. Her father tried to kill me earlier tonight."

"What? Are you serious?" He inched closer as if proximity would extract the truth.

"Yeah. I'm serious. And the guys he had with him were cartel guys. They had the same tats as the ones who killed Amy."

"Come on," Mike said with a last glance out across the country-side. "Let's get you inside. I'll make some coffee. You don't have to stay here, but—"

"No," I insisted. "It's late. You go back to bed. You have a busy life."

He laughed at that. "Gideon, I sold a multimillion-dollar company and bought a farm that I work on on my own time. I can wake up whenever I want."

Coffee did sound good.

I followed him into the kitchen, where he went about preparing the coffeemaker, ground the beans, and poured a pitcher of filtered water into the reservoir.

I sat at a wooden farm table in the center of the kitchen, watching him do his thing.

"So," Mike said when the coffee pot was dripping and the smell of fresh java began to waft through the house, "why would Amy's dad be in with the cartel? Doesn't seem believable."

"That's what I thought," I agreed. "But it happened."

"How did you get away?"

I froze for a second. Mike wasn't ready to hear everything Jesse and Jack knew. They were different. Jack had lived it firsthand. And Jesse was weird enough to believe it from the moment I met her.

"Lucky, I guess. I didn't have time to call the cops. Anyway, I know I can't trust him now."

Mike mulled over the information before speaking again. "You think he blames you for killing her?"

"I don't think it. I know. He said as much to me before he tried to shoot me." I almost slipped and said "before he shot me." A bullet figuratively dodged even though I didn't dodge the actual bullet.

"That's messed up." He focused on the table surface for a few seconds, then raised his eyes. Looking straight through me, he asked "What are you going to do? I know you didn't kill her."

"Thanks for that," I said. "Unfortunately, the feds think I did it. Jerry thinks so, which means so does her mother. But I didn't do it. I had to watch while Carrillo's men executed her. I can't say anything else, Mike, so don't ask. Okay? I'm not being weird about this. I just don't want to talk about it anymore."

"Okay, Gideon. Okay. I understand."

If only you did.

"I have a few leads I need to look into. One of them is Vernon Wells."

His eyebrows dipped. "What? You mean the television preacher with that huge church in town?"

"Yep," I said with a nod.

"What's he got to do with any of this?"

The coffee pot beeped suddenly, startling both of us.

Mike walked over to the cupboard, picked out two white mugs, and filled them three-quarters of the way to the top. He brought the coffee over and set the cups down on the table, sliding mine close.

"Thanks," I said, raising the mug to smell the fresh brew.

"No problem, compadre," he replied, raising the mug.

"I have no idea what the reverend has to do with Amy's murder, the cartel goons working with Jerry, or any of it. Call it a hunch."

He arched one eyebrow, unconvinced. "That's a pretty big hunch you're going with."

"I have insider information." That was all I'd give him.

"How do you—"

"I just need you to trust me on this one, Mikey. Okay?"

"Okay, Gideon. Okay. I trust you."

I picked up the coffee and took a long sip. "This is really good," I said, not realizing how much I actually wanted a cup.

"Local roaster here in town. Some good ones in the city, too, but I don't like to venture over that way too often. Too many tourists now, all wanting to see the honky-tonks."

"I hear you on that." My mind was stuck on Vernon Wells. "Has Wells ever gotten into any trouble with the media or the police?"

"Funny how you said media first. Seems like everyone's more afraid of them than the law these days."

"No kidding."

My friend shrugged. "I haven't heard anything bad about him. As far as I know, he's squeaky clean."

"No one is perfect," I countered. "Everyone has their hidden sins."

"That from the Bible?"

"Probably. Seems right."

He snorted a quick laugh, incredulous. "What are your secret sins, Gideon Wolf?"

If only he knew.

"That's between me and the Almighty." I offered a smug, *mind your business* look with the statement.

"Fair enough," he laughed. "It'll be hard to get to Wells. He's a busy man. Always doing charitable work or preaching. And his security entourage is always around."

"Security?" That caught my attention. "What kind of preacher needs a security detail?"

"You know how it is," Mike said. He pulled another drink from the mug and eased onto a stool next to me. His untucked flannel shirt draped over his brown belt and jeans. "They get a bunch of money, and all of a sudden everyone is all over them. It's like that with country singers, businesspeople, you name it. Once you hit that level of celebrity, there's no going back to a normal life."

"So, this pastor just walks around in malls and Applebee's with a bunch of Secret Service-looking dudes surrounding him?"

Mike spewed coffee from his lips. Luckily for me, he aimed to his left and I missed the splash zone.

"Jeez, Gideon. That's funny crap right there." Mike laughed hard for nearly a minute. "But I doubt he's going to Applebee's. Not sure you'll find one of those in Brentwood or Franklin, where he likes to hang out."

"What's wrong with Applebee's?"

"Nothing. Just saying, guys like him go to the fancier places."

"Oh." I waited until Mike was taking another drink. "Like Olive Garden."

The timing was perfect, and once more he spit coffee in a mist across the table to his left. "I swear, I'm going to spit it on you the next time," he said amid laughter.

"I won't do it again, then." I lowered my head and let the scent of coffee fill my nostrils. "I need to know where he lives."

Mike shook his head. "You're not going to his home."

He was right. That wasn't a good idea. Not yet, at least.

"No. I suppose not. I don't reckon I could get an appointment to see him in his office."

Mike chuckled. "Probably not."

"There has to be a way I can meet with him."

"What would that do? And why are you after him, anyway? Don't give me that bull about the hunch thing, either. What's going on, Gideon?"

I decided a half-truth was the right move. "I think that he and Jerry are somehow connected."

It wasn't a lie. Jerry working with cartel goons and Wells sending hitters after me, on top of the Sector and whoever those Division Three guys were. All of it was connected in some way. I just needed to figure out how.

Mike assessed my body language. He'd always been good at that, which made him hard to beat at poker. Fortunately, I was almost never on the other side of a table from him.

"If you want to dig up information about Wells, I don't suggest you approach the man."

"What do you have in mind?" I had to admit, my curiosity was piqued.

"I know a guy. He's the head of landscaping for Wells."

"The reverend has a head of landscaping? How big is his property?"

"Huge. Few hundred acres."

"Well, it's not the Dutton Ranch, but yeah, that's significant. How many people he have working there?"

Mike rolled his shoulders. "I think three or four, but my buddy Joey who runs it is full time and on salary."

"Wow." I would never have thought a pastor could pull that kind of coin.

"Okay, so you think your friend Joey will talk to me?"

"You bet. Just wait until the sun is up before you try contacting him. Okay?"

I nodded.

"Now, have you changed your mind about that bed in the guest room?"

I thought about it. Even with the coffee, I was starting to feel the siren call of sleep. "Yeah, maybe."

"What's the hesitation? No one knows you're here. I doubt Jerry had someone follow you."

He was right about that. If he had more goons working for him, there was no sign of them on my journey to the farm. There was no sign of any other cars, actually, once I turned off the interstate. The back country roads out here were lonely and quiet, perfectly suited to Mike's preferences.

"Stay the night. Have some breakfast in the morning, and I'll hook you up with my pal. I don't know if he can tell you anything that might help your little investigation, if that's what this is, but if there's been anything weird going on over at Wells' mansion, he'd have probably seen it."

I nodded, surrendering to the peer pressure. "Okay, Mike. I'll stay. And I appreciate it. Especially taking in Jack and Jesse. I feel bad about bringing them into this."

"Don't worry about them. Jack is always welcome here. He can stay as long as he wants. I heard his shop got torn up pretty bad." Mike took another draw from the mug.

"Yeah. It will be a few months before it's up and running again."

"Well, he'll be fine." Mike stood up and took his mug over to the sink. He rinsed it out and set it on the counter.

"Let me show you to your room, good sir, if you're ready." He talked in a goofy English accent that sounded like he'd combined three regions of the UK into one nearly unintelligible, yet lively, trill. I wondered if he'd slipped a little bourbon into that coffee mug of his.

"Yeah. I'm good." I stood up and took my cup to the sink, rinsed it out, and followed my friend down a hallway to the right.

This investigation was getting weirder by the minute. And now, apparently, I was going to talk to a landscaper about a potentially corrupt pastor who may or may not have been tied to one of the world's most ruthless drug lords.

As I followed Mike down the corridor, I couldn't help but wonder what was coming next.

19

I stopped the SUV at the guardhouse and waited as a security guard exited the little outbuilding. He wore a black windbreaker and matching hat, but unlike most security guards, his hat and jacket didn't have a logo for their company.

I immediately knew that meant this guy, and probably all the others on site, were hired directly by Wells. The other implication of that was that they were probably all former military of some kind.

The guard walked up to the car, and I rolled down my window. He held a tablet—an upgrade from days gone by when a dude like him would have had a clipboard. He looked at me then at the screen. "Name?"

"Actually, I don't have an appointment."

He looked at me like I was nuts. "No appointment, no entry."

"Yes, I know. I'm not here to see Reverend Wells," I said, hoping that my use of the formalized version of the pastor's name would help soften this guy a little.

Instead, he looked more puzzled. "Then who are you here to see?"

"Joey Philbin. Head of landscaping."

When I said that, he seemed to understand. Or at least he thought he did. "You here for a job?"

"Something like that."

He didn't seem to appreciate my curt, vague response, but he tucked the tablet under one arm and pressed a button on a radio attached to his upper left shoulder. "Guardhouse here, anyone see Joey?"

He released the button, and a few seconds later, the speaker crackled. "Roger that. He's in the maintenance shed right now."

The guard spoke into the radio again. "Can you verify if he has someone coming to talk about a job today?" He released the button. "What's your name?"

"Sid. Sid Patterson." I gave him the name Mike and I agreed upon, and the one he'd given Joey.

"Name is Sid Patterson," the guard added into the radio.

I waited patiently, hoping that Joey hadn't had a change of heart. The morning sun hid behind patchy blooms of white clouds lazily traversing the sky. At night, I could have simply killed the guard and broken down the gate with my bare hands. Right now, though, in human form, discretion seemed the more prudent approach.

"Joey says he's clear," the voice in the radio said.

"Looks like you're good to go," the guard informed me.

It was hard not to notice the red mist swirling around his feet—a signal that I was going into the belly of the beast.

The gate parted in the middle and slowly opened.

"Good luck on your job interview," the guard said. "Good place to work. The boss takes care of us here. Head down that way to the left. You'll find the maintenance building by the tree line."

"Thanks. Good to know," I said with a forced smile. He stepped back. I took that as my signal to drive ahead, so I did, passing through the iron gates.

Ahead, up the slight rise at the top of the hill, sat the gargantuan mansion belonging to Vernon Wells.

"So this is what tithe buys?" I said, sarcastically. I knew that wasn't the case with all churches. Probably not most of them. Definitely not with the Good Reverend.

Vernon Wells was reaping the fruits of someone's labor, and I couldn't help but wonder who his patrons might be. Right-wing oligarchs? Holy-warrior elements in the intelligence community? Or maybe "the Spirit" had urged Rev. Vernon Wells to take a humble pilgrimage and soothe his soul amid the faithful in Mexico. I followed the directions and veered to the left, driving down the hill toward a building that looked like it was half barn, half house.

The structure was only one story high, but took up a considerable footprint. Two pickup trucks and an SUV sat outside. Relief trickled through my torso at the sight of a different kind of vehicle than the ones that had attacked me the night before.

There was no way I could be certain that Wells hadn't hired the men who tried to kill me.

I pulled into the gravel parking area next to the maintenance building and got out of the car. The structure had a red wooden exterior with a tin roof. A porch wrapped around the front left quarter of the building. Four white rocking chairs sat under the shade near the entrance.

I closed the car door and walked over to the front. I paused, hearing laugher inside amid some conversation, and then knocked.

Through the glass panes of the door, I saw a man wearing a gray jacket standing inside. Brown cowboy boots covered his feet beneath faded blue jeans. No cowboy hat, though. Only a baseball cap with the words St. Pete Beach on the front. He came over and opened the door with a friendly grin on his face, nearly hidden under a reddish-brown beard that looked like it belonged to a young Santa Claus.

"You must be Sid," the guy said. His brown beard was perfectly manicured, and he looked every bit the part of a dude who spent most of his workdays outdoors. He was a veritable lumberjack, only not super tall as I envisioned them to be.

Still, he was about my height, which was slightly above average. His imposing physique, though, was what made him intimidating. At least to most people. Now, with my newfound power, I didn't feel intimidated by much.

I nodded and looked back over my shoulder. "I'm supposed to be."

He looked at me funny, cocking his head to the side. "What?"

"I'm going to level with you." I motioned to the side of the door and took a step away from it. He looked at me curiously, but followed along and let the door close.

When I knew the others couldn't hear, I spoke again. "I'm not here for a job. And my name isn't Sid. I'm friends with Mike Shepherd. And I'm conducting an investigation. It's an undercover kind of thing so I have to use an alias. I was just wondering if you'd have some time to answer a few questions.

"Questions?" He looked suspicious, and backed away a step like he'd seen a ghost. "Investigation? Am I under arrest?"

"No," I said. If he thought I was a cop, I wasn't going to correct that assumption. Not if it got me what I needed. "You're not in any trouble. But we're concerned your employer could be."

Fear struck Joey across the face. "What do you mean?" The color drained from his skin.

"We've been hearing rumors about suspicious activities going on here. You wouldn't happen to have seen anything suspicious, would you?"

He looked off toward the mansion, his eyes glazing over.

I knew I was being vague because the truth was I didn't have a thing on Wells. Not yet. But if this guy was friends with Mike, he couldn't be all bad. And besides, there was no red mist around him. I was learning what a relief that was, not to see that around people I liked, or who were connected to my little circle.

"Walk with me," he said. "I need to show you some of the things you'll be doing here if we decide to hire you."

I met his poker face stare and knew immediately what he was saying. "That would be great."

Joey led me down the porch steps and around behind the building where a red barn sat next to the wooden fence. He didn't say a word until we arrived at the fence next to the back corner of the building. He put his arm up over the railing and pointed into a rolling, green pasture where a dozen horses grazed.

"I'm going to point and motion around a bit to make it look like

I'm talking about the kind of work we do here. You nod and look serious."

I did.

"I don't know what Mr. Wells is up to," he began. "I know he makes a lot of money from his church. Don't get me wrong. I'm not one of these people who gripes and complains about a pastor getting rich. If that's the way of God blessing his messengers, fine by me. Don't bother me a bit." He pointed back up at the mansion, then around to the maintenance building. "But strange things go on here."

"Strange?" I faced him, but he wouldn't look at me.

"Come on. I'll show you the barn and some of the equipment."

We walked around the front of the barn. He stopped at a big door and slid it open. "All the animals are out to pasture. This is where they sleep and eat. Although they eat all the time, as you can imagine."

I nodded, playing along.

"Yeah. I always heard taking care of horses was an expensive venture."

"You could say that again." He closed the barn door and led me around the corner to where a work ATV sat. The dark green machine had a small cargo bed in the back, like a miniaturized version of a pickup truck. "Hop in. I'll show you some more of the property."

This guy really is paranoid about talking.

He started the engine, and we took off down the gravel path, which transformed into one made of two rows of beaten-down grass. Joey kept the ATV in the ruts and continued driving, pointing out areas of interest on the property and discussing the various chores required to keep the place going.

He stopped at the top of a knoll that gave a sweeping view of the rolling countryside. Joey killed the engine and stepped out of his seat, adjusted his pants, and crossed his arms before speaking.

"I've worked here nine years. Might not seem like a long time. Maybe it does. Once you've cut every blade of grass a few hundred times you start wondering what you're doing with your life, other than surviving."

I joined him near the back of the vehicle. "I suppose so."

He sucked in air through his nose and sighed. "I meant what I said about not knowing what's really going on here. But there's something. I can feel it. Every now and then I go in the house to take care of something or just to get a drink of water. Occasionally, the reverend will have lunch with us, but that's pretty rare. I think he does it to feel more like a man."

We shared a chuckle.

"Softest hands I've ever shaken," Joey added with another laugh. He looked down at the ground. "One night, I was working late, and my truck was parked behind the barn so no one up at the mansion realized I was still here. I'd left it there because we got a delivery that day, and I wanted to give the truck driver enough room to maneuver."

He paused, pressing his lips together as if contemplating whether or not he should keep going.

"I came back in from one of the fields. We'd had some issues with coyotes coming in, so I'd been out hunting for the rascals. Never found any that day." He looked off toward the mansion. "When I got back to the shed—that's what we call the maintenance building—I saw three white moving vans pull up into the front of the house."

"Moving vans?" That was odd. "Was the reverend getting rid of some old furniture?" I almost made a comment about him selling it and giving the money to the poor, but I had a sneaking suspicion that wasn't the direction this story was going. Not based on the look on Joey's face.

"No. The vans weren't empty when they arrived. And they weren't when they left."

I waited to hear the explanation.

He swallowed, then elaborated. "There were kids in the back of the vans," he said. The shock wave from the statement rippled through the valley. I said nothing and kept listening. "I wondered what they were doing, so I asked Mr. Wells about it the next time I saw him. He tried to tell me that it was part of some fun project they were doing with local churches."

He huffed and shook his head. "I didn't believe him."

"Because they bused a bunch of kids here in moving vans?"

"That's part of it. But I didn't mention to him what I saw his men loading onto the moving vans once the kids were gone."

The plot thickened, and I crossed my arms in anticipation.

"Crates of something wrapped in cellophane. They must have loaded a dozen pallets on those vans."

"Could you see what it was?" I pressed.

He shook his head. "No. Not clearly, but I didn't need to know what it was. The Good Reverend is double dealing. He's the epicenter of a human tracking ring, and a heroin ring."

20

I drove through the gates of the property and waved to the guard as I passed. What I wanted to do was rip his head off and punt it like a football, but it wasn't the time.

He only nodded at me as I went by, and the second I turned the corner probably went back to whatever he was doing. Probably staring at himself in the mirror.

Once I was into the town of Franklin, I found an open parking spot in front of a clothing boutique that specialized in selling country chic outfits to young wannabe country singers and movie stars.

I shifted the vehicle into park and did nothing. All I could think about was everything Joey had told me, about the heroin operation Wells was a part of, and the trafficking of children, mostly girls.

Joey hadn't been able to get close enough to clearly identify the children, but he saw that many of them looked Latino.

I'd heard stories about the cartel smuggling over a new cash crop through the years, but I'd chosen to put my head in the sand, hoping that it wasn't true. How could someone be so cruel to a child?

It was a question that had racked my brain for years when I first found out about human trafficking.

The answer, unfortunately, was irrevocably simple. Most people were greedy for two things: money and power. And if a hot commodity could bring them both, all the better. As sick as it was, it was true: child slaves were—disgustingly so—the hottest commodity on earth to those without regard to morality.

Now it seemed those rumors I'd heard years prior were being confirmed now. The cartel was doubling its profits by bringing in two forms of illicit cargo. And they were being assisted by Vernon Wells. Maybe *assisted* was the wrong word—because it was entirely possible that Wells was running everything. The man had power, money, influence, and a squeaky-clean veneer that, apparently, very few could see through.

As hard as that fact was to swallow, I needed to understand more about his operation and how he would cover up such a treacherous and despicable business. The guy was extremely high profile, about as famous as a pastor could be.

One of the things I couldn't figure out was, why risk it all? He'd built up a religious empire of devout followers. He was internationally recognized.

That also begged the question: Which came first? His mega success or the shady underworld dealings Joey described.

I sighed, unsure sitting there thinking about this stuff would give me the answers. I knew I was going to have to dig deeper, which meant infiltrating Wells' estate again, except this time not under the guise of a guy looking for some work.

I pulled out my phone and checked my messages. I only had one from Jack asking if I was okay and that he hadn't seen me at breakfast that morning.

I'd left early to meet with Joey and hadn't felt like dealing with questions or explanations. Guilt already pulled at my gut for bringing him and Jesse into this mess. Deep down, despite those feelings, something else told me that they had a bigger role to play in all of this, and that their paths merging with mine was no coincidence.

And then there was Amy's father. Jerry had shot me, "killing" me in cold blood in my own home. I could have understood that sort of revenge mindset if he had real, concrete evidence of my involvement in Amy's murder.

But something he'd said kept me from accepting it.

He said I was the one who was supposed to die. Not her.

What in the world had he meant by that?

The obvious, and morbid, implication was that he'd hired the cartel goons to kill me, not his daughter.

That was hardly a phone call between him and Carrillo that could have been misunderstood, if that's how it had gone down.

That meant Carrillo went off script. But why?

I sat there, trying to piece together the reasons for something that had seemed to defy any form of logic.

The same answer kept bubbling to the surface like a bobber on a fishing line, but that was impossible. And why would Jerry need me dead?

Unless...

"No," I muttered to myself. "That can't be."

The conclusion continued needling my brain over and over again —Amy and her father were looking for the medallion. That meant Carrillo must have seen the opportunity to take it for himself and seize all the power.

But why did *Jerry* want it? And how did any of this fit with the corrupt pastor who was running a heroin and human trafficking ring?

A knock on my passenger side window startled me so much I nearly jumped through the roof of the car.

I looked out the window and saw a familiar face. Then a shadow passed over me from the left, and I turned to find another one.

It was the two agents from Division Three.

I rolled down the driver's side window and slung my arm over the sill. "What's the problem, Officer?" I asked with a wry grin.

The agent standing next to my door smiled back. "You know we're not cops," he said. "I thought we made that clear."

"You did, Agent..." I paused for a second, trying to recall the usual names of the two men, "Keane, right?"

"Good memory."

"And that's Agent Miller over there, yeah?"

Keane nodded.

"He's the one with that funny first name, Az, right?"

"It's short for Azriel."

That name. I knew it from my Biblical studies. It was an ancient name; one that was associated with angels and holy wars between the sons of light and the sons of darkness before the Earth was created.

"Yeah," I said, stalling for a second. I didn't know why I felt the need to stall. I guess it was something about these two. They were suspicious—that much was easy to recognize—but they didn't come across as malicious. That didn't mean I was ready to trust them, but I needed more information, particularly on this mysterious Division Three they worked for.

"Azriel. I know that name," I said.

"I'd be surprised if you didn't," Agent Keane said. "Where you headed? You look like you're a little nervous. You in a hurry, Dr. Wolf?"

"No. I'm not in a hurry. And please, call me Gideon. I don't think I'll ever go back to being Dr. Wolf again."

Azriel stood up straight and turned his head down the street. People walked along the sidewalks with bags full of expensive clothing, jewelry, and accessories.

"There's never any going back, Gideon." His voice seemed to drown out all the street noise around us. "Only forward. A great man once said something to that effect. He said keep moving forward."

"Walt Disney," I clarified. "That quote is one of my favorites."

"I thought you might be a fan," he said.

"Oh? Why's that?"

"Call it a hunch."

It seemed I was dealing with a lot of hunches lately. Both my own and from others.

I looked over through the window at Agent Miller, then back to Keane. "He's keeping awful quiet," I noticed. "If I'm not under arrest, what can I do for you two?"

"We just want to talk," Keane hedged, returning his gaze to me. Something about his eyes were off. I couldn't put my finger on it, but the colors seemed to change and swirl in them. I suddenly realized I either hadn't paid attention to the color before or his irises were some kind of weird, alternating hue.

But that wasn't possible. Was it?

"We're talking right now," I observed. "Or by talk do you mean drive me out to the middle of nowhere, kill me, and dump my body in a shallow grave? Lot of places in Tennessee for that sort of thing, Agent Keane."

He smiled at me. "We're not going to kill you, Gideon. We're on your side."

I nodded and tore my eyes from him, focusing on the car parked in front of me along the sidewalk, then shifting to the pedestrians, the other cars passing by, anything but his chilly stare.

"Yeah, well, I'm not really sure I can trust you two." I looked back at him again. "I'm not sure who I can trust, other than my friends."

"Yes," he agreed. "You're right to reserve your trust for those closest to you. I would urge you to continue that caution in the future. There will be many tricks and traps thrown your way."

What was that supposed to mean? And what did this guy know about my future? Despite my gut telling me not to, I felt more and more inclined to sit down with these two and find out exactly what their Division Three organization was really all about.

I didn't know if they would tell me. Something about them following me, showing up right after I left Wells' estate, told me that they were looking for answers, had answers for me, or both.

I figured it was worth the risk to at least sit down for a cup of coffee with them.

"You guys ever had a good cortado?" I asked.

The two agents looked across the car at each other, and then Keane nodded. "They make a good one up the street from here at a local coffee house."

"You read my mind."

21

I sat down across from the two agents, my back to the wall so I could face the doorway. I'd started doing that lately, since the abduction in Mexico—always positioning the entrance in front of me in case there was an attack.

I couldn't believe I was having to think about such things. An attack? That wouldn't have even registered on my radar more than a week or two before. Now I was acting like some kind of special agent or a guy with military training, except I had none.

The truth was I was just trying to figure it all out as I went. I didn't have any training. But I had common sense, and I'd always heard from the experts that you should face the door in case there was trouble.

The two agents, on the other hand, didn't seem to care one bit that their backs were to the entrance.

They sat down across from me and placed the metal order number in the center of the table.

"Lucky number seven," I said, indicating the trifold aluminum placard.

I crossed my arms and looked at both the agents.

"So, you guys going to ever level with me or just keep playing these silly cloak-and-dagger games?"

Keane leaned forward and folded his hands on the table. He reminded me of Agent Smith from the movie *The Matrix*, except he looked nothing like that actor. His body language and demeanor, however, along with his way of speaking in a smooth, calm tone were similar to the agent from the movie.

One other big difference—I didn't feel like these were really the bad guys.

"What would you like to know?" Keane asked.

A curly-haired brunette in a black apron brought us our coffees—three cortados in clear tumblers set atop white serving dishes.

She placed the drinks in front of us and asked if we needed anything else.

"We're fine. Thank you so much," I replied, then pulled my beverage closer. I raised the cup and took a long sniff of the nutty, creamy liquid. "Cheers, gents," I said, raising the cup.

The agents nodded at me and raised their cups as well. Then we all took a sip.

Agent Miller was the first to set his back on the table. He stared through me, not in an intimidating way, but it didn't exactly make me feel at ease either.

"We can't divulge much about our agency to you, Gideon," Agent Miller said in his smooth, deep tone. "And due to jurisdiction restrictions, there isn't a whole lot we can do to interfere with what's going on."

I raised an eyebrow and took another sip of the hot liquid. "That's interesting. I didn't think you guys could tell me much about your agency, but the jurisdiction thing—I guess I just assumed that was never an issue when it came to big federal bureaus."

"We're not like the FBI," Keane corrected.

"And you're not like the CIA either," I added, "with all those international permissions and such."

"Correct."

I snorted and shook my head. These guys brought me here to give me some answers, or so I thought. Instead, more questions kept surfacing.

"What can you tell me?"

Keane smiled kindly. And it was a sincere, real expression—the same he might offer a child.

"Our agency has been around a long time," Keane answered.

"That doesn't really tell me much, does it?" I ran an index finger around the edge of the glass.

The smell of fresh coffee filled the air, along with the sound of the espresso maker steaming milk and a coffee grinder whipping up more freshly ground java.

A few patrons sat in the far corner of the building and another couple along the windows at the front. Those two looked out onto the busy street, talking about who knew what.

"We can tell you that you need to look deeper into Wells' activities," Miller answered.

I looked over at him, then to Keane. "I just left Wells' place."

"We know," Keane said.

"So, you two *have* been following me." It wasn't a question.

"Of course."

"Why? I haven't broken any laws. What do you two want with me? Just come out and say it. Huh? Why won't you just say it?"

I didn't often let my temper get the best of me, but I'd grown tired of the mind games and the charades that went along with it. "Would you give me something to go on?"

"You're not alone, Gideon. That's all I am permitted to tell you at the moment. Division Three represents what you would call the good guys. We are on your side."

"You have no idea what side I'm on. Or anything about me."

"Perhaps. Perhaps not."

That response threw me off.

"We know more about you than you might think," Miller offered. "We know about your past—your life as an archaeologist, your marriage, your life's work so far."

"You make it sound like I'm old," I responded. And the mention of my wife made me feel suddenly dejected. "And you know I'm not married anymore."

"We know you didn't kill your wife, Gideon."

The statement sent a shiver down my spine. I looked up at Keane and found no dishonesty in his eyes. "How do you know?"

"Strange thing to say for an innocent man talking to two special agents," Miller mused. "Usually, it goes the other way with these kinds of conversations."

I leaned back, setting my cup down, and crossed my arms. "I don't have to defend myself. I know I didn't kill my wife. Or do I need to call my attorney?"

"Up to you," Miller said, raising his shoulders for half a second. "Like we said, you're not under arrest, and we're not an agency that does that kind of thing."

I know I looked confused, and Keane clarified what his partner said. "Our agency doesn't arrest people, Gideon. Not usually. We're more hands-off."

"Hands-off?"

Keane tilted forward and cocked his head at an angle. "We're more interested in helping people who are trying to do good in the world."

I had no idea what that was supposed to mean. "Like Mother Theresa types? People who volunteer at soup kitchens? That sort of thing?"

"No. We appreciate what they do, and their work is important, probably the most important in the world."

"Your work," Miller took over, "is what we're interested in, Gideon."

"Archaeology?" I wasn't trying to be funny. I honestly had no idea what these two were getting at, but I had a bad feeling it didn't have anything to do with digging up old artifacts or pieces of lost cultures.

"In a manner of speaking," Keane continued. His eyes remained fixated on my neck. "That's a very unusual medallion you have there," he said.

I looked down, my face flushing with fire. I hadn't realized it, but the medallion had slipped out above my shirt and hung out over my chest for all the world to see.

I quickly stuffed it back under the cotton.

"Where, might I ask, did you find that one?" he demurred.

I shrugged, then took my glass and sipped the drink slowly, hoping I might buy some time. No luck.

I set the glass down clumsily, sloshing the brown liquid within— nearly spilling it over the edge.

"Found it," I said, hoping that would solve my issue.

"Yes. We're aware that you found it. That's why I asked where you found it."

"Oh." That's right. He had said that. I felt like an idiot, and lying certainly wasn't my forte. On top of that, I got the distinct feeling that these guys would know if I was lying—even if I was good at it.

"Something so valuable should be kept hidden," Miller advised. "Perhaps in a vault, or in a safety deposit box."

Now the two were creeping me out. *How did he know it was valuable?*

"I can't do that," I said, scrambling for answers. "I have to keep it with me."

"Interesting." Agent Keane took a drink and held his glass, sizing me up like a prize fighter pitted against a slab of meat for an opponent. "Well, take good care of it, Gideon. If you're the rightful owner, it would be a shame for someone else to get their hands on it."

I couldn't tell if that was a threat or a warning. So I said nothing, instead opting to tear my eyes from him for a moment and look out the window at the lively street. I hoped looking outside would buy me some time—or the right things to say for these two—but nothing came to mind.

Except one idea. Maybe I could turn this little interrogation on its head. If that's what it was.

"Tell me more about Division Three," I blurted. The tone was casual, but the demand hidden under the surface told both of them I was done screwing around. "You've been dancing around an explanation since we got here. I want to know what the division is."

The two agents looked at each other. Miller nodded. So did Keane.

"We're not at liberty to divulge all the details, Gideon," Keane explained.

"Oh, horse crap," I fired back. I tried to keep my voice down and leaned forward. "Look, if you two really know what happened to my wife, then why are you bothering me? Huh? If you believe I'm innocent, what is all this about?"

Keane measured his words before he responded. "We are watchers, Gideon. We observe the course of human events and make suggestions to those who have the power to change things for the better."

That was vague. And a little weird. "So, you talking like reality television or something? That kind of watching?"

"Make your jokes, Gideon. It's one of the things we like about you."

Miller cracked a smile. "That was a pretty good one, boss," he said with a sidelong glance at his partner.

Keane didn't seem amused, but he didn't seem angry either. The guy was a tough read, like an alligator at a poker table. I realized I tended to make a lot of comparisons to poker for someone who rarely got to play.

"Your wife was killed by Carrillo's men," Keane said plainly. I couldn't remember if I'd told them that when I first met them or if they had access to that information through some other means. What means, I had no idea. "And before you drive yourself crazy trying to recall if you told us that or not, it doesn't matter if you did or didn't. We knew because we see everything, Gideon. We hear everything." His voice was growing darker by the syllable.

"You know, you're really creepy when you talk like that, Agent Keane. You could scare small kids with that bit."

He reached into his jacket and removed something tiny and metallic. It looked like a chrome disc.

"What's that thing?" I asked.

"A gift," he said. "From a friend."

"Friend?" I wasn't sure how many friends I had left. Jack and Mike, sure. Jesse was a maybe at this point. I'd known her less than a day, so I felt compelled to file that one under acquaintance.

I reached out to take the little disc, but he let it go. I snatched at it to keep it from hitting the table and bouncing onto the floor. Tiny things like that seemed to bounce into the nether regions when they fell under tables. Instead of catching it, though, the disc hovered in midair.

For a few seconds, all I could do was stare at the thing as it levitated over the table. My eyes darted around the room to make sure no one else saw.

"They see nothing, Gideon," Keane informed. "Az has cloaked us. To them, this is nothing but an empty table."

"What if someone comes and sits down?" I asked, disconcerted by the floating metal.

"They won't."

"Did you make the table look dirty or something?"

Miller laughed. "Something like that."

"What am I supposed to do with that thing?" I wondered.

"Nothing," Keane said with a grin. "It knows what to do."

In a flash, the disc whizzed toward my face, then flipped up right before my eyes and dove into my shirt.

I grabbed at it with both hands, but the object was too fast. "What the?"

Then I heard a click.

"What did you guys just do to me?" I ran my fingers over my shirt like someone who'd accidentally walked through a spider web. "Where did it go? Where is it?"

"Relax," Miller laughed. "It's only a cloaking disc."

"Cloaking disc?"

"From your friend the shaman."

For twenty full seconds, I did nothing—said nothing—but stare at the men across from me.

When I finally mustered a response, I looked Keane dead straight in the eyes. "What did you just say?"

He offered a disarming smile. "The shaman asked us to give that to you."

That's what I thought he'd said. The shaman. But how did these two spooks know about that? I thought I was the only one who could see the mysterious guide.

"He gives you the cloaking disc as a gift and says sorry about all your other clothes," Miller added.

I snorted. "What? Is this thing supposed to fix that?"

"The cloaking disc will allow you to mirror clothing you normally wear. So now, if you want to wear your usual clothes, you simply allow the medallion to see them, and your guardian outfit will change to look like those."

It sounded impossible. Then again, so did finding an amulet that turned me into the Chupacabra. None of that mattered. "How did you find the shaman? How do you know about him? Where is he?"

"Around," Keane said. I guess it was his turn to be vague. "This device can also be of great use to you when you are in enemy territory."

My mind raced with the possibilities. But I had to know something. "What do you two want from me? Everyone wants something. Your agency, what do they want me to do for them? Huh?"

"To continue the mission, Gideon. Go to the home of Vernon Wells. Tonight, another shipment will arrive. You must save the children and destroy the product he's bringing in."

"Anything else?"

Keane blinked slowly, almost like a lizard, or a cat sitting by a warm fire. "Continue the fight, Guardian. We will always be with you. And we will always be watching."

The two stood up and started to leave.

"No. Hold on a second. You can't just say that and walk out the door. You know I'm a guardian? How did you know that?"

"We have always known," Miller said, as if the answer should have been obvious. "We've been watching you a long time, Gideon Wolf, son of the House of Claw and Fang."

"Okay, great. But what do I do when I do the thing at Wells' place, whatever that is?"

"You know exactly what you are to do with him," Keane said. "Obey the mist. When it is done, you will receive your next mission."

"Next mission? Okay fine," I said, walking after the two as they made their way over to the door. I figured we were done drinking the cortados, which was unfortunate because they were excellent. "But what about the other medallions of power? I thought I was supposed to track those down."

"You are," Miller said. He was almost getting annoying with that mischievous smirk he added on top of the tone.

"Okay, great. Care to tell me where to find the first one? Oh, and who am I supposed to give it to?"

Keane stopped at the door and looked around the room. People sipped coffee, talked to each other, nibbled on pastries. The workers behind the counter moved busily as if it were rush hour, even though no one stood in line and only one customer waited on her beverage.

"These people," Keane said, "need justice. They need someone who will stand up for them in the face of evil. For too long, the world has wallowed in darkness, consumed by greed, selfishness, hatred, fear, deception. Those things cause sickness and death. They cause families to be torn asunder and plunge the best of friendships into the abyss."

At the sound of the last word, Miller lowered his head, his eyes twitching for a second.

Then he was fine.

"Guardians bring balance to the world. We, as watchers, are not permitted to intervene. Only to advise, and offer a little help along the way."

"Great," I said. "You can help me take out Wells and his operation. What are your powers?"

Keane's eyes flamed. And not just like the expression. Literal tongues of flue fire licked the tops of his pupils. "We cannot intervene, Gideon," his voice thundered.

I snapped my head around the room, horrified that all the workers and patrons would be startled by the booming voice.

Instead, it was as if they'd heard nothing. They simply continued doing what they were doing before.

"Go to Wells' estate tonight. You will know what to do."

The two agents walked out onto the sidewalk, leaving me standing in the doorway. I hurried after them. "Wait. I have more questions," I insisted. "Please. How do you guys know about guardians? Please. Can we just—"

A large man in a gray T-shirt barged into me and knocked me backward a few steps.

"I am so sorry," he said, holding a bagel in one hand and a coffee in the other. "I wasn't watching where I was going."

"No problem," I said. I stepped around him, but when I looked down the sidewalk, the two agents were gone.

I quickly skirted the edge of the street and was forced to jump back up onto the curb as a black Maserati sedan speeding by nearly clipped me.

I hopped up on a park bench to see over the oddly dense crowd of people, but I couldn't find Agents Keane and Miller.

Resigned that they'd disappeared, I climbed back down from the park bench and sat for a minute. My questions about the clandestine agency known as the Sector would have to wait. Maybe these Division Three guys didn't know anything about them. Perhaps neither organization was aware of the other. My head spun with all the covert agencies suddenly thrust into my life, and that didn't include the FBI, which had been so welcoming upon my arrival back in the country.

Who were all these people? Where did they come from? How were they recruited into such shadowy organizations?

Right now, it seemed the only answers I was going to find had nothing to do with secret agents or covert operations.

Tonight would be as good a night as any to pay Wells a personal visit.

22

J ack didn't like the idea of me going back out without him. Jesse wasn't keen on it either, but since she was a new acquaintance, I wasn't going to give her as much say-so in the matter as my friend since childhood.

That said, he couldn't change my mind, either.

And there was no way he could stop me because I had no intentions of going back to Mike's farm. Not until after I took care of business.

I spent some time in Franklin, killing time in various shops until I'd run out of things to pretend to be interested in. Then I drove back to Nashville and hung out for the rest of the day.

If I'd gone back to the farm, both Mike and Jack would have insisted on coming with me or that I not go at all.

Just easier to avoid them and ignore most of Jack's texts asking where I was, when I was coming back, all that.

I only gave him one reply and chose not to respond to the rest.

"I'll be back later tonight" was all I'd told him.

Then I set my phone on Do Not Disturb and stopped looking at his responses.

When evening approached, I returned to Franklin and waited up the road from Wells' estate. I felt weird sitting there in my car like a cop on a sting. Seemed like I should have a big cup of coffee, a couple of donuts, and a partner in the passenger seat complaining about how long we'd been sitting there.

Maybe I'd watched the *Lethal Weapon* movies too many times.

No one paid any attention to me as I sat in my car, looking at my phone while I waited for the sun to set.

While most people would probably have been on social media or screwing around with their favorite time-suck app, I was doing research, and not the kind I was accustomed to.

I spent more than two hours reading about Vernon Wells and his rise to fame and power.

He'd grown up poor in the little town of Crossville, Tennessee. The son of a schoolteacher and an alcoholic father, his early troubles had taught him at a young age that he wanted more out of life—so the interview said.

The magazine was based in Nashville and had done a feature on Wells, selling it as a rags-to-riches story but with a spiritual spin. Because, after all, growing a church to the level Wells had wasn't about the money or the influence. It was about the Lord's Work.

I rolled my eyes.

There were plenty of good pastors out there, evangelists, too. People who truly believed in the message they were sharing, and who weren't trying to get rich from it.

It was difficult for me to think of something less Christian than what Wells was doing. Then again, I was a different kind of Christian.

I saw things differently than most, and tried to keep an open mind.

Good thing, too, because with the twist my life had taken in the last week, I found myself questioning things more than ever.

We'd been told to take things on faith, and that was good often enough. But it wasn't good enough. Not for me. Never had been. I wanted to understand why I believed what I believed. Now I had a whole new layer to pile on top of everything I'd ever trusted.

I was a monster. I wasn't a bad person, I hoped, but I had become something that my faith couldn't account for, and that made for a moat of confusion around my mind.

I sighed as I finished reading about Vernon Wells.

It was hard to hate the guy. I had to admit that. He'd done a lot of good in the community, and his charities had improved lives around the globe—feeding the hungry, housing the homeless, even prison ministries. He was checking all the right boxes from that verse in the Bible that talked about "When you've done these things to the least, you've done them for me."

But all of it was a cover for what was really going on.

Save a thousand kids from hunger and sell fifty kids for a cool million. Or whatever the going price was. I was willing to bet the pretty ones fetched even more. My stomach turned over.

That didn't even include the money he was raking in from heroin.

I flapped my lips at the thought.

There was no telling how much money Wells was making from his illegal ventures, let alone the cash his church brought in. He might have been worth a few hundred million, maybe more.

One thing was certain: a good chunk of that would be off the books.

Embers of anger sizzled in my gut the more I thought about it, and I found myself looking forward to the showdown with him.

I would relish this one.

The last glimpse of the sun dipped below the horizon. It was time to go.

I left the SUV and walked down the sidewalk. I looked back at the vehicle, wondering why no more of the Sector agents had shown up to antagonize me.

There had to be a tracking device on the SUV somewhere. I wasn't about to crawl around looking for it, but I assumed the thing was there. And if so, the agency's goons should have been swarming around me.

But they weren't. Maybe they learned their lesson.

I doubted that. More likely, they were amassing reinforcements to come at me full throttle. Or coming up with a new strategy instead of throwing as many bullets as possible my way.

Either way, if those spooks showed up, they'd find an empty vehicle with me more than a half mile away from it, taking out the trash.

I made my way along the sidewalk until it ended, and then continued on until I was in the town outskirts that blended into the Tennessee countryside.

I arrived at the gates to Wells' estate as the moon poked up over the horizon and stars began glittering in the darkening sky.

The guardhouse at the gate was occupied by the same guy from earlier in the day. I recognized his face in the bright light filling the shack.

"I guess Wells works his people long hours," I muttered.

I kept walking until I reached the door. As expected, the guy inside stood up when he saw me and came out to greet me.

"This is private property," he said.

Okay, so "greet me" was generous.

"Yeah. I know. I'm the guy who came by earlier about a job with the landscaping crew."

He frowned for a second before the realization hit him. Meanwhile, red mist wrapped around his ankles, shins, and knees, pulsing with crimson light.

"You forget something?" he asked, and not in a kind tone. It sounded like an insult.

"No. I just came back to take care of something."

"And what's that?"

"I'm here to kill your boss."

He snorted a laugh, looking at me with derision oozing from his eyes. "What?"

"I said I'm here to kill your boss."

"Get out of here, weirdo. I don't have time for this."

I didn't let up. "You've done things," I said. "Bad things. Haven't you?"

"Okay, nutjob. Time for you to go." He stepped toward me with his right hand extended.

I grabbed his wrist and twisted his hand down, then jerked it backward until I heard a crack in the forearm. Before he could scream, I chopped the bridge of my other hand into his throat until I felt something solid.

His windpipe crushed and his arm broken, the guard fell to the ground gasping for air that would not come.

I bent down on one knee, lifted his head, and snapped his neck.

His movements stopped, and the body went limp.

I moved around to his feet and picked his legs up by the ankles, then dragged the dead man into the open guardhouse. Once I was at the back wall, I dropped the man's feet and hovered over him for a minute.

The words of the Division Three agents rang in my ears about the disc they'd given me. The voice in my head concurred with the idea sprouting in my mind.

Yes, it said. *You can use it for that.*

I wasn't sure, but it was worth a shot.

I knelt down next to the dead man as the red fog hovered over him, slowly filtering into his nose. I pulled out the amulet and held it between thumb and forefinger, and stared at the man's uniform.

Suddenly, my clothes weren't my clothes anymore. They were the guard's uniform. I looked down at the blazer and pants.

"That is some crazy magic," I said.

The voice in my head told me it wasn't magic. *Science, Gideon. Higher science.*

Magic. Science. Whatever it was, I'd never seen anything like it before. And I was starting to realize that there was a lot more to this world, and to the universe around me, than I ever thought possible.

I stood up and walked to the door, then leaned over and pressed a button on the desk marked Gate.

After a quick check of the camera feeds on the four screens sitting atop the table, I walked out the door and closed it behind me.

The gate creaked open at a snail's pace, as if anticipating the mayhem to come and savoring every second of the prelude.

I sensed it, too, and the monster in me grew impatient, and I stalked through the open gate toward the mansion.

"Okay. Free the kids. Destroy the drugs. Take out Wells." I sighed. I never felt like a hero. But maybe a hero wasn't what the world needed. Maybe it needed the monster.

23

I walked up the driveway, doing my best to look casual. I couldn't help but think of the line in Return of the Jedi where Han told Chewie to fly casual as they sailed right by Darth Vader's star destroyer.

At the top of the hill, I walked by a guard standing at the base of the steps leading up to the mansion entrance. He nodded. I returned the gesture and kept going.

The disguise worked.

I still looked like me, as far as I knew, but what guards would know if I was a new guy or a trespasser?

My guess was none.

At the top of the steps, I nodded at the guard at the door, expecting him to treat me the same way the guy below had.

I was wrong.

"Who are you?" he asked, throwing in an H-E-double hockey stick in the middle.

"Name's Sid," I said, using the alias from before. "I'm new here."

"What, did you walk here from your house, Sid? Where's your car? You know they give us a spot down behind the pool house, right?"

"They do?" I feigned ignorance. And since I didn't actually know about the parking space, or the pool house for that matter, it was believable.

"Aw, jeez. These rookies," he complained in what had to be a Chicago accent. From the looks of the guy, he was probably retired law enforcement. Early sixties, graying hair, but he'd managed to stay fit, like the guys I'd see at the gym who worked out into their eighties and were somehow stronger than me in my prime. Well, not now. But before the medallion.

He pressed the button on his radio and called in to some unseen supervisor. "Hey, Mick, I got a new guy here named Sid who doesn't know about the parking area out back. Did we hire a new—"

I stopped him right there, grabbing him by the throat as the red mist spun around him. I lifted him up until his feet dangled uselessly in the air.

He kicked and struggled, swinging his fists at my arm as I pinned him to a portico column, squeezing the life from him.

"Jim? Do you copy? You're breaking up a little. You said something about a new guy named Sid? We didn't hire any new people today. Was he with the landscaping crew?"

Jim didn't answer. His eyes bulged from their sockets. His face turned from beet red to a plum-colored hue. Spittle burst from his lips as I strangled him.

When I felt the fight to survive leave him, I held him for another few seconds before tossing the body into the huge yew shrubs next to the porch. The dead man hit the ground with a thump.

I stepped to the door and pressed on the latch. It didn't open.

I grumbled. "Well, there goes the subtle way in."

A quick look to the left and right revealed no immediate threats. The cameras in the corners of the portico had seen everything, and it would only be seconds before the security guy on the other end of Jim's call would show up with a whole gaggle of mall cops.

I took one step back and then lowered my shoulder.

The door shuddered, but I bounced off it and staggered back. Frowning, I looked up at the cameras and mouthed, "Really?"

I shook my head, touched the medallion, and shifted into the Chupacabra. My grin must have looked terrifying as I stared at the camera over my right shoulder. Then, I took a step back, and this time charged right through the door.

The heavy wood splintered, ripping from its hinges and tearing the deadbolts out of their sockets. The entire wall buckled from the blow.

Dust and debris exploded into an opulent foyer and scattered across a white-and-black marble floor. Bright light sparkled from a crystal chandelier overhead.

I heard footsteps clicking louder and louder, the signal that more guards were on their way.

To my right and left, long hallways stretched out in both directions. Straight ahead, two staircases curled up to the second floor. Red carpet covered the dark hardwood steps.

I could run up the stairs and try to find Wells first, or I could take out all his security and then go find him when he had no one left to help.

Seemed like a waste of a good opportunity to cull the world of bad guys to just run up there and take out Wells. I figured that while I was here, I might as well make the most of it.

So, I stood there in the foyer, waiting as the sounds of guards approaching reached a crescendo.

I looked up at the chandelier again and noted it was held in place at a single point in the ceiling. It dredged up an old memory of the time I was visiting Cumberland Caverns and heard the tour guide talking about the massive chandelier in the dining hall. The thing hung what seemed like eighty feet above us. The guide had said it was held in place by a single bolt. I remembered thinking what a tragedy that would be if the bolt shook loose or broke. It was almost—

"Stop right there!" a man shouted from my right.

Two guards charged toward me. Then two more appeared down the left corridor. Four appeared in the doorway across from me in the foyer.

All of them were armed with pistols. I rolled my eyes in anticipation of the pain that would come with every bullet wound.

I also noted that all but one of the guards had red mist circling around them. The one who didn't made me wonder, but it wasn't for me to question. They were either marked for death, or they weren't.

"Put your hands on your head and get down on your knees!" the same guy barked.

I heard one of the others say, "What is that thing? It looks like some kind of dog-man."

"I'm a Chupacabra," I said, turning my head toward the guy.

"I said get down!" the first guard shouted again.

The glittering lights dancing around me on the floor gave me an idea. I put my hands up and on the back of my furry head and knelt down.

"Okay. Okay. Take it easy. This isn't what it looks like."

"I said shut up!"

"Actually, chief, no. You did not tell me to shut up. You said to—"

"Shut up!"

The guy looked like he was in his late forties and hardened by a good twenty years in the service. Which service, I didn't know, but I guessed Marine Corps. Maybe Army Rangers.

"Relax," I begged as he and the others closed in.

They surrounded me in a tightening circle with only the destroyed doorway behind me.

"Get your zip ties," the leader ordered. I didn't see which guy he was talking to.

Didn't matter to me.

"I'm telling you. This is not what it looks like," I continued, doing my best not to laugh.

"What it looks like, freak, is that you broke into the Reverend's home."

He inched closer until he was right next to me, his gun pointed at the back right side of my skull.

Then I felt the heel of his boot dig into my back as he tried to shove me down flat on the floor.

"I said... get... down."

He kicked harder, but my strength was too much for him to even make me budge. I decided to toy with him.

"Oh, sorry. You want me to lie flat on the floor? Like on my belly?"

He pressed the gun to the back of my head. "I don't know what you are," he said with a few expletives sprinkled in for good measure. "But if you don't get down on the floor right now, I will splatter your brains all over the room."

"Okay," I surrendered. "Just take it easy." I lowered myself to the floor, biding my time for all the men to get close enough to trigger my plan. "Would you believe I'm just doing my trick-or-treating a few months early?"

"Shut. Up!"

"Okay, like six months. But still..."

He shoved me again, and this time, I allowed myself to get pushed.

I felt one of the other guys wrapping the zip ties around my wrists.

"Oooh, that tickles," I said, giggling mockingly. "Stop it. Stop it." I laughed harder.

"Sit still or I will—"

"I know. Blow my brains all over the floor. Pretty sure the maids wouldn't appreciate that. Lot of cleaning that kind of thing causes."

"You're a real wise guy," he said. "Whatever you are, you freak." He looked at one of the other guards. "Take this guy's mask off," he ordered.

I snorted. "Good luck with that."

One of the guards stepped close and took a knee next to my face.

"Hey, you mind getting your foot away from my head? I don't know where that thing's been."

The guard tugged at my fur to no avail.

"Sir, this thing is really stuck," he said.

"Ow," I complained. It only hurt a little. "That's because it's not a mask, you nitwit."

"Get out of the way. I'll do it. Simpson, keep an eye on him. You move an inch, big boy, and you die."

"I sense a lot of anger in you."

He stood up and started to swap with the guard who'd tried to remove my "mask"—the only one without the red mist around him.

Before any of them could react, I broke free of the feeble bonds, bounced to my feet, and grabbed the young, innocent guard. "You should run, kid," I said, and threw him back down the hall to the left.

He slid on the marble tiles before rolling to a stop against a pedestal holding a bust of Vernon Wells.

Then I jumped high up to the ceiling while the others watched in rapt amazement until I grabbed onto the middle of the chandelier and swung from it like an ape in the jungle.

The guards opened fire, sending rounds zipping past me and causing extensive, and expensive, damage to the pricey fixture and the white-domed ceiling.

One of the bullets tore through my leg, and I howled in anger. But I felt the chandelier give a few inches, and I knew my plan would work.

I did one pull-up on the metal ring in the chandelier and then let myself drop down hard.

The beastly weight ripped the opulent fixture free from its housing and sent it cascading down toward the circle of seven guards below. I pushed away from it, letting myself fall to the side.

The heavy chandelier dropped onto the seven remaining men before they could get out of the way. The only one who managed to escape being killed by the gigantic fixture was the leader, who dove clear just in time—mostly.

His right leg got crushed by a bulky support ring and, from the looks of it, partially severed the limb.

He swore like the Marine I believed him to be and writhed around in obvious agony, grabbing at his leg.

I stood up and walked over to him, hovering above like a furry angel of death.

He grabbed a gun lying on the floor at his side, but I stepped on his hand and pressed it into the tile until it crunched.

The guard yelled as his nerves burned with pain. I knew within minutes he'd probably go into shock.

I looked back down the corridor where I'd thrown the innocent one and was glad to see the guy was gone. I didn't want to hurt one of the unmarked.

"Where are they?" I asked, still pinning the guard's hand to the floor.

He replied with an obscenity.

"Oh. That's not very nice. So, I'll ask again." I twisted my foot, sending a fresh round of nerve signals to his brain.

He screamed—at first. Sweat rolled down his blushing cheeks and red forehead. "Who? Who?" He couldn't ask the question fast enough.

I looked around for a second, pretending to look for something. "Is there an owl in here?" Then I looked down at him again. "Oh, it's just you. Ready to answer the question now?"

I leaned close so he could smell death on me. "Where are the children? Let's start with that. I can find the heroin on my own."

His eyes widened. "What are you?"

"Not the answer I was looking for, chief."

I started to twist my foot again, and he immediately shouted, "They're in the basement! They're in the basement!"

"Where in the basement?"

"Down the stairs," he said. "Over there." He turned his head to where the spiral staircase on the left continued down into the bowels of the building. "Once you're at the bottom, you go to the right."

"Which room?"

He chuckled, and that didn't do him any favors. "All the rooms."

I blinked at the staggering statement. "How many rooms?"

He replied with the same disrespectful obscenity referring to something I should do to myself.

I nodded. "You should be more creative with your insults," I mused. Then I kicked his head like a football. The blow was so strong it nearly ripped his head off. It definitely broke his neck, judging by the loud pop. But the blow to his brain might have also killed him.

I didn't care. He was clearly one of the wicked, and his death or its means weighed not on my conscience.

I ran over to the stairs in seconds, then bounded down them without giving care to whether or not more guards waited.

When I reached the bottom, two guards rushed me from both sides of the hall. Their pistols raised, they fired at me, but I dropped to the ground and lunged forward on all fours at the one to my left. I bit into his leg below the knee and tore it left and right, twisting my head like a wild animal.

His partner tried to shoot. Actually, he did shoot me in the back, but I swung my current victim around like a club in a dog's mouth. The club guard smashed into the other, sending them tumbling to the floor in a pile by the door leading out to the pool.

They scrambled to recover. The one with the wounded leg tried to keep pressure on it to stem the bleeding, but his face was already pale from the blood loss, shock, or both.

"What are you?" the one with two working legs asked.

He drew a switchblade and brandished it at me.

I cocked my head to the side and shook it in condescension. "Seriously? You brought a knife to a fight with a shape-shifter?"

Unfazed, he lunged at me, stabbing me in the gut. I looked down at him, my eyes holding the guy for a second. At first, the relief and thrill of victory coursed over him. But it quickly faded as he realized that the knife had done nothing but make me madder.

I grabbed him by the back of the head, then forced him to watch as I pulled the knife out of my abdomen, and then slowly worked the point toward the base of his throat.

"No." He shook his head fervently. "No. Please. No." He kicked at me, striking my legs with his knees. He swung his arms, punching me in the face—which was annoying but didn't hurt much. "No. No!"

I leaned close to him. "The mist says yes," I said. Then shoved the blade through his skin.

He grimaced, twitched, squirmed, and even cried. But there was no escaping death for him.

I dropped him to the ground unceremoniously and looked over at his partner. The guy was unconscious in a pool of blood. He may have already been dead. I must have hit an artery in his leg when I adjusted my bite, moving up above the knee just before I swung him.

I turned down the hall and walked to the first door on the left. I checked the knob, but it was locked.

I took a step back and was about to barge through it when I realized how terrifying it would be for the kids to see me in my monster form.

"Right," I said, catching myself.

I returned to the guard with the knife in his neck and checked him for keys. They hung on his belt. I snatched them up and returned to the door, then calmed the power coursing through me, touching the medallion to hurry the transformation.

I didn't know if that was what did it, but it seemed to help.

I also found myself back in my original T-shirt and jeans I'd been wearing when I left the farm earlier that day.

More questions spiked about Division Three, but they could wait for now.

I inserted the first key into the door, twisted it, and turned the knob. *Lucky guess.*

The door opened, and what I found inside was far more terrible than anything I'd seen or done so far.

A dozen kids were piled up in a one-hundred-square-foot room with blankets and pillows lining the floor. It was a prison.

Children ranging in ages from probably eleven or twelve up to thirteen occupied the room. They looked at me, terrified.

For a second, I wondered if I'd changed back into the Chupacabra. "I'm here to get you out," I said. "Follow me."

The kids looked around at each other, uncertain if they should believe me or not.

I repeated myself in Spanish since most of them looked like they spoke that language.

"Who are you?" a girl with long, black hair asked.

"Soy el Chupacabra," I said.

She smiled and shook her head. "No you're not. He's a monster."

I smiled back, disarming all of them. "Sometimes you need a monster to beat the bad guys." I extended my hand. "Come on. Let's get you out of here."

24

Thirty-six.

That's how many kids I found in the basement of Vernon Wells' mansion.

My first priority was getting them to safety, though I had no idea what that meant. I led the procession of children up the stairs and out through the front door. Fortunately for them, the bodies were gone—consumed by the mist.

I couldn't imagine how nightmarish that would look to a kid, stepping into the foyer where seven dead guys were lying around, crushed by a chandelier. It would be horrific, and they'd have carried that image with them their entire lives.

Instead, all they saw was the oversize light fixture destroyed on the floor.

"What happened?" one of the boys asked, walking by the pile of glittering crystal.

"Hard to say, kid," I said, leading them through the doorway and down the steps.

I took the phone out of the pocket in my guardian outfit and called Jack.

I hadn't wanted to bring him and Jesse into this, but I had no idea what to do with these kids.

"Where are you?" Jack asked. "I've texted. I've called. What are you doing?"

"Jack, I need some help. Any chance you can get a bus?"

"A what?"

"A bus. I need you to find a school bus, a big RV, something to carry thirty-six kids."

"Thirty what now? Did you just say thirty-six kids?"

"I don't have time to explain right now." I kept moving, leading the children down the mansion steps. I'd found some older kids in the last room. They looked like they were high school age, ranging from fifteen to eighteen.

I started to wonder how many had been brought through here and sold off as slaves of various kinds to disgusting elites all over the world. How many presidents or prime ministers or princes had paid Wells for his child slaves? I started to feel nauseated.

"I need you to get whatever you can and bring it over to Vernon Wells' place."

"What? Vernon Wells? Gideon, what did you do? What's going on?"

I kept walking toward the road with all the kids in tow.

"Jack, please. I need you to trust me. Get a bus, anything, and get over here now. You know where it is?"

"Yeah. But—"

"I'll be waiting down at the gate. Don't call the police," I warned. "I don't know who we can trust right now."

"Trust? Police? Why would I call the police?"

"Just don't. Okay? I'll see you soon."

"Wait. Gideon—"

I ended the call and cut him off.

"Who was that?" one little girl asked.

I looked down at her and smiled. Her black hair tossed in the breeze as we marched toward the gate. I kept looking for more guards, but none arrived.

At the base of the hill, I waited for nearly an hour for Jack to arrive. Some of the kids were impatient. Most of them were hungry. There was no telling how long it had been since they'd eaten.

I knew there was a burger joint not far from there that was still open. I'd seen softball and baseball teams there in the summer. It was always a pain in the rear to get behind one of those groups in line at the register.

I shook my head at the stupid observation. These kids were about to be sold into a life of who knows what, and I was complaining silently about waiting a few extra minutes to get a combo meal.

I silently told myself I wouldn't be so shallow in the future.

My patience was starting to wear thin, though, and I didn't know how long we could hang out here inside the gate before there was a changing of the guard. There could be a delivery on the way. That wouldn't be pleasant. The thought of three dozen kids watching me massacre a bunch of drug dealers might have been amusing if it hadn't been a real possibility.

Finally, I saw bus headlights coming our way. I didn't think Jack would get an actual yellow school bus, but there it was, rumbling down the road toward the gate.

He turned into the driveway and pulled the thing through the gate, careful not to scrape the pillars on either side.

Except when the bus brakes hissed and the door on the side unfolded, it wasn't Jack sitting in the driver's seat.

Jesse gave an upward tilt of her head in greeting.

"What's up," she said, coolly.

"Where's—"

Before I could finish my question, Jack poked his head into view from the seat behind Jesse.

"I hope you have a good explanation—wow!" He stopped whatever he was about to say when he saw the kids standing in the shadows of the guardhouse. "You weren't kidding," Jack said. "What are they all doin' there?"

I turned to one of the older girls and asked her to keep the others there for a second. She and the ones around her looked worried that I wasn't coming back, but I soothed them by putting out my hand and smiling. "I'll be right back," I said. "I need to make sure we can all fit."

I climbed into the bus, took a quick look back, and then inspected the bus—or camper, as it turned out.

"Um, Jack, is—"

"It's mine," Jesse said. "I like schoolies. Converted it myself a few years ago."

"It was the best I could do," Jack explained. "I mean, where am I going to get a bus at this hour?" He twisted his face, perplexed. "Or any hour for that matter."

"What's with all the kids?" Jesse asked. She managed to keep her tone matter of fact despite the seriousness implied in the question.

I took a breath. "Wells is involved in human trafficking."

"What?" they both blurted.

"That's not all," I said. "He's dealing heroin."

They looked at each other as if one could tell the other I was joking.

"That's pretty far-fetched, Gideon. Seriously," Jack pleaded. "What is going on?"

"You saw what I am. What I can do, Jack. I'd say we're living in the land of far-fetched now.

"Touché."

"You just gonna make those kids stand out there?"

"No," I said. "But I didn't want to bring it up in front of them."

"Where's Wells?" Jack asked. Concern filling his eyes.

"I don't know. I just wanted to get the kids out as quickly as possible."

I understood the gravity of my words, so I added, "I'm going back up to the house to look for him. Get the kids out of here."

"Where should we take them?"

"I don't know. A church?"

"Shouldn't we take them to the cops?" Jesse suggested.

"You think they can be trusted?"

Jesse nodded. "My brother can. And he's a cop."

"Good idea," I said. "Make that happen." I climbed off the bus and started ushering the kids on board. When all of them were in their seats, I stepped up onto the lower landing at the door. "Take care of them. Okay?"

"Where are you going?" Jack demanded.

I looked back up to the mansion. "If Wells is there, I have to find him. And he has some questions to answer."

"Questions?"

"I want his list of clients. And distributors."

Jack saw the fury in my eyes. "I'll come with you."

"No," I said. "Too dangerous. I don't know what he's up to. My guess is he's hiding in his office like Scarface with a pile of cocaine on his desk and a stupid one-liner to go with the gun that's bigger than he is."

"You really thought that one through, didn't you?"

I shrugged. "Was it good?"

Jack chuckled and nodded. "Yeah. It was. We'll get the kids to safety. Don't die. If that's possible."

"I won't," I said, and turned away from the bus.

I walked up the driveway again and looked over my shoulder as Jesse turned her renovated RV around and drove away.

I hoped the kids would be okay. I couldn't imagine what their parents must have been feeling.

The kids would be fine with Jack and Jesse. I reassured myself with that thought.

I just hoped that Wells hadn't managed to escape while I was getting the kids to safety. If the man was even here.

I kept walking, but picked up my pace. It soon turned into a trot. *Why hadn't Wells shown his face? Was he really sitting in his study waiting in ambush?*

If that was his plan, he was in for a bad evening. But without Wells on site, I'd be wasting my time going back in there.

Then again, I might find something useful if I did a little snooping.

I stopped, looked back up at the mansion, and made up my mind.

25

The inside of the mansion was way too quiet.

I stepped across the splintered threshold and looked around. Then I touched the medallion and shifted into the dog.

I calmed my breathing. Even my heart slowed down. I heard nothing in the immediate area.

"Reverend?" I shouted so my voice boomed through every corridor in the palatial home. "Where are you?" I did my best impression of De Niro in the remake of *Cape Fear* from the '90s.

No response.

I crept across the floor and then dropped down on all fours to run up the stairs to the next level.

I made it up in seconds and stayed down on my haunches as I looked both directions. *If I were a crooked piece of crap like Wells, where would I put my study?*

Down the hall to the right, I spotted closed double doors. "That looks like a good place to start," I growled.

If Wells was in that room, he sure was keeping quiet.

I sprinted down the hall to the closed oak door, then stood up on my hind legs. I leaned close, listening intently. Still nothing.

No reason not to take a peek.

I stepped forward and kicked in the door.

The heavy oak erupted into the room, shattering into splinters of wood and dust.

I stuck my head through the opening and looked left and right. The study was empty. Sort of.

Wells wasn't there. Neither was anyone else. But what I found made the trip up to the second floor worth the minimal effort.

I turned to close the door behind me, then remembered I'd destroyed it. I touched the amulet again, and in a blink, I was back to my human self.

I didn't want clumsy paws and claws breaking anything else in here because what I found looked like it was worth way more than a couple of doors.

Wells' study was a veritable museum. To the left, bookshelves formed a U-shape around the wall. Two leather chairs and an oak coffee table sat in the middle of the volumes. Between that and where I stood, multiple glass cases stood atop alabaster plinths, each containing priceless artifacts from ancient civilizations. Rome, Greece, Persia, and Babylon were all represented.

A worktable stood by a massive window that stretched from floor to ceiling. The table surface festooned with maps, scrolls, leather journals, and a few very old looking books.

The desk at the other end stood by itself with a couple of fancy candles sitting on either side. Behind it, a scimitar hung from the wall.

"What the?" I muttered. "Why does Vernon Wells have a scimitar."

It had long ago been a popular weapon in Middle Eastern cultures for centuries. But what the corrupt pastor was doing with it I had no idea.

I walked over to the worktable and pored over the items on the surface. One thing after another sent chills through my body.

I opened a leather journal closest to the edge. It sat next to a pen. The leather looked and felt newer than basically everything else in the room except the chairs. I figured that was a good enough place to start.

I looked back at the mangled doorway. The house was still completely silent.

"What are you up to, Reverend?" I said to myself.

I peeled open the journal's cover and got an answer I didn't expect.

"A man approached me today. He wore a suit like a fed, but I don't think he works for the government. He told me about strange things —relics that could turn humans into powerful creatures," I read the line at the top of the first page.

A chill shot through my spine. "Vernon Wells knows about us?" Then I noted a curious distinction in the line. It said Guardians *and* Monsters. If I wasn't a monster, then who was?

I turned the page and kept reading. The date was a week after the initial entry

Two men approached me today after my sermon. One of them was the same guy from before. I guess he thought he should bring his partner this time.

I went on.

These men offered no identification, and didn't threaten to arrest me. More evidence they weren't feds or cops.

Instead, they asked if I'd considered the relic thing.

I told them no. But they were insistent. Then they gave me a map and a set of clues to begin the search for what they claimed was an artifact of incredible power—a medallion they claimed to belong to the goddess Artemis.

Being a lover of history, I had to know more.

So, I began the hunt.

What I've learned in the last ten months has changed everything. Supernatural beings truly do walk among us. The pagan gods of the ancient world were superheroes of old. There were monsters, too. All the stuff I always believed to be fiction or legend turned out to be real, as hard as it was to believe.

These mythical creatures of old actually roamed the earth.

Some of them protected humanity. Perhaps they were misguided, those guardians. Those who sought to subdue the masses offered the peace and safety of servitude. It seemed to make sense to me.

People don't know what they want. They think they want freedom when all they really want is to either be better than someone else or have that person brought down to their level so they're both equal.

What people really want is to be ruled. The freedom they truly crave is the freedom of responsibility and accountability.

That, I knew, was the premise behind communism. Make the people believe that things are fair, and they'll eat crackers and broth three times a day in their tiny cubicle apartments—while the ones at the top eat filet mignon and drink the finest wine money can buy.

Sounds like a horrible system. Unless you're the one at the top.

I stopped reading for a second to take a look around. I didn't feel comfortable here, but I needed to find out what Wells was up to.

I turned the page to the next entry.

Every map. Every clue. Every one of those blasted books I bought hasn't given me what I needed. I know I'm close. I can feel it. The medallion of Artemis has to be here. It's somewhere in the Cyclades, but I can't figure out where.

There are so many islands, hundreds of them all throughout the Northern Mediterranean Sea.

I checked Andros Island. They have a small archaeology museum there, but the curator said they'd never heard of anything about a medallion dedicated to the goddess Artemis.

Idiot.

It wasn't just dedicated to her. Based on my findings, it embodied her power and would imbue its wearer with incredible abilities.

The Artemis amulet was the first one I investigated, so I have decided to dedicate all of my efforts to finding it. I don't need to be distracted with other pursuits.

Perhaps along the way I may find one of the other six.

A chill shot through me. "He knows about all of them," I breathed.

I turned the page and noted the date. It was a few months ago.

I've learned of another medallion of power, this one from the House of Claw and Fang. Dread filled me about where this was going. But I continued reading.

I recently discovered there are two archaeologists from Nashville working on a massive project in Mexico. I must come up with a way to get them to help me.

Perhaps my partner will have a connection down there.

"No," I said. "That can't be." I shook my head dramatically.

There was no denying it. The conclusion was obvious.

Jerry, Amy's father, was working with Vernon Wells.

I didn't need to read farther to know that. But I pressed on.

My partner says he can make arrangements, but it will be expensive. Like money matters at this point. I have the general location of the hidden temple. Now I just need the archaeologist, Gideon Wolf, to find it for me.

My partner wanted me to have him killed to motivate his daughter. I guess he doesn't realize she's been cheating on him for years. I've even had a go.

I felt a knot in my gut, but it wasn't as bad as before—like the first time I learned of Amy's indiscretions. It was shocking to learn about Wells and her, but then again, nothing was off the table.

She wasn't the woman I thought I knew.

Apparently, to Wells, she was expendable.

Now it was coming together. Jerry's comment about how I was the one who was supposed to die had confused me before. He'd believed Carrillo's men would kill me. Perhaps Jerry knew Amy didn't care about me, and that was his motivation. Or was it something else? Did Amy know?

That question shook me harder than the others.

Was she part of the plan to take me out and find this medallion for Wells?

The preacher had changed the rules, stabbing her in the back instead of killing me.

In a way, he'd been right. I doubted Amy would have ever found the hidden temple. She'd never been as good with interpreting clues. Pictionary was a disaster for her. She was a great research archaeologist. That was one of the things I admired about her. But when it came to the unconventional, doing things on gut instinct—she couldn't get out of her box.

I doubted Carrillo would have cared which one of us survived. That brought on a new sackful of questions.

Would Carrillo have given the medallion to Jerry? And if so, would Jerry have followed through and delivered it to Wells?

I had a feeling the answer to both was no.

The second one of those guys touched the medallion, they would have changed into the creature and been granted the same powers I now wielded.

I shuddered at the thought.

That was the end of the entries for that book.

I slid the journal off to the side and looked at the map. A red circle indicated the area he believed the hidden temple would be found in Mexico. I was shocked at how close he'd come.

I carefully unrolled one of the scrolls and read through the contents. It was written in Greek. The text talked about powerful beings who protected mankind from the forces of evil, and how these guardians would appear when the innocent needed them most.

More of the stuff I'd read before. I didn't need confirmation. I was living it.

I shifted the map to the side and looked at another one that featured the nation of Greece. He'd circled several locations there, including the island of Andros, but had no luck tracking down the Artemis medallion.

There were a few other islands circled.

I tilted my head, looking closely at the map.

Like the other, this map was extremely old—likely dating back at least a few hundred years. Based on the typography and the material, I guessed somewhere in the eighteenth century.

My eye caught something in the bottom right corner, below the compass drawn onto the surface.

It was writing, but the script made no sense.

The text may has well have been Elvish.

Something looked familiar about it, though I couldn't put my finger on it.

I continued looking through the evidence Wells had collected. Ancient drawings, notes from explorers and historians, and even some more modern theories taken from books or websites, all cluttered the worktable.

One scroll was of particular interest to me. The top of it read Jadah, Guardian Slayer.

"Guardian Slayer?" I echoed.

"What kind of person would—"

The wicked, the voice in my head replied.

Right.

That was a dumb question.

The forces of evil intended to rid the world of guardians so they could have their way with the people, and from what I'd read, that meant total enslavement.

The strange words at the bottom of the Greek map pulled my attention back. What was it about that? It wasn't a language I'd ever seen before, and I'd seen many.

A thought occurred to me.

I looked around the room and found a small mirror hanging on the wall near the doorway.

I quickly walked over to it and removed the frame from the wall. Without fanfare, I raised it high and let it fall to the hardwood floor.

It shattered into several pieces with a crash.

I picked up one of the larger shards and returned to the map. Bending down, I carefully held the edge of the mirror close to the script in the corner.

My eyes widened with excitement as the text suddenly made sense. It was written upside down so only a mirror could reveal what it said.

The script was in English, written long ago. And it was one word.

Delos.

26

"Delos?" I said.

I scrolled up the map and found a small island labeled with the same name. It wasn't one of the ones Wells had circled. Clearly, he hadn't figured out the hidden message.

I picked up the map despite all my training telling me not to do so without protective gloves.

I needed to know who this map belonged to.

Sometimes, not always, cartographers would put their initials on maps they'd created. And now and then, I'd come across several that belonged to ship captains who also put their own names on them, usually on the backside.

Sure enough, I found the name in the top left corner.

It was one I'd seen more times than I could recall throughout my career, including when I was in high school.

Sir Francis Drake.

"This can't be real," I said, scanning the room again out of paranoia.

I scoured the notes again, the maps, everything I could find, just to make sure I was looking at this correctly.

None of that stuff could change the fact that the name on the back of the map was written in the man's own hand.

Francis Drake had been one of my favorite historical figures growing up. Naturally, as a boy, I loved playing pirate games, pretending to be a scallywag in search of buried treasure all over the world.

While Drake wasn't officially a pirate, he was a privateer licensed by the Crown of England to wreak havoc on as many enemy ships as possible.

In Drake's case, that meant the Spanish.

He'd loathed the Spaniards since he was a young man, viewing them as a sort of evil empire.

I recalled looking at maps of his exploration but didn't recall seeing anything into the Mediterranean.

Now, as the realization set in, I took out my phone and did a quick search. I checked the first link and saw what I needed—a map of the routes used by Drake in his voyage around the world, and the other voyages he'd taken to antagonize the Spanish Armada.

The map on my phone showed exactly what I believed—nothing into the Mediterranean. The man had gone almost everywhere around the entire planet, yet he hadn't ventured into one of the more famous seas in history.

I'd never really considered it before, but now the fact struck me as extremely odd.

The famous navigator—perhaps the Queen's favorite—had been almost everywhere. And he'd fought everyone—especially the Spanish. But based on the routes I was looking at, he'd never ventured beyond the Strait of Gibraltar.

Why?

Pirates had roamed the waters of the Med for millennia, raiding merchant vessels whenever they could. That tradition would have carried into the time of Drake, but pirates hadn't bothered him. The man had been afraid of nothing. Heck, he took on the Spanish Armada against incredible odds.

So, why not the Mediterranean?

Unless...

The question wasn't why he didn't take a voyage beyond Gibraltar. It was why did he have a map of the Cyclades Islands in the first place?

If a man—a world-famous navigator—hadn't visited this area, then why the interest? Was he plotting a trip to explore the ancient chain of islands and just didn't have time? Or was the truth far more scintillating?

Had Drake actually visited Greece and simply kept it secret? And if so, why? He'd need funding for a trip like that.

Or would he?

The questions and answers going back and forth in my head were like watching a tennis match.

"No," I said out loud. "He wouldn't need funding."

He had all the money he needed and the full support and authority of the British Crown. He'd been given privateer papers, which meant he could take what he needed from whoever, though his favorite targets were the Spaniards.

Money, to Sir Francis Drake, was a nonissue.

That begged the question: Why didn't he explore the Mediterranean?

Was it because the sea had been traveled for thousands of years, mapped by countless voyagers, or because every stone had been turned on every island?

That was possible. And I had to consider Occam's Razor when it came to this. But something in my gut said none of that was the real reason.

I'd sifted through all the documents on the table but still hadn't found all the answers. Although I had a great place to start: Delos.

Unfortunately, I didn't know much about the island, so I'd need to brush up.

I looked over to the desk and noticed Wells had left his laptop open. I didn't know if the man took off in a hurry, or if that was how he rolled.

The fact Wells wasn't here still needled me. The hour was getting late, and I expected he'd have to return home soon.

Unless he was out of town, or somewhere else in town.

The man had vices. Everyone does. It could have been he was indulging one of those in the city at this very moment and would return home to the surprise of finding all his men gone and his home a wreck.

I snapped out of the thoughts about Wells. The reverend's computer was calling me.

I crossed the room and sat down in the leather chair behind the desk, then pressed the mouse pad with my finger. The screen blinked to life. To my surprise, Wells didn't use a password to protect the screen.

So, everything he'd been looking at was still there.

The web browser overflowed with over a dozen tabs open. I'd been guilty of that myself on more than one occasion.

Whenever I was researching multiple topics or ideas I hated closing windows, so I simply opened another tab over and over until my browser was full of them.

I skipped over the ones for Wells' email account, though I thought it might behoove me to give that a look at some point. I doubted the man would be dumb enough to send anything damning through email. Then again, he was stupid enough to leave his laptop open without a password.

I'd clicked on the tabs and arrived at the third one from the end on the right. When I clicked this, I found more information about Sir Francis Drake. This page contained stories and histories about Drake that I'd never read before.

I clicked the last two tabs, and they offered other strange facts about the famous captain. The Spanish Armada was the mightiest navy on the seas in the sixteenth century, but they grew to fear the captain the Spaniards called *El Draque*, or the dragon.

According to the websites, the Spanish started to believe that Drake was practicing witchcraft or using other supernatural means to achieve his unlikely victories at sea.

Witnesses testified that no man should have been able to do the things he did with a ship. Some believed he was immortal. Others thought he was in league with the devil himself.

No one ever found out for certain.

I let out a hmmm. "The Spanish believed that Drake was supernatural. I wonder if he was a guardian."

The voice in my head didn't answer. I wasn't sure if the silence meant yes or no. But I was pretty certain the fact I was debating this in my head meant I was losing it.

I continued scrolling down the page on the last tab and stopped when I saw a portrait of Drake. I studied the image for nearly a minute.

"It can't be," I said. Then I clicked on a new tab and did a quick web search for more images.

The results popped up immediately, and I didn't have to look far to notice something out of the ordinary.

In more than one portrait—each with different outfits—the legendary captain wore an amulet.

I shook my head. "No. That's impossible."

You're impossible, too, the voice in my head finally chimed in.

It was true. My new existence defied logic and what we knew of science. Those dogmas were going out the window in a hurry.

And it seemed history was about to experience a similar upheaval.

I stood there reading through the pages until I'd absorbed everything. When I was done, I nodded.

I'd discovered an amazing truth... or Wells had, but he wasn't going to get to live to tell anyone about it.

And I was going to do everything in my power to make sure no one found out.

Sir Francis Drake—iconic figure in history—had been a guardian.

"A fascinating truth, isn't it, Gideon Wolf?"

I instinctively spun around and searched the room, ready to transform. But I saw no one.

"You don't think I would be so stupid to show up there on my own, do you, Gideon?"

I recognized the voice of Vernon Wells, but I didn't see him anywhere. I snapped my head around, making sure he wasn't hiding behind a curtain like a six-year-old playing hide-and-seek.

"Alexa?" I replied.

"You're a funny man, Gideon. Unfortunately, that won't save you now."

"Where are you, Reverend? I killed all your men. Got to the last one on my list and found you weren't here. I hate to leave checklists unfinished. It's one of my few OCD qualities."

"Yes, well, sorry to spoil your little plan. But I wasn't about to sit there in my study and wait for a supernatural to show up and murder me. I know what you are, Gideon. You wear the medallion of Xolotl, and wield the power of the Chupacabra. Impressive, I must say, that you were able to locate it."

"Yeah, and I kind of have you to thank for that. You were working with the cartel."

"Oh, Gideon. So easily misled. But that's all well and good. The medallion will be mine soon enough. And you'll be dead."

I twisted around, anticipating an attack, but heard nothing, saw no one.

"You look panicked, Gideon. Why don't you shape-shift into that magnificent creature? Not that it will do you any good. The monster needs air to breathe, just like the rest of us."

What did he mean by that?

"Not to worry, Gideon. You'll just feel a little sleepy at first. Then, when you wake up... Well, you won't have to worry about anything much longer. I'll leave it at that."

"Wells!" I thundered.

His nauseating laugher filled the room. Then something else did.

Gray fog poured out of the vents in the ceiling.

Reality hit me hard. He was going to gas me. As far as I recalled, the shaman didn't say anything about being immune to such things.

I left the desk and ran for the door. When I reached the door, I found the same fog filling the hallway outside.

I coughed at the irritant in the air. Grimacing, I plunged forward to the stairwell. I had to get out of the house and into the... into the fresh...

No. I wouldn't let myself slip out of consciousness. If I did, I was a dead man.

I sprinted to the left toward the end of the corridor where a huge window opened up to the eastern side of the property.

My legs felt heavy, and it took every ounce of strength I could summon to jump.

I crashed into the window as my body went through the transformation into the Chupacabra. Glass shattered all around me, and I felt the unsettling sense of nothing beneath me as I fell toward the ground.

Just before I landed, I managed to whip my feet out beneath my body, and landed with remarkable balance in an upright position. I sucked in huge gulps of air to cleanse my lungs and my brain from the gas, or whatever Wells was using to knock me out.

The cool, clean air sent a shock wave of clarity and energy through me.

Pausing, I looked back up at the house and noted the two security cameras—one mounted to each corner just under the roof.

I wanted Wells to know I knew he was still watching me. I didn't know if the guy had a direct feed to the outside cameras or not.

I took off into the darkness and circled around the property down toward the road and the gatehouse.

There was other unfinished business to attend to.

I wanted to know what was going on with Amy's parents. And then there was still the matter of the Parthenon. The museum would be closed right now, so I'd have to either go back during the day or I would need to sneak in.

It just so happened that I knew one of the curators who worked there, and I figured a call might get me in for a private tour.

Once I reached my car, I would make the call. Visiting Amy's parents' house could wait a few more hours.

27

I watched my friend Alan pull into a parking space outside the Parthenon. He climbed out of his car and looked around the lot until he spotted me. I waved and walked in his direction, carefully looking to the left and right to make sure I wasn't being watched.

I had no idea how to tell if I was being followed. I mean it seemed like a sort of self-explanatory kind of thing, but I felt like I needed some kind of training. It seemed impossible that the world's best agents and operators weren't given some kind of additional lessons on how to spot a tail and how to lose one.

Then again, I had no idea. Maybe it really was as simple as keeping a watchful eye out for anything unusual or suspicious.

For now, I didn't see anything out of the ordinary and so approached my friend with a disarming smile on my face.

"Well, well, well. The prodigal son has returned," Alan said as he approached. His crooked smile was every bit a part of his brand as the long, dramatic gait he walked with.

Alan Whitney towered over me by at least six inches. He'd played college basketball at Austin Peay State University and still carried that big athletic frame.

I wondered if he'd been in many fights in his life and what that kind of foray would look like. I'd known Alan for at least twenty years and never seen him even get upset about anything, so I doubted hand-to-hand combat was in his dossier.

Dossier? What was I thinking?

Checking for tails, using agency-type terms. I was starting to sound like a wannabe spook.

"Thanks so much for coming out here at this weird time of night," I replied and clapped my friend's hand to shake it.

Instead, he reeled me in for a big hug and slapped me on the back. "Good to see you, Gideon. We need to hang out more often."

"I know. I know."

"You're out of town so dang much. When you called, I thought you might still be down in Mexico." He crossed his arms and stopped talking, ready to listen. That was one thing about Alan. He was a great listener. And not just in the way people say on their online dating profiles. He was the genuine article.

I'd seen the guy at parties, listening to girls in the corner as they gave him their sob stories about why the quarterback wasn't into them or how they'd been dumped by their boyfriend or who knew what else.

I pitied him in many ways. He would have given his left thumb to be with any of those girls, but they were never into him. Not until he got to Peay.

There, he became a campus star overnight.

"You still with Marci?" I asked.

He grinned. "Yeah. Been together three years now."

"Wow. That's a long time. You thinking about...."

"Yes. I am. Haven't asked, but that's coming. We've talked about it."

It was my turn to grin back up at him. "Sounds like you're doing well, my friend. I'm glad to hear it."

"I am. What about you? Where's Amy?"

Just when I thought I was turning a corner on that issue, a new knife dug its way into my gut.

"You didn't hear?" At least genuine curiosity worked as a numbing salve for the issue. I couldn't believe Alan didn't know.

"Hear what?"

I filled him in on everything that happened—the trip to Mexico, the gala, the murder, and my return to the States.

Alan wasn't the same as Jack with his unflappable open-mindedness to the ancient world. Alan was a traditionalist. He viewed history the way he read it in high school and college, and if something came along to change that perspective, he instinctively dug his feet in and fought tooth and nail.

I appreciated that about him, even if I often didn't agree. I'd learned there was way more to history than what we'd been led to believe. And the last week or so had hammered that fact home.

When I finished filling him in on the tragic life of Gideon Wolf, Alan merely stood there with pain drawing the corners of his eyes toward the earth.

"Gideon. I'm so sorry. I didn't know."

I appreciated the gesture, but I was beyond sorry now. Amy had betrayed me. And based on what I'd heard about her father, I wasn't sure I'd dug down to the depth of that betrayal yet.

"It's okay. I... I'm working through it."

"I can't imagine."

"I know." I offered him a nod that told him he'd done all he could. "Seriously. I'll be okay."

He looked over at the museum, keeping his eyes fixed on it for a few seconds—probably to buy a little time to think of what he should say next.

"This why you wanted to meet me?" He brought his focus back to hear my answer.

"No." I tipped my head toward the Parthenon. "I'm curious about something with this place."

"Curious?" Alan sounded intrigued and cautious at the same time. "About what?"

"Don't worry, Al. I'm not going to break anything. I just want to have a look around without the throngs of tourists here."

I knew that rang his bell. Alan appreciated others enjoying history or their learning about people and civilizations from the past, but he also wasn't a people person. He preferred to be in his study or on a couch reading a book or in a lab doing research.

"I can certainly understand that," he said, predictably.

"I don't want to get you in any trouble," I added. "If you're not comfortable doing this, then don't worry about it."

He looked at me disparagingly. "Get in trouble? Gideon, I'm head of the museum here now and on, like, three historical preservation committees. No one is going to get me in trouble for popping by the office after hours." He leaned emphatically toward the employee entrance. "Come on."

I followed him to the back door, where he swiped an access card. The door clicked and beeped. Alan turned the latch and held the door open for me. I looked out across the huge lawns that surrounded the building. Normally, there would have been cars lining the street or people milling around, taking in the sights surrounding the replica.

It was just us here now.

I spied the camera hanging from the wall as I walked through. I didn't want the attention, and I had a bad feeling that feed would somehow end up in the hands of my enemies.

I shook my head at the thought. *Enemies.* I'd never had any real enemies in my life. Not that I knew of. I'd always tried to be nice to people, not cause trouble, and always say what I thought without talking badly about someone behind their back.

My grandmother taught me that—the old cliché that seemed to be the guide stone for generations. *If you can't say something nice about someone, don't say anything at all.*

I'd lived that to the best of my ability, but now I found myself with more enemies than I ever thought possible. And they all wanted me dead.

Inside the Parthenon, the air smelled different. It was the scent I'd noticed in every museum I'd ever visited. Bookstores and libraries had a similar odor. It was the scent of old things, of history.

Alan let the door close behind us and passed me to shut off the alarm with a key code on a panel on the interior wall.

"So," he said, business handled, "what was it you wanted to have a look at?"

"I'm not sure, actually."

His eyebrows raised slightly. "Oh?"

"I know that sounds weird. And me calling you here in the night to just have a look around makes me a bad friend. But I'm working on something I think is connected to ancient Greece, and I think that part of the answers I'm looking for could be here, in this place."

He shook his head, more confused than he was a few seconds before. "But this isn't the Parthenon, Gideon. You know that. It's a replica. The only authentic things here are the molds they used to make it look like the real thing. And of course, some of the art and artifacts we keep on display."

"I know. And I know it must sound crazy. But because it was done to look as much like the original as possible, I'm thinking it's worth lookin' around before I buy a plane ticket and fly all the way to Athens."

He seemed to accept that answer.

"So, what is it you're looking for again?"

"Like I said, I don't really know." I knew I was going to have to give him more than that. Alan wasn't stupid, and I wasn't about to treat him like he was. "I believe, and please don't judge me, that there could be some kind of artifact here that was supposedly sacred. A relic of power, so to speak."

It was a risky thing to use that term. If I didn't watch it, Alan would shut off and wouldn't listen to a thing I said for the rest of my life. He always blew off everything Jack said when the three of us hung out.

Jack didn't take offense to it. A good sport, Jack actually went the other direction with Alan's disparagement. He viewed it as a challenge, almost like a missionary seeking to convert a nonbeliever.

"That doesn't sound like you," Alan said, his suspicions still present. "What kind of artifact is it?"

"It could be a sacred object to Athena," I said. "Or perhaps one of the other gods, maybe even one of her favorite warriors."

"Where did you find the evidence for this search? I know you, Gideon. You wouldn't just jump at some random tidbit you found in an online forum."

"You're right," I agreed. "And I appreciate you trust that about me." I paused before I went on. "Let me ask you something. What do you know about monsters in Greek mythology?"

He shrugged. "I know about most of that stuff. You talking about the ones from Homer's writings?"

"Yeah. But beyond that. We've all read that stuff. I have a pretty good foundation. But I was wondering if there are other legends, stories that are lesser known. Stuff that isn't always mentioned in schools."

He considered the question carefully, pinching his lips between a finger and thumb as he stared at the floor. "I mean, every culture has forgotten legends like that. Heck, the stories about when the Titans ruled the earth were blunted and somewhat lost when they were replaced by the Olympian mythology. But I don't know about many others. What are *you* talking about?"

"I don't know," I said, rolling my shoulders. "I just thought if anyone knew, you would." An idea popped in my mind. "Actually. Think about Bigfoot," I said. "Bigfoot is a local legend."

He snorted a laugh. "Local to like five or six different areas of the continent. There have been 'sightings' all over the place, according to witnesses." He used air quotes to emphasize the supposed evidence.

"Yeah, I know. It's crazy." I said the words uneasily and hoped he didn't notice. "But were there any stories like that in Greek legends?"

That one stumped him, and I could see the consternation on his face. "Huh. That's a good one, actually. I mean yes. Sure. Every region and town had local legends. Probably ghost stories for the most part. That's a tradition as old as time. And you know how people were thousands of years ago. They were way more superstitious than now. Well, except for baseball players."

I laughed at the joke. He was right about that. Baseball players really were some of the most paranoid, superstitious people I'd known.

"As far as specific ones," he continued, "I don't really know about many. Although," he stopped himself for a second. His eyes lit with a flicker of excitement. "There was a story about powerful artifacts that were imbued with certain powers of the gods. Strength, speed, invisibility, those kinds of things. Obviously, we've never found anything like that before."

"Right. Because it's myth. But still, it's interesting."

"What does any of that have to do with what you want to see here?" Alan asked, getting straight to the point.

It was a fair question. I owed him an answer. Problem was, I couldn't think of one that didn't make me sound like a raving lunatic.

"The shield and other articles," I said, remembering my last visit to the Parthenon. "Would it be possible to go look at those?"

"Sure," Alan said. "You're talking about the statue, right?"

"Yeah. Sorry. Could we get a closer look at Athena?"

"Of course. Follow me."

Alan led me into the main hall where the impressive statue of the Greek goddess towered over the floor. Most of the lights were off, but a few glowed brightly off the gold-leaf layer coating the shield, spear, and the elegant robe flowing to her feet.

A golden serpent sat upright to her left, looking out at those who would dare enter the sanctuary of Athena.

She held an angelic figure in her right palm.

The sculpture was completed in 1990 as part of the restoration efforts on the Parthenon. I recalled reading about it, but I'd been preoccupied with other things at the time since I was just a boy.

"Impressive, isn't it?" Alan said, pride radiating from his face.

We approached the sculpture and stopped just short of the rope that blocked the rest of the way.

"Yes. Very." I looked up at the face of the goddess staring out at the other end of the building. The roof overhead was designed like a pergola, with beams crisscrossing in perfect squares.

I wondered what it must have been like to be in the real temple in

Athens thousands of years ago, back before light or noise pollution, when life was simpler and places like this could really be appreciated.

Alan cocked his head to the side, analyzing the statue with a fresh perspective.

"You know, I said before that I didn't know much about the monster stuff in some of the older legends, but I guess I've gotten so accustomed to being around this thing that I forgot about some that were out in the open."

"What?" I suddenly felt a dash of hope spring up in my gut. "What are you talking about?"

He indicated the serpent first. "That was a monster," Alan explained. "And there are others represented here. A sphinx, gryphons, gorgons, winged horses... All that stuff is present here. They represent some of the challenges and trials Athena had to go through to achieve lasting peace and victory. Essentially, they're primitive forces she domesticated."

"Primitive forces," I said in a whisper. "Fascinating."

"Yeah. I don't know if that's the sort of thing you were talking about, but it's here if you want to take a closer look."

"Sure. Yes. You don't mind me crossing the rope?"

Alan looked back over his shoulder. When he turned to face me, he wore mischief across his face. "Pretty sure you're not going to get in trouble. Just don't break anything. Okay?"

I nodded.

"I'm going to run back to the office real quick to check something. You need anything?" He pointed at me.

"No. I'm good. Thanks, Alan. I really appreciate this."

"Happy to help, my friend." He turned and made his way back down the main aisle in the room, then disappeared around the corner to the right.

It felt weird to be in this place by myself. And at night. It would have been more surreal if it were the original temple, where people had come to worship or seek insight thousands of years before.

That sort of thing always got to me.

I shook off the nostalgia and crossed under the velvet rope, inching my way closer to the pedestal upon which the goddess and the serpent stood.

The forward-facing relief depicted Greek people engaged in various stages of life, but all coming to rest at the feet of Athena.

I stared up at the snake, the pet of the goddess.

The thing was ghastly, although well crafted. I'd never cared much for snakes. And this golden one was no different. I felt like at any moment the thing could spring to life and try to devour me.

I told myself that wasn't going to happen. But what did I know? I was the freakin' Chupacabra, for crying out loud.

I stepped closer to the pedestal, admiring the intricate craftsman-ship of the figures on the relief.

Chariots, animals, and people all in various stages of life were represented.

But none of that helped me with my question.

My feet carried me almost unconsciously around to the right, where I saw the designs on the enormous shield more clearly.

A woman's face stared out from the center, circled by twisting serpents. Outside the inner circle, dozens of warriors with shields and spears raged in battle. Some had already succumbed to their wounds and lay on their backs facing the heavens.

I paused for a second, assessing the expertly carved design, then walked back around to the front. There at the corner, I stopped and looked up at the shield's inside.

The interior was decorated differently than the exterior.

Instead of carved and layered in gold, the textured figures, warriors, and monsters on the inside were painted on, depicting incredible battles. Some of the fights were between men and beasts, others between men, and a few others included what looked like deities.

I found myself wishing I'd studied the sculpture in greater detail before coming here.

"Pretty remarkable, isn't it?" Alan asked.

His voice startled me in the silence of the great room, and I nearly jumped out of my shoes.

"Yes," I agreed. "It really is spectacular."

"The sculptor had the same name as me. Alan. Last name was different, though. LeQuire."

Alan joined me at the base of the statue and looked up, admiring it. "He really did an incredible job with all this."

"Yes. It's amazing we have something like this in our state. Such a cool tribute."

"Indeed."

Alan stared up into the statue's eyes for a long minute before asking, "Did you find what you were looking for?"

"Maybe," I hedged. "That shield has some interesting designs on it."

"Great battles between man and monster, and sometimes the gods make an appearance as well."

"I noticed."

I couldn't help but wonder if some of the people in the imagery were guardians of ancient days. Guardians like me.

28

We stood there for a few minutes, taking in the sight of the impressive sculpture before I walked around to the left corner and continued my inspection. I needed to know if there was anything here, something that could be related to the book I'd read at Jack's shop.

"You don't look satisfied," Alan observed.

"Is it that obvious?"

He chuckled. "I've known you a long time, Gideon. I know you better than most. You gonna tell me what's really going on? Or you just plan on keeping me in the dark?" He waited as I kept my eyes locked on the sculpture. "I can't help you if you won't tell me what you're up to."

I sucked in a deep breath through my nose and exhaled. "Honestly, I don't know what I'm looking for. I thought maybe there would be something here, hidden from plain view."

"Like in a secret compartment?" He sounded sincere.

"I don't know. I guess." I felt foolish for the admission. I knew how he viewed things like that.

To my surprise, he didn't say anything snarky. "Well, if there is something hidden here, I've never noticed it before."

I resigned to the fact that if there really was something concealed within the confines of the Parthenon, Alan or someone else would have surely found it by now.

"It was worth a shot," I said.

"You're not going to tell me what you were looking for. Are you?" Alan pressed the question, but there was no malice in it—only curiosity.

"I read a book about ancient relics," I said.

"You mentioned that."

"I did?" Honestly, I couldn't recall if I had or not. The days were running together now, and the hours and minutes blurred by. "I guess I did. Anyway, this book spoke about powerful relics from the ancient world."

"Are you talking about weapons or other items?" Alan asked.

He seemed intrigued, so I decided to feed him a little more— without adding in the part about me being a monster.

"Some of them were weapons. Others were things like good luck charms. Some of it was armor. I even read about the shackles of the Titans."

"Ah," Alan said with an understanding nod. "Yes, that one is an interesting one. The chains used to shackle the Titans in the abyss for a thousand years."

"You know about those?"

"Of course. I think that component was included in a video game in recent years. The chains were used by Zeus to restrain the Titans and keep them from returning to the realm of men. Can't have a bunch of giant monsters running amok." He said the last part cheerily—his own way of blowing off the legend as nothing more than an old story parents told their kids thousands of years ago.

"I'm interested in things like that," I said, pushing the envelope a touch further. "Artifacts that were so rooted in religion or even day-to-day life that have vanished from antiquity. Like the priestly breast-plate from the Old Testament."

"The one with the Urim and the Thummim?"

"The very same. Everyone focuses on the Ark of the Covenant or the place where Jesus may have been buried. Famous things like that. But what about some of the other powerful artifacts from the scriptures?"

"And that's just one religion," Alan added. "Every single one of them contains items like that. Could you imagine if those things were actually real and worked as described in the histories and scriptures?" He laughed. "We'd have chaos on a global scale. Destruction everywhere."

"Well, some of them are real," I suggested.

"Sure," he said with a shrug. "I've never seen any of these kinds of artifacts, but that doesn't mean they aren't out there somewhere, hidden from mankind."

"I appreciate your open-mindedness."

He smirked. "Look, I want to believe in stuff like that. I just haven't seen any evidence for it so far. Doesn't mean it isn't out there. But I like proof. I'm big on having something I can see and touch. Tangible evidence tells the story, I believe."

"Understandable," I said. I looked closely at the relief, studying the figures on the façade.

"Was there anything else you wanted to look at in here?" Alan asked.

"I suppose not. I appreciate you coming down here to let me in. I'm sorry it was a waste of your time."

"Hanging out with you is never a waste of time, my friend." He said the words with a kind, sincere tone that I'd grown accustomed to over the years. "You want to grab a beer or something?"

A beer sounded pretty good. Heaven knew I could use something to take the edge off. But I knew I couldn't. Not tonight. Not with Wells out there running around still alive. I'd mangled his home and taken out his entire security detail. But there was still work to be done. I needed to get to Amy's parents' place and find out what I could about their involvement with all this.

I hoped her mother wasn't a part of it. She'd always been kind to me, at least on the surface, but she was a hard one to read. There could have been a shark lurking under that calm surface, and I'd have never known it.

"No, I can't right now. I need to do a few more things before I head back to the house for the night." I kept it vague, knowing Alan wasn't going to pry.

"Have you been back there since you returned?"

I wasn't going to count that as prying, especially since he asked the question more out of concern than anything else.

"Yeah. I have."

"Must have been difficult. I can't imagine."

I nodded. "We had some good times there at our home. Lot of memories to sort through. But things weren't what they seemed in our marriage, Alan. That's the way life goes more often than not. We think things are one way, and they turn out to be something else completely."

"Isn't that the truth," he said, his voice trailing off with his own thoughts.

I knew where his mind was going. He'd lost a sister in a hiking accident when we were in college. She'd been out at one of the state parks walking too close to the cliffs. I knew the spot well since I'd been there rock climbing on a few occasions.

It had been a careless moment. One little slip of judgment. That's all it took.

Her boyfriend had jumped first over a narrow gap in the rocks. The opening was less than three feet across. Yet somehow, she didn't make it over to the other side.

She fell eighty feet to her death, right there in front of two friends and her boyfriend.

That loss still haunted Alan to this day.

"You okay?" I asked.

He nodded. "Yep. I'm fine. Just thinking." He looked around the huge room and bobbed his head again. "If you don't want to take a look at anything else, I can—" He stopped in mid-sentence, his eyes locked on something beyond the statue.

"What?" I asked. Then I followed his eyes.

"What is that back there?" he wondered.

His feet started moving on their own, carrying him toward the rear of the long building.

"What in the world?" His legs moved faster.

I followed close behind, now seeing something on the floor I hadn't noticed before.

It was hidden behind the pedestal from the other angles where we'd been standing.

As I reached the back corner, every suspicion I'd had about this place was immediately confirmed.

Debris sprayed across the floor. Chunks of white stone and piles of dust littered the surface around the base of the pedestal, all from a jagged hole in the side.

"What in the world happened here?" Alan looked over at me, flabbergasted and furious.

"I have no idea. I'm seeing it for the first time, too." I looked over at the other side of the statue. "I didn't notice this from that vantage point."

I squatted down in front of the hole. It was at least three feet wide, more than enough to fit a person through. A tight fit, sure, but still big enough for me to get through.

"This is..." Alan faltered, unable to come up with the words to describe his fury, his loathing for whoever had desecrated this incredible work of art. "Why? Why would someone do this?"

I took out my phone and turned on the flashlight, then pointed it into the cavity. Within the base was hollow. But it wasn't empty. Not entirely.

"I'm going in there," I said, getting down on my belly amid the jagged chunks that had been broken from the pedestal.

"What? No. We need to call the police. And I need to have someone look at the security footage from the cameras. We have to catch whoever did this."

I looked up at him with deadly seriousness in my eyes. "You're not going to catch the people who did this, Alan. Go through the footage if you want to, but you won't find anything. They'll have been masked. And on top of that, you're probably dealing with someone who has the ability to shut off your security cameras."

"Why do you think that?" He had his phone in his hands, ready to call the cops.

"Did the alarm go off at any point tonight?"

He thought about it for three seconds longer than he should have. "No. No, I guess not."

"Right. That means they disarmed it. And it was armed when we got here earlier, right?"

He nodded. "Yes. I... Well, I think it was. I mean, now that you mention it, I don't recall the system beeping when I deactivated it."

"Bingo."

He shook his head, trying to find clarity in the now-murky reality. "What are you saying, Gideon? Someone broke in here and busted a hole in the base of this sculpture? For what? Why should they do that?"

"Take a look for yourself."

I rolled to the side and kept the light pointed into the hole so he could see. Alan squatted next to me and craned his head to the right to get a better view.

His face drained, replaced with confusion. "I don't understand. What is that?"

Inside the vacant pedestal were two stone blocks, each with a knob sticking up in the center.

I didn't need to crawl in there after all. I could see everything just fine. And I doubted there was anything else to find. The robbers had taken whatever had been placed in there.

I shifted onto my knees and swiped away some of the dust on the floor. "Look," I said, pointing at the shiny tiles underfoot. "Looks like someone dragged something out of here."

Scrapes and gouges in the floor ran all the way to the back of the room toward the emergency exit.

"I don't understand," Alan confessed. His voice was in another state now, miles away from here. "Who would do such a thing? And for what?"

I leaned closer to the floor to examine some of the scrapes. "Whatever they took from in there was heavy, made of metal, most likely."

"What?" Alan looked down at me, totally unprepared to do any kind of investigation.

At least *that* was part of my job. Not typically this sort of thing, but closer to my area of expertise than vigilante or secret agent stuff.

"Look closer," I advised. "You see these grooves right here?"

"Barely. How did you spot that?"

"I noticed some of the debris was dragged out away from the pedestal." I pointed toward the emergency exit. "You can see the lines of dust get thinner until they disappear. That means they were pulling something. And from the scrapes on the floor tiles, I'd say it was pretty hefty. Maybe a few hundred pounds."

I was guessing on the weight, but if it was too heavy to carry out of here, the conclusion was logical.

"Oh," Alan realized. "I guess you're right."

His head twisted back and forth on a swivel. "But I still don't understand. What was in there? I doubt the artist knew about that."

"Maybe," I said. "Maybe not."

"Are you saying the sculptor put something in the base of Athena? Like what?"

I shook my head, my lips curling in dissatisfaction at the lack of answers. "No. I'm not saying that. But it could be what happened. Someone put it there. As to what it could be? I have no clue. I can tell you this, though, Alan. I'm going to figure out who did this, and what they took."

29

I stopped outside Amy's parents' house and looked around.

The luxurious subdivision boasted enormous, opulent houses with so many square feet I had to wonder if the owners ever got lost inside.

People from other walks of life usually wondered how home-owners of such gigantic places ever kept them clean.

I knew the secret: a maid who worked twenty hours a week.

Jerry Hanlon had made enough money with all his ventures that hiring a maid to work even forty hours a week wouldn't register on his spending radar. The guy was worth at least fifty or sixty million, as far as I could tell. But it was possible his net worth was much greater due to illegal activities.

I still didn't have much proof to go on in the way of tangible evidence, but the testimony was pretty damning. And the fact he tried to kill me only reinforced Jerry's willingness to do whatever he felt necessary. Or in my case, take revenge into his own hands regard-less of the consequences.

Usually, people like that didn't often face consequences. They could buy their way out of trouble. And they did it with constant regularity, and without guilt or regret.

No cars sat in the circular driveway that looped around in front of the white brick mansion. The porticos in the front towered up to the second floor, where the balcony looked out over the neighborhood.

I doubted Jerry had ever even used it.

I'd often thought about how nice it would be to sit out there at sunrise, sipping a cup of coffee in the cool of morning.

It was possible Amy's mom spent time out there. She seemed the sort to enjoy relaxing that way. But not her father.

He'd always been too intense, perpetually focused on getting things done—even when he was on vacation.

I got out of the car and walked around to the side of the house, recalling the last time I'd been on a family trip with the Hanlons.

We'd gone to Palm Springs and stayed at an all-inclusive five-star place. I wasn't used to stuff like that—people waiting on me hand and foot. The golf course, La Quinta, had been one of the nicest I'd ever played in my life.

I enjoyed the game and always made it a point to visit a course when I was traveling abroad. But that didn't mean I got to play all the best courses. It was usually a local club, and most of the time a public one unless one of my contacts in the area had a connection.

No connection was needed when you were with Jerry Hanlon.

He took care of everything with money, and he paid for everything. I tried to help pay the bill for a couple of meals here and there, but he always refused and told me that my money was no good.

I wondered how he felt about paying for all those things now.

He blamed me for his daughter's death, but that was only the surface of it. He'd said I was the one who was supposed to die that night in Mexico. Not Amy. And there'd been more confirmation of that plan.

It made me sick to my stomach. But like all the other crazy turmoil spinning in my life, I was getting used to it.

Before I got any closer to the mansion, I slipped a mask over my face and pulled a black baseball cap down low to shield my eyes. Jerry had cameras all over the place. I'd always thought him paranoid, especially living in this neighborhood. There was never any crime, no people checking car doors to see if they were locked or any home invasions.

Criminals left this part of the city off their radar.

I skirted the side of the house, making my way around back. I kept to the shadows in case one of the nosy neighbors happened to be looking out their window or on their deck enjoying the stars, or maybe a cigar and bourbon.

Jerry had me over a few times for that. We'd smoked the best cigars money could buy and had drunk bourbon poured from crystal decanters into crystal tumblers. He knew how to impress.

And it was all a show.

The successful, wealthy husband and father was a monster.

I rounded the back corner and stopped at the steps to the massive three-level deck that overlooked a full acre of gardens, lawns, and ornamental shrubbery. A pool abutted the lower level and was surrounded by a black metal fence. The gray stone tiles, coping, and pillars supporting gas lanterns must have cost a fortune to bring in.

Then again, Jerry wasn't one to spare expense. And now that I was seeing things in a new light, I had to wonder if some of his frivolous spending *had* to be done.

I'd always noticed he was an extremely generous tipper. More than once I saw him tip a bartender or the kid cleaning our golf clubs a hundred bucks. Other than the occasional bourbon and cigar, I knew Jerry didn't like me. So it was a confounding thing to try and understand if he really was a nice guy or simply liked how it felt to appear wealthy.

Now I realized it was probably a tax thing more than anything else. He had to spend that money. And it was usually in cash. Heck, the more I thought about it, the more I realized it was almost always in cash.

The whole thing struck me as odd now.

I shook off the thoughts as I walked around to the gate into the pool area. I stopped for a second and looked over at the cameras on the corners of the house. I knew Jerry would see me. I just hoped they bought my story.

The second I walked into view of one of the cameras, he would get an alert. I figured I probably had about thirty seconds after that before he would be able to access the video feed. I'd avoided the ones on the front of the house, but there would be none of that the rest of the way in.

Once he looked at the feed, he'd call the cavalry.

I was willing to risk it.

And I was hedging all my bets against him calling the cops.

Jerry was a killer, or at least an attempted one. He was involved with the cartels in multiple schemes, and that was possibly all just on the surface.

He wouldn't call the cops for a little breaking and entering unless he had them in his back pocket, which was a possibility I couldn't discount. Men like Jerry Hanlon forged relationships with all the "right" people. It was how they never saw a minute of jail time no matter what horrible things they'd done.

I pulled my hat down tighter and opened the gate. I scurried across the patch of grass between the house and pool deck. I stopped at three rocks stacked neatly in the corner. Each bore a Japanese inscription on the surface.

Jerry didn't know a thing about Japanese culture. Not that I knew of. I guess he thought the rocks looked cool here in the corner, like some kind of makeshift shrine or something.

Either way, I knew what it really was.

He kept his spare key hidden there.

I lifted the center rock and found the lone key lying on the tile. After I took the key, I replaced the stone and walked over to the door.

I looked inside to the den where the Hanlons had several workout machines—an exercise bike, a rower, some weights, and an elliptical.

The keypad to disarm the alarm hung on the wall to the left, just inside the door. Jerry had given me the code in case Amy and I ever wanted to come over to use the pool since ours was often crowded with young children or twentysomethings throwing down on the weekends.

I inserted the key and unlocked the door, stepped inside, and shifted over to the keypad. I entered the four digits and then waited for the beeping to stop.

Beep. Beep. Beep. Beep.

The elongated notes continued.

I frowned. This was about to be the shortest break-in in history if Jerry had changed the code.

I took a step closer and this time, slowly, deliberately entered the code again.

I held my breath as I waited. Then, to my relief, the panel let out a quick staccato of beeps, then the light turned green.

I exhaled and looked around the room.

A billiard table sat a few feet away to my right. A big black wrap-around couch on the far side of the room provided a comfortable place to watch movies or sports.

I'd spent a few nights hanging out down here with Amy's parents, though most of those were early on in our relationship.

I wondered how genuine their cordiality had been at the time, but there was no reason to go down that path now.

Jerry had tried to have me killed. Then he'd pulled the trigger himself to make sure the job was done.

I'd never been anything but good to their family, and to their daughter. That told me all I needed to know. I was expendable. And Jerry Hanlon had no problem with disposing of me.

I walked across the room and over to the hallway that stretched into the other parts of the downstairs. There were guest rooms, I knew, along with an office where Amy's mother made jewelry and clothing.

I'd always been impressed with her ability to make nice things, though I didn't get the impression her husband had the same appreciation for her work.

I rounded the bottom of the stairs and climbed up to the main floor, hurried around the next corner, and continued up to the second floor.

Nothing stirred in the house except for me. A haunting silence filled the cavernous corridors, rooms, and antechambers. I stopped on the landing between floors and listened. A grandfather clock down on the main floor ticked away the seconds. The clicking sound echoed through the foyer and down the corridors, all the way up to the cathedral ceiling.

Satisfied no one else was in the house yet, I continued to the top of the stairs and rushed down the corridor to Jerry's study.

He kept a vault there, though he didn't know I was aware of it. One time on a visit, I'd seen the secret safe hidden behind a tall painting—a portrait of Jerry and his labrador. The picture was meant to look like the two had been off hunting quail, but I knew it was just a painting. Jerry was no more an expert hunter than I was a chocolatier.

I cut to the left and into the study through the big double doors and stopped once I was inside. Jerry's desk sat straight ahead with a huge window behind him that opened up to the view of the property behind the house.

To the left, hanging on the wall, was the portrait of Jerry and his dog.

The dog was long gone, put down a few years before due to old age. Now, I was thinking it might be time to do the same with Jerry.

The painting stood nearly six feet tall and four feet wide. I'd always thought the thing garish and awkward, especially where he positioned it on the wall, but it wasn't my office.

I stalked over to the portrait and pulled it back away from the wall. It hung on hinges and swung open like a door to reveal the tall vault behind it.

The safe was locked. No shocker there. And I knew that at any second, whoever Jerry had called to take care of the intruder in his home would be on their way.

That didn't give me much time. And I was anything but a master thief with the ability to easily crack safes. I knew, too, that it would take more than just his wife's birthday or a favorite number as the combination. No way he'd be that stupid.

I took a closer step to the vault and turned the wheel. To my surprise, it spun easily. I heard a click, and realized that the safe wasn't locked after all.

I looked back over my shoulder, certain this was a trap similar to the one at Wells' place, but I heard no guards charging down the halls, and no alarm rang out to announce my trespassing.

I didn't trust it, but I would change into the beast if needed.

I continued pulling the safe door until it was wide open.

All I could do was stare at the treasures within. Stacks of cash two and three feet tall filled the back of the safe. There must have been ten or twenty of them, all hundred-dollar bills from what I could tell.

It was like something out of a movie scene. And that was just the cash.

Stacks of tightly wrapped bags of white powder sat in the forefront to the left. A few more packages with a dark yellow powder occupied the front right.

Three AR15 rifles hung from across the back. Two pistols dangled on the inner right wall.

A shelf near the top housed several other items. Upon closer inspection, I realized they were passports from other countries, false papers, bonds, and some other financial documents I didn't understand, but appeared to be from foreign banks.

I flipped through the passports and found they were all assigned to Jerry, although his name differed on the documents. He'd established a series of aliases, with addresses in three different counties to support the fake identification.

"He had a whole other life going on," I realized, shaking my head. "But what about Mrs. Hanlon?"

I didn't see anything for her in there, and I wondered if she'd been left out of the whole operation. Or did she simply keep her own things separate from his?

I found myself wanting to believe she wasn't involved, that she didn't know about the seedy underworld operation Jerry was a part of, but how could she not?

I searched the rest of the safe's contents, but I found nothing in the way of balance sheets or anything that would show cash flow relating to the illegal activities Jerry was obviously conducting.

The only question that remained, who was the one pulling the strings? Was it Vernon Wells? Or was it Jerry Hanlon?

A third possibility percolated in my mind.

The two men could have been equal partners in the business. They each had a different set of skills and connections that could make the two of them stronger together.

I knew arrangements like that didn't often last long. Eventually, one person always let greed overcome them, and they would bump their partner out of the business—one way or the other.

I turned around and found Jerry's cigar humidor on the corner of the desk. A fancy lighter sat next to it—one of those things that had a brass lever on the side. I pulled the handle and watched the flame flicker to life atop the wick.

Then I looked back at the safe and the illicit contents inside.

An idea struck me, and I smiled at the thought.

If Jerry were going to send someone to check on his place, it would have to be soon.

I looked around the area for something to put the money in but found nothing useful. Then I recalled seeing some boxes in one of the closets down the hall on a previous visit. I didn't remember what was in them because I hadn't looked, but I knew those would serve nicely.

I hurried back down the hall, turned right into one of the guest rooms, and opened the closet door.

Just as I expected, a stack of cardboard boxes towered from the floor almost to the ceiling on the right. On the left, four storage bins stacked one on top of the other.

"Even better," I said.

I dumped out photo albums and an assortment of stuff the Hanlons had accumulated over the years, and carried two of the bins back down the hall to the study.

There, I rapidly stuffed stacks of hundred-dollar bills into the boxes until they were brimming.

I returned to the closet and retrieved two more boxes, getting every last dollar into the bins before I was done.

When I was satisfied with the packing, I shifted into the Chupacabra and carried the bins downstairs, two at a time. However, on this trip I went out the front door and out to the car on the street.

After dropping off the boxes in the back of my ride, I rushed back into the mansion to get the last two.

Once I was back in the study, I stormed over to the windows and ripped down the linen curtains hanging from a dark bronze rod over-head. I returned to the safe and piled the curtain inside, then took a newspaper from the desk and wadded it up before tossing it into the safe as well.

With my kindling ready, I arranged the packages of drugs on top of the flammable materials and then took the lighter from the desk, pulled the lever, and set it ablaze.

Flames began dancing within the vault. I knew that soon the foul stench of drugs would fill the room along with a thick, gray smoke.

I hurried over to the window once more, lit the flame again, and touched it to the bottom of the remaining curtain on the right-hand side.

Within seconds, the flames hungrily licked at the fabric, climbing higher and higher until they nearly reached the ceiling.

Fire alarms would go off any second, and I knew that once that happened I wouldn't have much time to get away—depending on the response time of emergency crews.

With the fires burning, I picked up the remaining boxes and hurried down the hall, descended the stairs, and made for the front door.

Just as I crossed the threshold out into fresh air, a cacophony of noise filled my way-too-sensitive ears.

The klaxons blared their warning of fire in the building, but no one was there except me. And I was just leaving.

30

I wanted to watch the place burn.

More accurately, I wanted to run to the nearest grocery store, grab a packet of Jet-Puffed marshmallows and a roasting stick, and come back over here to enjoy the blaze. Seemed like a good night for s'mores.

Of course, those were fanciful thoughts and beyond realistic.

Still, they were fun to think about. Especially in the mind-movie where Jerry showed up and found me sitting by his burning home holding a stick with a marshmallow on it.

The fire department would arrive on the scene in time to douse most of the flames and spare the majority of the mansion from damage, but it made me feel good that I'd at least done a small part to take away deadly drugs from the streets of Nashville and who knew what other parts of Tennessee.

We had enough issues with the opioid crisis. The last thing we needed was harder stuff coming into the state.

I passed the fire trucks and police cars a few minutes after leaving the subdivision. They had no idea the arsonist responsible had simply driven right by them.

I watched them in the rearview mirror. It was an instinct, like slowing down when you pass a cop and looking back to make sure they weren't turning around to give you a ticket for speeding.

I kept driving, heading into the city with the pile of money in the back. Normally, having more than five hundred dollars in my pocket would have made me nervous, but nothing felt like a threat now.

No one knew I had the money, but on top of that, if someone wanted to try to mug the Chupacabra, well, best of luck with that.

I kept driving, replaying the events of the last week in my head.

I needed to find Wells.

Jerry was a part of all this, but I felt like Wells was the one pulling the strings.

It made sense based on everything I'd seen of Jerry.

More memories flooded my mind as I steered the car toward the interstate.

Amy's father had always been one of those types to try to keep up with the Joneses. Like a kid who saw their friend get a new bicycle and demanded the same or better from their parents.

He had fancy cars, a boat on the river, a beach house, all those things that he thought would bring him status or make him happy.

To be fair, a beach house would have made me pretty happy, too. But I wasn't naïve enough to believe that material things would bring me some kind of lasting peace or contentment.

Burning Jerry's house, even a part of it, would send him through the roof. His possessions meant way too much to him, and it would be a slap in the face that someone went after him.

I sighed, wondering where in the world he could be.

My first thought was he headed to Mexico, perhaps to broker a new deal with the cartel. Except that there would be no cartel for him to meet. Sure, there were others. The second one weed was cut down, another grew up right in its place.

But he didn't have connections to the other cartels. And if he were dumb enough to try to work out a new deal with a different organization, the second they found out he'd been Carrillo's guy, they'd probably hang him from a bridge in Juarez.

That thought gave me almost as much pleasure as the marsh-mallows.

I turned on the blinker and merged onto the ramp leading up to the interstate. The clock on the dash told me it was almost eleven.

The same thought kept interrupting all the others as I merged onto the highway amid sparse traffic: *Where is Vernon Wells?*

He'd tried to lay a trap for me, but I'd escaped.

It was evident that Wells knew who I really was, at least the beast part. He'd been researching the medallions and had come close to finding the one around my neck. What really shocked me was the trap itself.

Had he been planning on that for a while? Or was that simply one of his defensive measures in place in the event someone broke into his house and tried to steal something important or valuable?

I had to assume it was the latter.

For now, I had somewhere I needed to be. After I dropped off this money, I'd head back to the farm and regroup. In the morning, maybe my friends could help me figure out where Wells might have gone.

Mike might know someone who could access passenger manifests or flight plans. I was certain Wells had his own private jet. He had everything else.

I shook my head at the thought. "Crazy money," I muttered.

I looked in the back of the car at the bins stacked across the back seat. The other two were in the trunk.

That was more money than I'd seen in my lifetime. Probably more than anyone would ever see.

It had to be a few million bucks, just based on the stacks. Of course, I didn't know what that amount of money looked like. I just assumed.

I recalled a scene from one of my favorite movies where Ben Stiller offered Vince Vaughn a hundred grand to quit the dodgeball tournament. He'd opened a metal briefcase, and inside was a single stack of bills.

The memory made me smile.

It was one of the first times I'd truly felt humor since Amy was murdered, and since I'd learned of her indiscretions. It felt good to laugh. And the more I thought about the scene in that movie, the more the laughter swelled.

I needed that.

I turned on the radio and found a station playing classic rock and turned it up loud as I sped down the highway.

Jimi Hendrix blared from the speakers. I knew he didn't write "All Along the Watchtower," but I liked his version better than any others. And right now, it felt like the most appropriate song for the moment.

I was a guardian, watching out for the people who couldn't defend themselves. It was like I was the one on the watchtower.

I drove another twenty minutes until I reached the lights of downtown Nashville. I looped around on the various interchanges until I made it to the exit I was looking for, then steered the vehicle down the ramp and hung a right.

Many parts of the city and the surrounding metro area had been cleaned up and improved. New houses and apartments were going up all over the place.

But the refurbishing of Nashville hadn't reached this street yet.

Here, people still lived in squalor. The buildings were dilapidated. Some of the rooftops still showed damage from the tornadoes that hit the area more than a year before. Blue plastic covered some portions of homes.

I'd heard about how some of the insurance companies didn't pay out what they should have. But here, in this part of town, I knew most of the people either didn't have good insurance or had no insurance at all.

I passed an old church with a sign out front that quoted one of my favorite Bible verses. "Cast all your cares on Him because He cares for you, 1 Peter 5:7."

That verse always had powerful meaning for me. It told me I wasn't alone in the universe.

Now, I felt that more personally. I had been given a gift, a special power that enabled me to mete out justice and to help those who couldn't help themselves.

That just so happened to be the purpose of this boring little drive into the city.

A few people milled around on porches smoking cigarettes. Scant others walked aimlessly along the sidewalks. I caught more than a few questioning glances from folks, probably wondering what I was doing there or why I was driving through a rough area like that so late at night.

Up ahead, what passed for an old strip mall stood on the side of the road to the left. Eight years ago, I imagined it was more like a main street. The brick buildings stacked in a neat row faced the street and another church across the way. I turned into the crumbling parking lot and parked my car in front of the two-story brick structure with a sign over the entrance that read Grace Mission.

Homeless people sat around on the sidewalk outside the building. Some leaned against the façade.

They were, all of them, the picture of abject poverty and total lack of hope. Life had beaten them down and stood over them like a championship fighter, waiting for them to try to get up again just so it could punch them one more time.

I killed the engine and climbed out of the car with vapid eyes staring at me. Most of the people looked on with curiosity. A few held exhausted disdain.

I spotted a couple of guys who looked like they were probably in their early thirties. That saddened me more than the others. To be so young and have given up all hope must have been the worst thing to endure.

I tried to imagine what it would be like. After all, I was in my mid-thirties, and I couldn't grasp having nothing, not even a couple of changes of clean clothes.

Homelessness had always been something I wanted to address, to help with. I'd volunteered in years past, but now my career kept me from doing much of anything to help the community except for the occasional talk at local school.

"Hey," I said to the two guys huddled together against the wall.

They were passing a joint back and forth to each other.

"Would you two mind helping me with this?"

The guy with dark hair in long dreadlocks looked at me like I was crazy. "Pfft. Why, man?"

The other one seemed to be more amicable to the opportunity. He had short dirty blond hair with smears of filth on his face. But there was kindness in his gray-blue eyes, and even though life had kicked him while he was in the gutter, I saw that hope wasn't gone completely from him yet.

"Sure, man. I can help. What do you need?"

I smiled at him and opened the back door, pulled out one of the bins, and handed it to him. "Careful," I cautioned. "It's kind of heavy."

When he took the crate in his hands, his torso doubled over slightly despite the warning.

"Told you," I said with a smile.

He quickly adjusted. "Not too bad. What's in this thing?"

"Supplies for the shelter," I said.

"Oh. That's very kind of you."

I smiled at him and nodded, then picked up the other box in the back and led the way to the glass door.

A woman stood just inside the entrance and saw us approaching. She pushed the door open and stepped out to hold it for us.

"What you got in them boxes, honey?" she asked with a cheery curiosity.

"Supplies. You mind pointing me to the manager's office?"

"Sure. Just down the hall there. First door on the left." She raised a bony finger and pointed in the prescribed direction.

My temporary assistant and I carried the bins down to the open door. I stopped just outside and saw the young woman sitting behind her desk with a pen in her hand.

She looked worn out, with big circles under her eyes and pale skin that looked as if she hadn't been out in the sun for months.

"Little late to be working, isn't it?" I asked.

She exhaled and rubbed the bridge of her nose. "Little late to be making deliveries isn't it?"

"You can set that over there," I said to my helper and indicated some floorspace in the right corner.

"Excuse me?" she said, standing up.

The guy helping me looked at her, then me, then back to her.

"May he please set this box down over there? They're kind of heavy. He's not superhuman."

She rolled her eyes. "Fine. Whatever. What's in them?"

The helper nodded his thanks and set the box down in the corner.

"Much obliged," I said.

"You're welcome. Any others?" The guy seemed like a genuinely nice person, which made me feel even worse about his current lot in life.

He slipped by me and back out into the hall.

"You gonna answer my question?" the manager pressed.

The office was small, and everything from the chairs to the desk to the shelves along the far wall looked like relics from a 1960s principal's office.

The vinyl chair upholstery had more cracks than surface, and the foam poked out in multiple places.

"Let me get the other two boxes, and I'll explain."

The woman obviously didn't understand. And who could blame her? Random guy shows up with storage bins and asks if he can set them in her office? I'd have been a little thrown off, too.

"Look," I said. "I really need to bring the others in. I'll tell you what's going on when I come back."

She took a deep breath and sighed. She looked famished, like she hadn't had a good meal in a week. "Fine," she surrendered.

I hurried out the door, not fully comfortable with leaving all that money in the trunk. I walked out the building and found the car left alone. The guy who'd helped me had resumed his spot on the concrete and took a puff from a proffered joint the guy with dreads passed to him.

The air filled with the sweet and pungent aroma, reminding me of concerts I'd been to in my younger days when the smell of cannabis wafted through music halls and amphitheaters.

"Thanks again for your help," I said.

He nodded as he exhaled. "No problemo, man."

I snorted a laugh. He sounded like a stoned Bart Simpson.

I opened the trunk and removed the last two boxes, set them on the ground to close the hatch, then picked them up easily.

The guy who'd helped looked at me in awe. "Man, how are you strong enough to carry both of those at the same time? You don't look that strong."

"Thanks?" I said with a laugh.

"No offense, man."

"None taken. You're right. I don't look strong enough. Sometimes we have more strength on the inside than on the outside."

He bobbed his head. "Far out, man. Far out."

"Hey, man," Dreadlocks said to his friend, "who is that guy? Some kind of philosopher or something?"

I shook my head and carried the boxes through the open door.

Once back in the office, I found the manager about to open one of the bins.

"Not yet," I said upon entering.

"Oh. You startled me." She nearly jumped out of her shoes, the universal sign for someone who'd been surprised.

"Sorry about that."

She shook it off. "It's fine." She frowned at the boxes as I stacked them on top of the other two. "What's in those anyway?"

"Mind if I close the door?" I asked, pointing at the exit.

"Actually, I do. I don't know you. And I have an open-door policy. That doesn't mean people can just come in and talk whenever they want. It also means when someone is visiting, the door stays open.

"Smart," I said. "I know a guidance counselor who has the exact same policy. Keeps him from ever being accused of anything."

On top of that, this young woman had a natural beauty to her. She didn't wear makeup, or if she did there wasn't much. But she didn't need it.

"Fine," I said, happy to continue. "However, I think when I show you what's in the bins, you'll probably want to close the door."

She looked even more confused now.

I stepped over to the nearest box and flipped off the lid. I looked back at her, and the last remnants of color left her face, replaced with wide-eyed wonder and more than a little concern.

"What is all that?" she asked, rushing to the door and closing it as fast as possible.

"Before you ask your next question, this is a donation." I pointed to the boxes.

"Where did you get it?"

"I'm not going to lie to you. It came from my father-in-law, Jerry Hanlon."

She wrinkled her nose and lowered her eyebrows, thinking about whether or not she'd heard that name before. "Jerry Hanlon?"

"Yeah. He's not famous. But he's got money to throw around."

"Why didn't he just write a cashier's check or something?"

I knew that question was coming, and I'd already considered the answer. "Jerry is an eccentric. Anyone who knows him or knows of him is aware of that. He keeps cash on hand at all times. Heck, when he's taken me golfing, out to dinner, whatever, he always pays with cash. It's just how he does things."

She seemed to accept the answer. "Okay. But what am I supposed to do with this? I can't keep it here, and the banks are all closed."

"Do you have a safe?"

She nodded. "Yeah. I mean, it's not that big. I might be able to get all that in there."

"Put whatever you can in the safe," I suggested. "Then if you're comfortable with it, take the rest home and lock it up until you can get it to the bank."

She swallowed, suddenly very nervous about having all that money in her possession. "Okay. Okay. I think I can do that." Her eyes wandered back to the boxes. "How... how much—"

"How much is in there?" I finished. "Honestly, I don't know. I just collected the boxes and brought them here. I didn't ask how much."

She took a deep breath and nodded. "Okay. Wow. It looks like a lot."

"It is. Probably best not to think about it, actually. Just treat it like it's a hundred-dollar donation."

She blurted out a laugh. "That is way more than a hundred. Are those all hundreds?"

I grimaced. "Again, best not to think about it."

For a second, I thought the young woman might faint, but she kept her balance. "All right. I'll put as much as I can in the safe here. Pretty sure I can get most of it in there." She gave me a funny look, then asked, "Does he want a receipt?"

I shook my head, smiling. "Best to keep this donation anonymous. And besides, one of the reasons he uses cash all the time is so he won't have to keep receipts."

She accepted the explanation with a deep breath and exhaled.

"I have to get going," I said. "Please, get that into a safe as soon as possible."

"I will." She couldn't take her eyes off the bins. "Wait," she stopped me as I made for the door. "What's your name?"

I grinned pleasantly at her. "Don't worry about that. Use this money to help those who need it. I always wanted to start a shelter that focused on career counseling and rehab for homeless people. Build some new dorm rooms. Get some new beds. Show them how to reenter society as functional adults." I looked around the office. "And use some of it to get yourself a new office. You've earned it."

I opened the door and walked out, leaving her there with mouth agape.

As I got to the car, I felt my phone vibrating in my pocket and fished it out before sliding into the driver's seat. I closed the door and started the engine, then looked at the screen. It was Jack.

"Hey, man," I said. "What's going on?"

"Hello, Gideon." That was a different voice than expected. And immediately, all the joy of doing a good deed evaporated in my chest.

31

"You must be surprised to find me using your friend's phone. It's simple, really. They're with me now. At their little farm. And I highly suggest you meet me back here within the next hour, or I start taking fingers and toes."

I clenched my jaw and gritted my teeth. Anger pulsed through me.

"What do you want, Vernon?"

He answered with a sickening chuckle. It was an unnerving sound, one that made my blood curdle. "You know exactly what I want, Gideon. Bring me the medallion. And come unarmed."

I snickered back at him, partially to unbind my brain from the concern clouding my judgment. "If you know anything about the medallion, you know I don't need to be armed."

"Touché," he replied. "Not that it matters. If you do anything, try anything with your powers, I will kill all your friends right before your eyes. Just like when Carrillo killed your wife."

The barb stung, and the replay of the events of that night crashed into me again.

"I'm going to kill you, Vernon. I hope you realize that."

He laughed at the threat. "Oh, Gideon. It's so cliché to say such a thing. How exactly are you going to do that when I have your head on my wall? I know that to take your medallion, I have to take your head first."

"Then why don't you come downtown and try?"

"I'm sure you'd like that. Then you could eliminate me and rescue your friends. I'm not stupid, Gideon."

"No. But you *are* a coward, hiding behind innocent people like that."

"Oh please. Like you're so different. You mete out your own brand of justice, playing the role of judge, jury, and executioner with your newfound powers like you're some kind of god. You're just a man. Without that amulet, you are nothing. No one."

"And what's your plan for the medallion?"

"I'm sure you'd like to know. But that is none of your concern. Your only priority is to bring me the necklace. Immediately. Perhaps I'll let your friends live. If you play nice."

Anger burned within me, but there was nothing I could do. He'd played his hand and backed me into a corner. I had no choice but to comply.

I didn't think for a second that he'd actually let my friends go. Not alive, anyway. The second I was dead, he'd kill them, too. They were loose ends. Can't have those lying around.

Still, I had to try.

"I'll need your word that you won't harm them, and that you'll let them go free."

"My word? What are we, in the nineteenth century? Fine. I'll give you my word."

I knew he didn't mean it. And even if he did, there were a million ways around that. He could have his men kill them or let them go free and then kill them from a distance. All of them were as good as dead unless I could figure out a way to rescue them from his clutches.

An idea emerged in the angry, murky fog of my brain. I didn't like it. But it was the only way I could see. And it would take a massive leap of faith.

"Okay, Vernon. I'll be there. As long as my friends are unharmed, I'll keep the beast under control."

"Excellent," he exclaimed. "I'm so glad you see things my way."

"Whatever. I'll be there in thirty."

"I'll be waiting."

I ended the call and looked around the parking lot for a minute, trying to think of another way to get out of this mess—specifically how to get my friends out of it. But the only path seemed to be the path of surrender.

I sighed and started the engine, steered the car out onto the road, and drove back toward the interstate with a pantheon full of emotions racking my entire body.

I was going to put myself in the hands of a madman, a murderer, a guy who'd done every evil thing in the book, all while masquerading as a minister in front of thousands every weekend, and even more on television.

Wells operated under the guise of being a shepherd to the lost, and that was probably the thing that made me hate him most. The outright lie he lived was to the level of blasphemous. And if everyone knew what he was up to...

I shook my head at the thought. No one would ever believe it.

I guided the car up the ramp and onto the highway, losing everything passing around me to a swirling vortex of memories and thoughts.

My life was about to end. Nothing could change that now.

Sure, I'd faced death many times since that fateful night in Mexico. Now, however, it seemed certain.

I was dealing with a man who knew exactly how to kill me. He knew about the medallions. And more than likely, he'd continue searching for the others once I was dead.

But why? Why did he want them all?

He had money, power, influence, and an underground crime operation that I knew would never get investigated. The man was untouchable.

I'd set my phone in the passenger seat after getting off the call with Wells. Now it vibrated incessantly.

I pressed the green button and tapped the speaker icon so I could speak while keeping my hands on the wheel. Well, except for the two seconds it took to hit those buttons.

"Hello?"

"Hello, Gideon." The voice was masculine and vaguely familiar, though on the phone it was hard to tell who it belonged to.

"Sorry, I'm driving, and you're on speaker phone. Who is this?"

"Agent Keane."

"Oh, hey there. Good to hear from you again." I knew my tone sounded mocking, but at this point I didn't care. These guys seemed to be an impotent arm of the government, unwilling or unable to interfere in the chaotic events storming through my life.

"Where are you going?"

"Uh, why do you care?"

"Because you're making a mistake."

I frowned at the comment. "What?"

"You're making a mistake," he repeated.

"The only mistake I made, as far as I can tell, was marrying the wrong girl."

"Cynicism is so unlike you, Gideon."

I huffed. "You don't know me."

"Better than you realize. And I'm asking you not to give that medallion to Vernon Wells."

Breath caught in my throat, and I couldn't swallow for a few seconds. How had he known that?

"Did you guys tap my phone or something? Because that's creepy. And not just a little creepy. It's very creepy. Also, probably illegal."

"Nothing we do is illegal," Keane said. And I thought I heard a chuckle out of him. "As we've said before, we're not permitted to intervene directly."

"Yeah, I recall that. And it doesn't exactly make your agency all that helpful. Whatever it is your agency does."

"Right now, what we do is ask you not to give up the medallion. At any cost."

I swerved around a slow-moving sedan in the right lane. "Yeah, that's cool. Except if I don't, then my friends will die."

"Yes. That is true. Wells will kill your friends. Nothing can stop that now."

What kind of talk was that from an ultra-covert agent?

"But you can make sure their deaths aren't in vain, Gideon. You can eliminate him and everyone in his operation."

I shook my head. "I have to try to save them, Keane. You telling me that if it were your friends, you would be okay with watching them die? No offense, but I've already watched one person I loved get executed right in front of me. I don't feel like doing that again."

"I know. But if you let him kill you, he will simply kill them seconds later. You cannot trust him."

"You think I don't know that? I am very much aware I can't trust Vernon Wells."

"Then why are you going? Your sacrifice will not save your friends. But theirs can save many."

I didn't like the way he rationalized that, in part because it made sense. And I didn't want it to. But that didn't matter. I wasn't going to just stand by and let my friends die, especially for something they didn't sign up for.

"I was given this responsibility for a reason, Agent Keane. Anyone could have taken up this mantle. But it was handed to me. That means I have to make the calls. For good or bad. Right or wrong. You want to decide what happens with the medallion? Then take it from me."

I let the gravity of the words hang around his neck for a couple of seconds before I continued. "I'm going to handle this. I don't want Wells to have this medallion any more than you do."

"And yet you're going to just give it to him?"

"I didn't say that."

"So, what's your plan?"

"I'm working on it."

There was a pause. Then, "You're working on it? You have one of the most powerful artifacts in the world around your neck, and you're going into an ambush with a man who knows what he has to do to kill you, and you're telling me you're working on it?"

"Yeah. Look, I'm not sure what I'm going to do, but I'll think of something."

"You're just full of bad ideas today, aren't you?"

"I guess so. Look, Agent Keane, if your outfit can't lift a finger to help, then I don't know why we're even having this conversation."

"We help by directing. And right now, I'm directing you not to let Wells take the amulet."

"Thanks for the advice," I drawled. "I'll keep that in mind."

"I'm serious, Gideon. You know what happens if a man like Wells gets control of that medallion."

"Bad things. I know."

I ended the call and kept driving. The city lights faded into the background, casting a dim glow into the night sky, blurring the stars twinkling in the heavens. The moon beamed over the hills to the south, poking out behind thin strips of cirrus clouds streaking across the dark canvas.

When I pulled into the driveway at Mike's farm, I slowed down and surveyed the area. I'd expected some of Wells' goons to be at the base of the gravel drive, but it was vacant except for the black mailbox standing next to the road.

I kept driving until I reached the farmhouse. That's when I found several white SUVs, including a brand new Cadillac Escalade with black rims.

"At least he's got good taste in vehicles," I muttered as I tapped the brakes and parked next to the big SUV.

Four armed men stood by the walkway leading up to the farm-house. The irony of a preacher with armed guards wasn't lost on me.

I turned off the motor and grabbed the keys, and as I climbed out of the vehicle casually let the key scratch a fresh line down the side of the passenger door of the Escalade as I walked toward the guards.

"Hey there, fellas. There a poker game going on here or something?"

I heard a muted pop. Then I felt a thump and a sting in my neck. I spun around, the beast within suddenly raging to life.

I grabbed at my neck and found something protruding from it. I winced and jerked out a tranquilizer dart.

The world around me started spinning. I felt my body trying to change, but also resisting the shift at the same time.

The man with the tranquilizer gun stepped out of the shadows of the big shed twenty feet away. He kept the weapon trained on me even as I felt gravity sucking me toward the ground.

Everything felt heavy.

The four men by the walkway closed in around me.

I fought—the drugs burning through my veins, the goons surrounding me, everything. I swung my fists but only struck air.

Some of them laughed at me.

Then I heard the sound of Vernon Wells' voice as everything in my vision blurred.

"So, it looks like you can teach an old dog new tricks," he said.

32

D aggers of ice sliced across my face and neck.

One second, I'd been trying to escape Wells' mansion. The next, I woke up to a bucket of ice-cold water being splashed over me.

Blinding light radiated so harshly against my eyes, I thought I was staring straight into the sun. As the seconds passed, my eyes adjusted, and I realized there were four horizontal LED lights overhead causing the problem.

I winced and lowered my head, but my chin was stopped by something cold and metal. My eyes continued to focus until I could take in everything and everyone around me.

"Quite the gathering here," I spat.

Someone punched me in the face. It hurt. Not like it would have if I were an ordinary person, but it still stung, and my cheek bone ached.

I looked up into the eyes of the man who'd hit me. He looked like one of Carrillo's goons, one of the dozens I'd taken from this world.

Five other guys stood around who looked just like him. And then there was the other one.

He stood off to the side, next to the barren cinder block wall close to a door. He remained in shadow even though the room drowned in bright light. Darkness surrounded him like an ethereal entourage. Except for the red mist that circled around his ankles.

"Good to see the Sector is helping out with a human-trafficking, heroin-dealing fake pastor," I sneered.

The man didn't respond. He simply stared at me from black eyes under cropped black hair. Even his pale complexion didn't seem to reflect the light in the room.

Another punch from the opposite side jarred my senses for a second. I shook my head to clear the cobwebs, only now realizing I was bound to a wooden chair with chains—heavy, old chains with links the size of my fist.

I struggled against the bonds but found I was unable to break free.

I focused on the medallion, closed my eyes, and waited for the shift to happen, but when I opened my eyes again, I was still in human form. My head dropped immediately, and I checked to make sure the amulet was where it belonged—around my neck.

Tepid relief fluttered through my chest, but why wasn't the thing working?

"There's no use in trying to activate it," a disturbingly familiar voice filled my ears from behind. "Those chains binding you to the chair are enchanted."

I scowled at the sound of the man's voice. *Had he said the shackles were enchanted?*

Slow, methodical footsteps clicked on the floor.

I didn't have to wait more than a few seconds for Vernon Wells to come into view. I recognized him from the billboards, the television, and from the smell of someone who spent too much money on fancy cologne, which he also used excessively.

"Those chains have contained monsters far stronger than you, my friend." He looked at me as if assessing a cut of meat. Ambition filled his eyes. It was a look I'd seen now and then, though usually from potential investors for my various projects.

I turned my head to get a glimpse of the shackles. I noted ancient

Greek key patterns engraved into the links, along with lightning bolts set within each key.

Then it hit me. "It was you," I said.

He raised an eyebrow, momentarily confused.

"You broke into the pedestal at the Parthenon. These are the shackles of the Titans."

His lips parted into a crooked grin. "Yes. Very good, Gideon. Nice of you to catch up."

"But how did you—"

"How did I know it was there?"

I exhaled through my nose and bobbed my head once.

"Oh, your friend Jack was quite helpful in that regard."

My heart sank into my chest. "What did you just say?"

"Your friend." His grin grew wider and more wicked, if that was possible. The red mist glowed so bright it reflected in his eyes. It gave him a demonic look that shook me to my core. "If not for his cooperation, I wouldn't have been able to find this magnificent artifact. And it's a good thing I did. We can't have a monster like you running around."

"Why didn't you just kill me, Vernon? You one of those types who takes pleasure in staring people in the eyes before you kill them?"

He snorted derisively. "You know, I have to admit that is part of it. Some people pay good money to torture or execute others. But I get to do it for free. It's one of those little perks of the position."

I felt my stomach turn. I'd heard of things like that, places where uber wealthy wretches paid big money to do whatever they wanted to other human beings. I'd never spent time on the dark web, but as I understood it, that was one of the places to find such horrors— among many others.

I wrestled my disgust into submission and tried to change topics. If for no other reason than to keep this guy talking so I could find a way out of this mess.

"I can't believe I'm finally getting a chance to meet you. This is so amazing." I twitched my nose. "Wow. You smell great. What is that?

No wait. Let me guess. Christian Dior, right? Get it? Because you're a—"

"You must consider yourself a funny man, Gideon."

"Some people think so. I have to say, that's a nice sword you have there." I nodded toward the scimitar hanging in his right hand. It was the same blade that had hung over his desk in the study.

For the first time since I'd acquired my powers, I felt a very real sense of fear rush through me.

The man before me—the guy who I was pretty sure was behind my wife's murder and who had done any number of horrible things —held in his hand the one thing that could kill me outside of dropping me in a volcano.

"You should maybe go easy on the cologne," I offered. "Only one pump. Two at most. And I mean at most. That stuff can get pretty strong."

He smiled at me with condescension dripping from his eyes. He was shorter than I expected, but I knew being on stage added at least six inches.

"Do you know what this is?" Wells asked, ignoring my sarcasm.

I shrugged but was barely able to move against the strength of the chains. "A scimitar. Popular weapon in the Middle East for a long time. That sword basically conquered half the known world at one point."

He shook his head and rolled his eyes, disappointed I wouldn't give up. "It's more than that. This is one of the most powerful weapons in history." He noticed me struggling. "Gideon, I already explained you won't be able to escape those chains, so you can stop wriggling. Do you have any idea where they came from?"

The only answers that came to mind were the kind that used to get me in trouble in high school. The smart aleck in me seemed to have grown even stronger with the arrival of my new powers and heightened sense of confidence.

Instead, I only shook my head. "No. I only know where you found them."

"And here I thought you had been to Crete."

"I have—" I stopped. That made sense, in the new nonsensical world in which I now found myself. There were more than one set of shackles, based on my loose understanding of them. The legend— more like an ancient rumor—was that they'd been forged by the hands of Zeus's blacksmith, Hephaestus. But I'd never heard about where they might have been hidden.

A greater trouble rumbled under that curious surface. If the shackles were real, did that mean the Titans were too?

"Yes," he continued. "Impressive, aren't they? These chains supposedly bound the infamous Minotaur in his labyrinthine prison in Minoa. And now, they contain another powerful specimen."

I didn't like the way he called me that. It gave rise to thoughts about laboratories and experiments with needles or prodding. My experience was limited, but I didn't think I would enjoy either.

"What do you want, Wells?"

He laughed. "That's a silly question, my boy. You know exactly what I want. Heck, you looked over all the things in my office. You know what I'm up to. Don't you? Or are you dumber than I thought?"

"You can't have it," I countered. "The medallion belongs in my family."

"Oh please. Spare me the sob story. You know," he wagged his finger at me, "I knew you were going to try something like that." He put his free hand up in the air and shook it around. "Oh, look at me. I'm from the House of Claw and Fang. The medallion belongs to me."

He backhanded me across the face. "Wake up, boy. The real world plays out according to those who plan. Not dumb luck."

I said nothing, resigned to staring at the floor. The red mist wrapping around Wells' feet pulsed angrily, but I could do nothing but sit and await my fate.

"You just gonna let him do this?" I asked, turning my head to the spook by the stairwell door.

The Sector agent merely gave a single nod in response.

"You're a real talker."

And as was his brand, I received silence for my effort.

"Never mind him," Wells said. He held up the sword and eyed it with pride, probably enjoying his own reflection on the broadside of the blade. "You never answered my question, Gideon."

"Sorry," I said. "Just a little distracted. You know, with the six hired guns standing around, the weirdo from the government by the door, and you and that cologne. My goodness, man. Did you just duck your head in a bucket of that stuff?"

Another backhand stung my skin. The garish gold ring on his index finger cut across my flesh and opened a gash.

I winced at the pain, but that was all he'd get out of me.

Within seconds, I felt the wound closing.

"Remarkable," Wells said, observing the miraculous healing. "Absolutely incredible."

He turned to the other men in the room. "Did y'all see that? His skin just healed itself."

He shook his head, and for a second I thought he was going to say "Ain't that the darndest thing?"

But he didn't. Thankfully.

The men nodded, staring wide eyed at the freak of nature in the chair before them.

"The sword," I said, steering my attention away from being slapped. "I know you didn't get that from Crete."

"Very astute observation, Gideon. And you're right. I did not get it from there. This little beauty came from the Middle East, as you alluded to before. It's very old, as I'm sure you can tell. Heck, you probably know exactly where it was made seeing how you're an expert on such things. Of course, I knew you were the clever one. You know, between you and your pretty wife."

My eyes narrowed to penny slots. The rage within me burned off quickly, though, as had most emotions regarding Amy.

He saw the rage burning in my eyes. He had to. I didn't try to conceal it.

"Yeah," he goaded. "She sure was pretty. Always smelled good, too. I got everything I wanted from her, though. If you catch my meaning."

I blinked away the dagger. I knew exactly what he insinuated.

"Why did you have her killed?" I asked pointedly. "I was the one the cartel was supposed to eliminate. Not Amy."

I asked the question with pain in my voice, but I honestly felt none. I only used it now to leverage Wells for information. I needed to know what Jerry's part in all this was. And not just from what I'd learned so far. I wanted to hear it from this guy's mouth.

"Oh. That. Yes, well, lucky you. Well. It was lucky you. Now you and she can be together. Though, let's be honest, Gideon. Would you really want that now? After you learned the truth about her... indiscretions?"

It was starting to seem like everyone knew about that but me. I didn't like being the sucker in the room, but right now it was the only part to play.

"Gideon, I knew you had a better chance at finding the temple than your wife. And seeing how she'd been cheating on you... Well, I decided that maybe her time on this earth was up."

"Who made you God?" I snarled.

He cocked his head and glowered at me. "Quite the thing to say for someone like you, Gideon. Or perhaps you don't know what you are." He inclined his head and stared down his nose at me.

"I know what I am," I said. "And I haven't forgotten *who* I am."

Wells pulled his head back, pretending to be surprised. "Well, that is just beautiful, Gideon. I mean, you're going to die now, so I guess that's fitting your last words were so eloquent."

He raised the sword high, a devilish grin stretching across his face. The weapon looked like it took all his strength to lift it, but gravity would help him drop it onto my neck.

I couldn't believe I was about to be beheaded. Such an old-school, gruesome way to go.

"This blade," Wells said, lowering again so that the sharp edge sliced the back of my neck, teasing me with death, "is known as a Guardian Slayer. Funny. I never thought I would need it for that. I always figured I would be the first to find the medallion, and all the others. But I guess it's good I keep some of these old relics around."

More relics of power, I thought. *How many of those things are out there?*

The thought unnerved me almost as much as having a sword against the back of my head while the wielder lined up his death blow.

"With this, the weapon forged in shadow, I receive the medallion of Xolotl," he said, his voice in a trance-like state.

He used both hands to raise the weapon high over his head once more. All the men in the room watched. And I noticed the spook by the door seemed to be particularly enjoying the display.

"Wait," I said.

"There is nothing you can say to stop this, Gideon," Wells soothed. "Let it happen. It'll be okay. I mean, you'll be dead. But hey, that's the breaks."

"You kill me, and you'll lose any chance you ever had of finding the other medallions."

He froze for a second. Then he rolled his eyes. "What?"

I gazed back at him with a petulant smile. "You know exactly what I mean. Don't you, Reverend?"

He lowered the hefty sword, peering into my eyes to search for the lie he suspected was there.

He wouldn't find it. At least not a full lie.

I knew better than he where the next medallion could be found. He'd danced all around it. Now, however, I knew there was an opportunity.

"Where is it?" he demanded.

I huffed. "You don't even know which medallion I'm talking about. I would think that might be your first question."

"Very well." He sounded frustrated. "Which one?"

"You were so close," I said, shaking my head in disappointment. "I looked at your maps, your journals, all the documents in your office."

"I know. I saw."

"Yep," I nodded, unaffected. "I figured the cameras in there caught me snooping around. Only way you would have known I was there.

Clever, by the way, putting the speakers in there so you could try to scare me."

"You should be scared," Wells said. "You should be terrified. I'm going to kill you and take that medallion from you."

"I doubt you'd say that if I didn't have these chains holding me back."

"And I doubt you'd be so brave if you didn't have your medallion around your neck."

"Touché." I had to give him credit for that one. Even though I wanted to rip his head off. "I'll tell you what, Reverend, you let all the kids go that you have in your little network, and I'll tell you where to find the next medallion."

He narrowed his eyes, staring at me curiously. "Do you really think that I need your help that much? That I would give up all that money to get a little help from you? You underestimate my ability, and my resolve."

I strained against the bonds and felt them barely move against my strength. I would have lunged forward and pounced, ravaging him from limb to limb until there was nothing left.

"How does someone like you become so evil, Vernon?" I asked. "What happened to you?"

"Evil? Good? None of it is real," he said. "Oh, sure, there are sides to every war, every fight, everything in life. But I choose the side that helps me most."

"So you made a deal with the devil."

He seemed amused by the comment. "We're all cattle, Gideon," he said. "Every single one of us a pawn in a grand game, a game you probably have no idea is even going on. All we can do is try to get what we can. You can be one of the cattle. Or you can prosper from the game if you understand how to play it. It's not that complicated, really. And it's nothing personal. It's just business."

"It's not just business for those kids. And their families."

"Yes. And you managed to free—temporarily—my current stock."

I didn't like how he said the words "temporarily" and "stock."

"Not to worry," he continued. "I'll get them back. And there are always plenty more where they came from."

I steamed at the statement. But I didn't let him see it. "Good luck with that," I offered. "But I don't think you're ever going to get those kids back. They're long gone."

"Is that so?"

Something about his foreboding tone unsettled me.

"My shipments will continue. Business will go on as usual. You wrecked my home. So, I'll let you die with that little victory. Of course, it was the price I was willing to pay to take you down. I did what I had to do. Clearly, you don't have any idea where the next medallion is. So I'm going to kill you now. Guardian."

He raised the blade and held it over my neck, then lifted it high.

"Artemis," I said. "The medallion of Artemis. I know where you can find it."

33

Wells stopped and grinned down at me.

I hung my head in shame.

"Where? Tell me where." He sounded greedy, hungry almost.

Even the spook by the door seemed to perk up at the statement.

"I'll need some assurances," I countered.

He snorted. "Like what? I don't kill you and you tell me where it is? You can't be that stupid. You know the second you tell me where it is I'm going to kill you anyway. I can't have a guardian roaming around. And besides, I have to kill you to take your medallion."

We both knew the only way he could take it from me was by removing my head. That plan didn't really work for me.

"Destroy whatever heroin is here on your property. And leave the children I released earlier alone. Let them go. I won't try to make you promise to never deal in that business again because I know an oath from a liar is no oath at all."

He hummed, as if considering the offer. "You would give me the location simply to let a few dozen kids go?"

"And burn whatever drugs are stockpiled around here."

The agent at the door cleared his throat, beckoning Wells to his side.

Wells complied and walked over to the door. The two whispered for a few seconds. I heard everything, but I didn't understand it.

The spook said, "It's a trick."

"Maybe, but I have to know."

"He doesn't know where it is. He's only stalling, trying to buy time."

Wells looked back at me, and I knew he was trying to assess whether or not I was lying.

"I believe you," Wells said and turned back toward me as he addressed the spook. "But he's one of the top archaeologists in the world. If he thinks he's found something, we should at least hear him out. Your boss would want that."

"My boss wants him dead."

"I am aware of what your boss wants. But he's not exactly been very helpful with the locations of the other medallions."

"You know as well as I do that our agency is not privy to that information. The medallions are hidden, even from our eyes." The spook sounded irritated, and the look in his eyes matched the sound.

"That's something that bothers me about your boss," Wells said. "If he's so powerful, why can't he find these precious artifacts? Hmm? And what is his priority? Killing Wolf or finding the medallions of power?"

I clenched my jaw. "What are you two talking about?" I asked, feigning ignorance.

Wells rounded on me. "I was just discussing your terms."

He walked back to the door and disappeared up the staircase. The Sector agent stood there staring at me with a long, hard warning in his eyes, then turned and followed up the steps.

The rest of the men followed except for two, who stayed by the door to guard the prisoner.

I struggled against the chains, but I may as well have been trying to move a mountain with my finger.

"Either of you guys mind loosening these chains for me?" I asked.

Both simply glared back at me.

"No? They're a little uncomfortable. Kind of chafing my wrists. You know?"

I heard footsteps coming back down the stairs. "See?" I said. "They're coming back down to tell you to let me out of these chains."

One of the other guards appeared in the doorway. "We're to take him up to the study."

"Ha!" I laughed out loud. "Good luck with that."

He looked over at me with vapid eyes. "We moved you down here, gringo," he said. "We can move you again."

Turns out he was correct about that.

The goon walked over to me and jabbed a needle in my neck. The syringe looked like it came from a farm, and judging by its size, I couldn't refute that might have actually been its origin.

Within seconds, the tranquilizer kicked in and I felt myself drifting into the darkness.

PASSING OUT IS A STRANGE EXPERIENCE. One second, you're there, doing your thing. The next, you're waking up in a different place, groggy and staring across the room at your friends who are tied up in chairs with gunmen standing behind them.

"Nice of you to wake up and join us, Gideon," Wells' annoyingly familiar voice said from somewhere behind me.

I didn't know how much time had passed, but it still appeared to be dark outside, though it was difficult to tell through the drug haze my mind struggled to crawl out of.

"I guess you see your friends are here now. They have you to thank for that."

I hadn't realized it, but there they were. Jack, Jesse, and Mike all tied up in wooden chairs directly across from me. The mind fog had blinded me to pretty much everything for a minute. I also noticed we were in Wells' office. The familiar setting looked much the way I'd left it. Except the noxious gas was no longer present.

"I'm sorry, Gideon," Jack said, looking me in the eyes.

The haze in my mind cleared, and I knew how I had to play this.

"Save it, Jack. Wells told me you helped him."

Jack shook his head. "What? No. That isn't true." He looked to Wells, struggling against the ropes keeping him stuck to the chair. His face flushed red, and fire burned in his eyes. "You're lying."

"Oh, Jack. I'm not lying at all. You helped me find those fancy shackles keeping your friend from turning into that creature."

Jack's head kept turning side to side. "No." He looked to me, pleading for me to believe him. "He's lying, Gideon. I would never do that to you."

My face drew long, darkening with betrayal and rage. "Save it, Jack," I spat back at him. "I see the red mist surrounding you. The mist doesn't lie, pal." I said the last word with a lethal amount of vitriol.

I narrowed my eyes at him, and for a second, Jack didn't seem to understand what was happening. Then he kept shaking his head. "Please. I'm your best friend, Gid. How long have we known each other? Huh? Our entire lives. You know me. You know I wouldn't do this."

"You have to believe him," Jesse said. "Jack would never betray you."

"She's right," Mike added. He looked the roughest of the three. A black right eye decorated his face, accompanied by a busted lip and a cut on his cheek. "You know Jack. He would never do that."

"The mist doesn't lie," I repeated. "The wicked must be punished."

Wells snapped his head around and stared at me. His eyes widened with a lust for violence.

"Oh my. What have we here? A little squabble among friends?" Wells teased all of us.

"How else could he have known about the location of these chains, Jack? You sentenced us all to die when you told him what we talked about. You gave him my idea. And now all of us are going to die."

"No. Gideon. I swear. It isn't true."

"Save it, liar."

"If the two of you don't mind, we have a little matter to discuss, Gideon. Remember? That's why we're here. You were going to tell us where the medallion of Artemis is located. Unless you were lying. If that's the case, I'll just start killing your friends the same way Carrillo's men killed your wife."

He gave an upward nod, and three of his goons stepped forward, raising pistols at the backs of my friends' skulls.

Two guards stood by the door. And I felt the presence of another two behind me, both standing close in case I tried to escape.

"Where is it, Gideon?" Wells pressed.

I snorted. "Why don't you ask my friend over there? He seems to be your go-to resource now."

"Gideon. Please. You have to believe me. What is wrong with you, man? I would never betray you."

I looked Wells in the eyes. "I have a new offer for you, Vernon."

"Oh?" he asked, genuine curiosity showing on his face. "And what might that be? I don't know if you're really in a position to make any deals right now."

"I am," I replied. "I'll give you the location of the Artemis medallion. But I want you to let Jesse and Mike go."

Wells rolled his eyes. "You know I can't do that. They're loose ends, Gideon. But what I can promise you is that they will die quickly. They won't suffer. And in the end, isn't that really all anyone can ask for? We're all heading to the same destination, the same fate. Making that as easy as possible should be a goal, should it not?"

I nodded absently. "Fine. I don't want them to suffer. But I want you to kill Jack first. And I want to see it."

Both of the pastor's eyebrows lifted at that statement. "Really, now? I have to say, I didn't see that coming."

"Jack must die. The mist doesn't lie."

Wells shivered his shoulders as if a chill shot through the room. "Oooh, such a dark rhyme that is. Very well, Gideon. Jack dies first.

But I want the name of the place where I can find the second medallion."

I blinked slowly; my eyes locked on Jack. Tears formed in his, and he kept shaking his head in denial.

"Ephesus," I blurted. "The medallion is in Ephesus."

"Where in Ephesus?"

I sighed. "Where do you think, Vernon?"

The blank look on his face told me he really didn't have a clue.

"The temple of Artemis is there. At least the ruins of it. But that's where you'll find the hidden temple. At sunrise, the door will only open for a moment."

"No, Gideon. Stop," Jack urged. "Don't tell this guy anything. You can't let him have the amulets."

"Shut up, Jack," I barked. "You'll be dead soon. So you don't have to worry about any of this."

"I have to worry about the world. I have to worry about the innocent people this man has killed or ruined. How much worse will it be when he has your medallion? Let alone the Artemis one? He will be unstoppable."

"You know, I like the sound of that," Wells interjected. "Unstoppable." He turned to me. "He's right, you know. I will be. Nothing will stand in my way."

"I don't care anymore," I spat. "It seems nothing is sacred. Not even lifelong friendships."

Jack huffed a laugh. "Maybe you're not who I thought you were," he demurred. "I thought you were my friend. I thought you knew me."

"Well, this has been a real treat," Wells said. "But now that I know where to find the next medallion, I don't need any of you anymore. So, Gideon? A deal's a deal." He looked at the guard standing behind Jack with the gun to my friend's head. "Kill him first. Unless he has anything else he'd like to add. Jack, you don't know where any of the other medallions are, do you?"

Jack breathed in and out, collecting his final thoughts before his execution. "Gideon. If the last thing I say to you is this, then so be it. But you have to know the truth."

I listened to him, but my focus was on the three men behind my friends. The red mist swirled around them like crimson-clouded serpents.

I slowly closed my eyes and remembered the dream I'd had. Maybe it was a vision. But it felt as real as anything.

I'd seen the man in the interrogation room talking to agents from the Sector. He was one of Carrillo's men, and he was about to tell the agents about the monster who'd decimated all of Carrillo's forces.

He alone had survived.

Until the crimson mist took him.

I opened my eyes and stared across the room. I reached into the depths of my soul and drew out the power, willing the mist to do my bidding.

"Well, if that's all you have to say, and it seems like your friend has no response, I guess it's time for you to die, Jack. Oh, and Gideon?" Wells looked over at me. "He didn't tell me anything. I had his book-store under surveillance." He turned and faced Jack. "You really should have been more wary about your hobbies and the books you read, Jack. But I guess that doesn't matter now."

I heard all of it, but I already knew Jack hadn't lied to me. I knew from the beginning. He was my best friend. He'd never betray me. I had to play it up and work the angle to buy a few more seconds.

Now, though, I could feel the mist swirling around the gunmen— as if I held it by invisible reins.

I blinked lazily and focused my thoughts on the gunman behind Jack. The man's finger tensed on the trigger, but it didn't squeeze.

He frowned and tried to pull.

The goon couldn't see the mist wrapping around his hands and forearms, pushing back against his trigger finger.

"Kill him," Wells ordered. "And the girl next."

The guard's scowl deepened. "I... I can't. Something's wrong with my hand."

I commanded the mist again, and the gunman's pistol started to rise, turning toward Wells.

"What are you doing?" Wells demanded. "Are you insane? Shoot him." He sounded nervous but stood his ground.

"I'm trying! Something is making me do this!"

"What? What are you talking about? Get control of yourself."

His hands continued to lift the weapon.

"Don't point that at me!" Wells pointed at the other two. "Take that gun from him," he ordered.

The other two started to move. They could not.

Fear splashed across their faces as they both raised their pistols, turning to the gunman in the middle.

"What is the matter with you people?" Wells roared.

The cartel thug in the center shook his head, his eyes welling with sheer terror. "It's not me. It's not me. I swear. Something is controlling me!"

Wells looked over at me, and for the first time in a minute, I took my gaze from the three gunmen and glared back at him. "Even the chains of the Titans can't control me, Vernon."

"No!" Wells shouted and dove through the open balcony door as the center gunman fired his pistol.

The round blasted into the wall where Wells had stood only a second before. Then the other two men fired their weapons.

The bullets zipped through the guy in the middle and struck each in the face, dropping all three at once.

The guards at the door drew their pistols, aiming them at my three friends. The two behind me stepped back, and I felt them put muzzles to the back of my skull.

They spoke in panicked Spanish. One of them kept saying the same thing over and over.

"He is the devil. He is the devil that killed everyone in Santa Rojo."

"Shut up," the other one behind me snapped. "Kill them. Kill them all."

I shook my head and controlled the mist around the two by the door as they tried to unload their magazines at my friends.

Like the others, their fingers wouldn't work. The fog wrapping around their hands constricted their movement like a paralysis.

"What is the matter with you? Kill them!" The same guard issued the order, but then I heard a quiver in his voice. "What the—? No. No!"

The two by the door began to turn their pistols on each other. Slowly, as if possessed, they fought with every ounce of strength to keep from turning, but the mist was too strong.

"No," one of them said, shaking his head. "Stop."

"You stop. I'm not doing this," the other countered.

"Drop your guns," the guy behind me ordered. "Drop them now!"

"They can't," I said.

"No!" One of the guys by the door yelled as both he and his partner raised their guns high, muzzles pointed directly at each other's heads.

"Drop your—" The twin reports rocked the room with a deafening pop.

The two guards fell at the threshold, dead before they hit the floor.

"What kind of devilish magic is this?" the quieter of the two behind me asked.

"It's the devil," the other replied in Spanish. "Shoot him. He's doing this."

They pulled their triggers, and I felt the bullets drill though the back of my skull and out of my forehead.

It was probably one of the most unpleasant, nauseating kinds of pain I had ever experienced.

My head slumped forward until my chin rested on my chest, and I let my body go limp.

The guards stood there for a moment. I imagined they were staring at me, watching with caution.

"No!" Mike yelled.

Jesse cried.

Jack did nothing. He knew bullets couldn't kill me.

The two goons stepped around in front of me, lowering their weapons. The mouthy one grabbed my chin and raised it so he could look at the exit wounds.

"He's dead," the guy wrongly declared.

Then I felt the grisly wound healing.

He watched in paralyzed horror. I let him. And then I blinked.

He jumped back, terrified. The other guy standing next to him raised his pistol to fire again and finish the job.

Both men tried to squeeze their triggers, but the mist had them, and it wouldn't let go.

The red fog wrapped around their throats and squeezed exactly as I imagined it. The clouds swirling around their hands pushed back against their attempts to shoot me again.

"What are you doing? Shoot him!" the guy on the left shouted.

"I'm trying!"

I grinned fiendishly at them, then slowly turned their weapons against each other.

"Stop. What's happening to me?" The goon on the right asked the question with fear trickling through his voice. "What is this?"

Anger poured out of me, and the mist twisted them in a sudden burst of movement, jerking them toward each other.

"No. Don't squeeze the trigger, Pedro. Don't do it."

"You don't do it," the one on the left countered.

One of the men yelled as he tried to force his muscles to resist the power gripping him. It was futile.

"No!"

Tandem bangs rang through the study as the men shot each other in the head. Their bodies fell at my feet.

I breathed hard, strained from the exertion of controlling the strange mist. Sweat dripped off my nose onto the floor.

"Gideon?" Jack said. "You okay?"

I nodded, half consciously. "Yeah. Just... tired. Do you think you can get me out of these chains?"

34

J ack and the others wriggled for minutes. Jesse was the first one to get free of the tight ropes binding her to the chair.

Once she was loose, she untied Jack and then went to Mike while Jack hurried over and lifted the chains off me.

I felt renewed strength pulse through me the second the heavy, enchanted metal was off me.

"I thought you really believed I stabbed you in the back for a second there," Jack said.

I stood up, feeling like a thousand pounds had been lifted off my shoulders. "No way, pal. I know better than that. But I had to play along. Sorry about that. I hoped you could see it was a ruse."

"You should go into acting."

"Maybe later." I turned and hurried over to the balcony. Wells was gone.

I leaned over the railing but didn't see a sign of the guy. The others joined me, each taking a different spot on the overlook to see if they could find Wells, but no such luck.

"Where did he go?" Jesse asked.

"I don't know, but I'm going after him."

"Let me come with you," Jack insisted.

"Me too. I'm coming," Mike added.

"Me three," Jesse finished.

"No. I need you three to contact the police and tell them what's going on with Wells. They may not listen. But you have to try. And here." I fished Agent Keane's card out of my pocket. "Call this guy. He can help, too."

"What about all the—" Mike stopped cold as he looked back into the room and saw the bodies evaporating before his eyes, as if they were never really there. "What the—?"

I sighed. "Jack will have to fill you in on that. I have to find Wells."

Without another word, I vaulted over the balcony and landed on my feet below. I searched the immediate area, but there was no sign of Wells anywhere.

The pool vacuum gurgled in the corner near the steps. Then I heard a car engine rev to life. I doubted my friends heard it. They might have heard the tires squealing on the pavement. I didn't stick around to find out.

I sprinted to the gate, shifting into the beast as I ran.

I leaped over the black aluminum fence and kept going. I still heard the car racing away and the sound of the wind blowing through my ears.

When I reached the front of the house, two guards appeared at the front steps, both standing by a white SUV.

I snarled at them. They instantly opened fire with twin Heckler & Koch submachine guns. Bullets streaked past me as I leaped into the shadows behind the corner of the house.

The men spoke to each other in Spanish, asking each other, "Did you get him?"

"I don't know," one responded.

They had not.

I knew they'd come looking, so I jumped up onto the wraparound porch, between the portico columns, and hid until the two clowns came into view. My assumption that they wouldn't think I could make the fifteen-foot vertical jump up to the landing proved correct.

The two gunmen moved together, one sweeping the area to the

left with his weapon braced against his shoulder. The other checked the edge of the house, probably thinking I might be hiding in the bushes.

I grinned hungrily, watching them from above. It was almost comical.

When they'd passed my position, I ordered the mist to freeze them in place.

The men stopped abruptly.

"What's happening?" the one on the left asked, suddenly terrified.

"I don't know. I can't move."

Panic filled their voices. And rightly so.

I dropped down from my perch and landed with a thud right behind them. I felt them strain against the invisible bonds that gripped them.

"What was that?" the one on the right asked.

I smelled the fear on them. It was a pungent odor, like a combination of sweat and mildew.

"It's the Chupacabra," one of them stammered.

"Sí," I said, stopping just behind the two men. "I am."

I grabbed them by their belts and jumped high into the air. It took every ounce of strength I could summon, but we soared nearly twenty feet up before gravity started pulling us back to earth.

At the apex of the climb, I grabbed the screaming men by the back of their necks, and forced their heads down as we descended.

Their cries muted the second their heads struck the concrete path. I felt their necks break at the same time—dull pops from their spines that reverberated through my fingers.

I stood up and looked down at the two to make sure they were dead. Neither moved. They simply stared lifelessly at each other; their heads twisted at an awkward angle.

The sound of the car was gone now.

I cursed myself for letting these two idiots distract me, but I had to deal with them. If I'd left them, they could have hurt my friends.

I wondered if there were any others inside the house, and if I should stay and make sure or go after Wells.

The choice was clear. My friends were armed now. I'd seen them scoop up some of the weapons from the dead men in Wells' study. I knew Mike could certainly handle himself, even if he was a little banged up. And Jesse struck me as the kind of gal who didn't take crap from anyone.

They'd be fine.

My mind made up, I sprinted to the remaining white SUV and flung open the door. Thankfully, the keys were inside.

"Better than chasing him on foot," I said.

I got in, slammed the door, and pressed the ignition button.

Three seconds later I fishtailed the big vehicle around the circular drive, corrected, and aimed down the hill toward the guardhouse and gate.

From the high vantage point, I could see the road stretching out in both directions. To the right, the lights of Franklin glowed into the atmosphere, but the road that direction was empty.

To the left, however, two headlamps raced away from the mansion, speeding down the main road toward the countryside.

"Got you."

I hammered the gas pedal and roared through the open gate, then feathered the brakes before I spun the steering wheel and guided the vehicle out onto the road.

I could no longer see the other SUV ahead, but I knew which way he was going. The only question was, what was his plan?

The answer hit me.

A small airport was only fifteen minutes away. At this speed, maybe ten.

I kept my foot to the floor, using the SUV's V-8 to its limits—within reason. The thing handled like a log wagon, but it had power for days.

Opulent mansions blurred by on either side of the road until they were replaced by farms and rolling hills of empty land.

As fast as I was going, I couldn't believe I hadn't caught up to Wells yet, but he had a good half-mile head start on me. Maybe more.

I preferred to think of it in kilometers. That didn't make it sound so bad.

But I also didn't know the exact calculation.

So stupid.

I was chasing a drug-dealing, human-trafficking phony pastor who just tried to kill me and my friends, and I was having an internal debate about standard forms of measurement.

I blamed the Xolotl voice in my head.

It's not me, I heard.

I shook it off and kept going, wishing I could squeeze a few more horses out of this thing.

But if I went much faster, I'd lose control on the twisty, turning roads.

I peered into the night, desperately hoping Wells hadn't turned off on some backwoods county road. There were several of those out here, and I'd already passed two within a few minutes of leaving the mansion.

I knew there were more ahead. Any one of those could have been the perfect detour for Wells. But those roads didn't lead to the airport.

The man would be desperate now. He'd lost his little army, and now with my friends free he would lose everything.

Sure, he could fight the scandal in court, but things like this never went away. He'd never be able to show his face anywhere again.

In the court of public opinion, people of high stature like Wells were always guilty until proven innocent.

"There you are," I said. As I reached the peak of a small hill, I saw two taillights dipping and weaving along the road.

That confirmed it. He was heading to the private airport.

I gripped the wheel, finally assured that I was catching up, albeit slowly.

At this pace, Wells would reach the airport before me. There was no way he had time to call a pilot, which meant Wells either knew how to fly a plane or he thought he did.

Two more minutes passed, and I'd barely made a dent in the gap between the vehicles. It was just as well. He didn't know I was behind him. Not yet, at least, although it was possible he'd seen my head lights in his rearview mirror.

Now that I knew for certain what Wells' plan was, I let off the gas —realizing that if he spotted me, he might shut off his lights and make a detour. Then I'd lose him.

Another blue metal sign whizzed by on the side of the road. It displayed a white airplane on it with a white arrow pointing to the right just underneath the aircraft.

Unlike major airports, this one didn't have thousands of bright lights illuminating the night. Instead, there were a few windsocks, a dozen hangars, and a modest control tower.

I wondered if anyone would even be there right now.

Doubtful.

Not that it mattered to Wells. Whatever regulations and rules there might have been for flying out of that airport at this time of night was about to be thrown out the window.

I saw the other SUV's lights reflecting off the trees that lined the other side of the road across from the airport.

Wells wasn't far ahead of me now.

And I had him right where I wanted.

35

I whipped the SUV around the turn to the right and corrected it as the heavy vehicle struggled to keep its balance against momentum.

The thousand feet to the entrance of the airport went by in a flash.

I tapped on the brakes and steered the SUV into the entrance where a chain-link fence protected the boundary around the airport.

A gate had stood here before, but now only a mangled, bent remnant of its former self lay trampled on the pavement in front of the control tower.

"He just ran right through the gate," I said, also realizing that if the gate was closed, then no one would be occupying the tower.

I ran over the destroyed gate and steered around to the right, following the asphalt toward the airstrip.

I turned the corner and spotted Wells' SUV as I reached a T in the path. He'd parked just to the side of an open hangar. A white twin turboprop plane sat inside.

My foot stomped on the gas. The engine growled as I shot through the little intersection and out onto the tarmac.

Wells had gotten out of his vehicle and was scurrying toward the plane and the steps leading up to the fuselage.

He looked at me as I sped directly at him.

The headlights gleamed in his eyes. He still had the sword with him in his left hand, and a pistol in his right.

He raised the firearm and started shooting. Bullets peppered the windshield. One struck the mirror on the right side. Another round punctured the passenger side seat cushion.

"That's a crime right there, Wells," I said. "Ruining good leather like that."

I tightened my grip as the onslaught of bullets continued with decreasing accuracy until Wells' magazine ran dry.

I closed the gap between us, aiming the SUV straight for him.

Fear washed over his face. I could see it plainly, even from a hundred feet away.

He stood there, petrified, unable to tear himself from his spot until, at the last second, he dove out of the way just before I was about to hit him.

That was of no consequence. Part of my plan was to trash his plane.

I opened the door and leaped out, letting the SUV continue on its course.

My left shoulder hit the tarmac with a crunch, and I rolled to a stop twenty feet from where I'd originally landed.

The SUV plowed into the aircraft with a deafening crunch. I scrambled to my feet and jumped clear of the entrance just as something ignited the jet fuel.

The blast was the loudest thing I'd ever heard in my life. I felt the air sucked out of my chest in an unexpected and painful way. The hangar roof blew into the sky in huge fragments.

Flames shot out of the opening in the front, and I crouched down, covering my head instinctively. The ground shuddered.

And then all fell silent save for the roar of the blaze inside the hangar.

I heard a door slam shut and looked to Wells' SUV. The taillights flashed, signaling he'd shifted the truck into drive again.

"Oh no you don't," I said.

I charged at the vehicle as the back tires squealed, kicking out debris and a puff of white smoke.

Wells gave it everything he could, but it wasn't enough.

As he accelerated, so did I, until I was running at a speed I'd never imaged before. The wind blew hard in my ears and in my eyes.

Halfway across the tarmac, I got within fifteen feet of the vehicle and then leaped as hard as I could.

I flew through the air and landed on top of the roof with a thud.

Wells definitely heard me and reacted by jerking the wheel one way and then the other.

Keeping my balance was impossible, so I lowered myself down onto my belly and used the cargo rails on either side to keep me from sailing off.

With every turn, my legs whipped from one rail to the other, and even with my supernatural strength I found it difficult to keep myself static. My muscles strained against every countermove he made, almost as if I were wrestling the machine like a bear.

Wells turned the vehicle hard to the right, aiming it down the runway. I slid to the side, then corrected as he accelerated.

What does he think he's—

The question never fully formed in my head because the answer came too soon.

The driver slammed on the brakes. I felt the truck tip forward first. Then my legs flipped over my head.

Only an instantaneous reaction saved me as inertia pulled me forward. I switched my grip on the rails and grabbed them by the backside of the front housing and anchored myself to them.

I smacked against the windshield. My feet slammed into the hood with a loud thud that probably left a couple of dents in the metal.

I looked through the glass into Wells' terrified eyes. They were illuminated by the red mist churning inside the vehicle.

I reared back my right hand, made a fist, and punched through the windshield. My fingers wrapped around Wells' throat, but he spun the steering wheel and accelerated.

The maneuver caught me off guard, and I felt the solid surface of the vehicle leave me in exchange for that frightening feeling of nothing but air all around you.

I hit the tarmac and rolled to a stop, breathing hard from the exertion.

As I panted for air, I watched Wells drive down the tarmac. The brake lights brightened, and he turned around, aiming the grill straight at me.

I knew what was coming next.

The SUV lurched forward to the screech of the rear tires. Wells stared me down like a steak at a vegan potluck. Even from a hundred yards away I could see his eyes, wide with madness and "righteous" anger.

I watched, waiting to dive out of the way, until I saw him stick the sword out the window.

"You have to be kidding me," I muttered.

"Okay, Vernon. Have it your way."

The vehicle bore down on me at top speed. But I held my ground.

He veered slightly to my left, the scimitar still sticking out the window.

I'd have to time this just right.

He closed in on me. Fifty yards. Thirty. Twenty.

At the last second, I rolled onto the surface toward the center of the vehicle, and as it passed over me, I did one hard push-up.

The SUV's undercarriage cut into my back, ripping through my monster flesh, but the plan worked.

I howled in pain as I looked over my shoulder.

The SUV flipped end over end and tumbled to a stop on its roof a hundred feet away.

Fluid poured out of the vehicle's engine block. Smoke and steam gushed from the hood.

I exhaled slowly, focusing on healing instead of the intense pain from my back. Seconds later, I felt the wounds healing themselves, and the agony numbed.

Staring at the wrecked SUV, I stalked toward it, deliberately—like a horror movie bad guy who always catches their quarry no matter how fast the prey might run.

The driver's door flung open as I neared. Wells fell out. The sword clanked onto the ground. He stayed on all fours for a second, then saw me approaching.

He clawed at the tarmac, reaching for the blade. A cut on the side of his head oozed blood down his cheek.

Wells gripped the sword and stood up, wobbling like a newborn foal. The weapon looked heavy in his hands, but he held it up at his side, as if ready to strike.

"Right now is probably when you're thinking about saying something clever, Vernon," I mused. "Or maybe you're trying to figure out how this all came unraveled when you were soooo prepared."

I took a step toward him, and he retreated one.

"Gideon. Let's think this through. Okay? There's no reason either one of us has to die. We can work together."

I snorted my derision, baring my fangs.

"You have no idea how much money my operation pulls in. I'll split it with you. Fifty-fifty. Yeah? How does that sound?"

"Sounds like you're desperate."

He shook his head. "Don't be a fool, Gideon. My empire pulls in more than you ever imagined. Think of what you could do with all those millions. And you don't have to lift a finger. Or claw."

I took another step closer and inclined my chin, peering at him over my nose. "If I didn't know better, Vernon, I'd say you were wanting to partner up."

He nodded. "Yes. Yes. A partnership. Think of it. You help me find the Artemis medallion in Ephesus, and I split everything with you. We'll be unstoppable."

"You're serious, aren't you?" I asked.

"Yes. Yes, I'm serious."

"You think that I would come to work for you, the guy who

ordered my wife to be murdered? The guy who runs a human-trafficking and heroin ring?"

He replied with a shrug. It was a gesture that said, "What's a guy to do, huh?"

"No, I don't think so, Reverend," I declined. "I'm not like you, consumed by power and greed. I'm a guardian." I looked down at the ground for a second, then said, "Oh, by the way. The medallion isn't in Ephesus. It's on the island of Delos, at an ancient temple to the goddess Artemis."

Red mist spun around his feet and ankles. But I wasn't going to use it on him like I had with his men. This one was personal.

His head turned dramatically from side to side. "Don't be a fool, Gideon. Join me. And we will—"

I decided maybe I should use the mist after all and willed it to wrap around his throat. It squeezed like a boa constrictor, tightening until his voice shut off.

He grasped at his neck with his left hand, still holding the scimitar with the right.

"Sss... stop." He managed through his teeth. "It doesn't have to be this way."

"Yes, it does," I said. Then I loosened my grip so he could take a breath. "Who are those guys from the Sector?" I asked. "What are they doing with you?"

Hope flashed in Wells' eyes. He saw the chance for an escape from death, and he ran with it.

"The Sector? If I tell you, will you let me live?"

I cocked my head to the side. "Maybe. Letting you rot in a prison cell for the rest of your life might be just as good as killing you."

He nodded eagerly. "Yes. Yes, that will do. What do you want to know?"

"Who are they? Why are they always hanging around you? What is it their agency does, exactly?"

Wells puzzled at the question. "What? Are you serious? You don't know who they are?"

My eyelids tightened to slits. "No. Should I?"

He started laughing. It was a disturbing, borderline demonic sound. "You really don't know who they are?" Wells looked around the empty airstrip.

Sirens whined in the distance. Apparently, someone had noticed either the explosion at the airfield, the break-in, or both.

"Running out of time, Reverend."

He looked me in the eyes, his laughter ceasing. "They control everything. They make anyone who allies with them. And break anyone who refuses."

"You sure are saying a lot without telling me what I want to know." I took another step and stopped right in front of him, only a few feet away. "Who are they?"

Wells grinned devilishly. "You know exactly who they—"

I heard a loud click. The left side of Wells' head burst open, and he fell to the ground, wide eyes staring vacantly down the runway.

I turned toward where the shot had come from, but I didn't see anyone. The trees in the forest beyond the fence offered no answers.

The sirens swelled, and I knew I didn't have time to hang out here at the airfield, much less hunt for the mysterious sniper.

The red fog settled around Wells' body. Soon, the corpse would be gone, and the first responders would be left to wonder what happened.

I sighed.

The real monster was dead, but I had more questions than answers.

Before I went to Greece in search of the Artemis medallion, I'd need to return to the place where all this began.

36

I sat on Mike's front porch with a cup of coffee in my hand, staring out at the rolling hills leading toward the city. The sun blazed brightly in the cloudless morning sky to the east.

A tablet on the little wooden table next to me displayed a headline about megachurch pastor Vernon Wells' mysterious disappearance after one of his SUVs was found wrecked at a regional airport the night before.

There'd been no evidence other than the wreckage, and investigators from multiple agencies were embroiled in the search for the missing preacher.

I knew, of course, they'd never find him. His body disappeared within minutes of my leaving the airfield.

I'd run on foot, using my superhuman speed to get far enough away from the airport that no one would suspect I had anything to do with the wreck.

On top of that, the NTSB was on the scene investigating the destroyed airplane in the hangar.

I knew it would be the single most fruitless endeavor those agents had ever endured. They'd soon learn that the other SUV, the one that had struck the plane, was also registered to Wells. But without any bodies at the crime scene, they wouldn't know what to call it.

Arson?

I didn't know, and didn't care. I wasn't a lawyer or with the feds. Let them figure out how to sweep it under the rug. That's what they did when they didn't have answers.

And sometimes when they did have them.

"What are you thinking about?" Jack asked, taking a sip of his coffee.

"Yeah," Jesse added. "You seem pensive."

I let out a chuckle. "Just trying to figure out the next move. I need to go to Greece. I think one of the medallions is there on the island of Delos."

"Based on what?" Jack pressed.

"I looked over some documents in Wells' office. He had a lot of good stuff in there, actually. Shame I couldn't collect some of it."

Jesse and Jack shared a mischievous glance.

"What?" I asked. "What was that look?"

Jack shrugged and said, "We might have recovered some of it."

"Nice." I nodded in approval.

"And that sword you found," Mike jumped in, "will be safe here until you can find a better place to keep it."

"Thanks, Mike. I appreciate that. I don't mean to be a pain."

"Not at all, brother," he said, then raised his coffee mug toward me.

"So, you're going to Greece next?" Jack asked.

I sighed. "No. Not yet. I need to go back to Mexico. There are still questions that need answers, and I don't think I'll find them here."

"Why Mexico?" Jesse wondered.

I rubbed my right leg and listened to the birds chirping in nearby trees. A gentle breeze rolled across the field beyond a barb wire fence.

"There's someone there I need to see. And someone there I want to see."

Jack snickered. "Sounds like you're going to see a girl. Little soon for that, isn't it?"

He wasn't wrong. My wife had been dead for a week. But I couldn't deny the fact that my thoughts had constantly returned to Vero since the moment I met her. Even with every crazy thing going on in my world.

"She's just a friend," I said. "She helped me figure some things out when I was down there before. And I need to see someone else, too."

"Someone else?" Mike chimed in.

"Yes. She's a... like a guide, I guess." It was the only way I could describe Myra. The truth was I wondered if she was some kind of oracle, like the ones from ancient cultures.

"A guide?"

"I don't know how else to put it, but yeah. Something like that. She helped me while I was there. I need to make sure those two are okay. When I left, the Carrillo cartel was in shambles, but that only means someone else is going to step in and take their place."

"Kind of like you cut off the head of the snake, and two new heads appear," Jack offered.

"Exactly."

Silence descended onto the farm, and for a few minutes, all we did was sit and drink our coffee.

I watched the steam rise from my mug, glad to see that kind of fog instead of the crimson that enshrouded the wicked.

Finally, Jack broke the quiet. "I really thought you were going to let me die back there," he said, his eyes locked on some nonspecific landmark in the distance.

"Yeah?" I snorted. "Seriously?"

"For a second. Yeah. I mean, I didn't know what that medallion had done to you. I thought maybe it was messing with your head. Then when you said you saw the mist around me—"

"I had to play it up, buy time. Then it hit me how to take them down." I took another drink.

"How did you do that?" Jesse asked. Fear littered her curiosity.

I took a long breath and sighed. "Um... I don't know. I guess I just sort of feel it, and command it with my mind."

"When did you know you could do that sort of thing?"

"I didn't. I mean, I had a dream or a vision. I honestly don't know which. But there was a guy, one of Carrillo's men. He was the one that got away the night I took down Carrillo and his army."

"A dream?" Jack huffed.

"Yeah. I don't know. It was weird. It was like I was really there in the interrogation room. Two guys in suits were talking to him. Asking him questions about what happened in Mexico. None of the media outlets were talking about it."

"Shocker," Mike blurted.

He was right about that. More and more, media outlets that were supposed to cover the news merely offered spin or cover-ups for one side or the other.

"Anyway, they looked like feds, the two guys talking to him. Then I saw the mist in the room surrounding Carrillo's guy."

"What about the feds?" Jesse wondered. "Did the fog surround them, too?"

That was a good question. I struggled to recall if it had, but couldn't see it clearly. "I don't know. Maybe. I was focused on the prisoner. Something about that scene connected me to the mist in a way I hadn't experienced before. I still don't know if it's real or if it was part of my subconscious imagination, but I killed him before he was able to tell the spooks who I was." I swallowed another sip. "Not that it matters. I think they found me anyway."

"The feds?" Mike seemed hung up on them, but he was always suspicious of government agencies. He was the conspiracy theorist of the bunch.

"Yeah." I left out the part that the same guys I'd seen in my dream had approached me in Nashville.

They were from the Sector. And just as Wells was about to give up the goods on that little operation, someone had shot him.

I found it odd they hadn't fired at me. Maybe they were wise to the fact that had they done that, I would have hunted them down.

It didn't matter now. I'd have to figure out the sniper's identity some other time. My immediate priority was locating the Artemis medallion and the guardian who was meant to wear it.

That was the primary reason for returning to Mexico. I needed to meet with Myra and find out everything she knew. And if I were lucky, the shaman would make an appearance.

The guy still creeped me out. And I couldn't figure how he was able to appear and then vanish right in front of me. I wondered if I'd accidentally gotten into some peyote, but that wasn't the strangest thing that happened in the last week.

I'd come to accept that bizarre now had a permanent place in my life.

"I'm coming with you," Jack said.

It reminded me of the night before when he'd used those exact words just before I ran after Wells.

"What?" I laughed.

"To Greece. I'm coming with you. My store won't be open for weeks. So, when you get back from Mexico, I want to go with you."

I shook my head at the offer. "You know I love you, man. But I can't let you do that. I thought I'd lost you guys. I had no way of knowing I'd be able to get out of that situation. I don't ever want to put you in harm's way again."

None of the other three said anything, but I could see they understood.

"Besides," I added, "I have another job for you, my novel friend."

"I see what you did there." He lowered his eyebrows at me.

"Sorry. Couldn't resist. But yes, I need you to do something for me."

"Anything," Jack said, waving a hand like, "Name it."

"I need you to keep an eye out for more books about these relics, the guardians, all of it. Anything you find, buy it, and I'll pay you back later."

"You don't have to pay me back."

"Fine. Whatever. Just collect all you can. The more you can find, the better. If we're going to locate these other medallions, then we're going to need as much information as possible."

"You got it." He gave a determined nod.

I eased back into the chair and held the mug close to my face so I could take in the aroma.

No one said a word for a long time as we looked out over the farm and the rolling hills beyond.

That was another way I knew these three were true friends. They didn't bother me with questions about the beast within, the medallion, the power. They just let me drink my coffee in peace.

At that moment, experiencing something normal made me feel something more powerful than that amulet ever had.

I felt grateful—for good friends, good coffee, fresh Tennessee air, and the responsibility I'd been given to fight back against evil.

37

A man in a white lab coat walked across the tarmac at a small airfield. I recognized the airport immediately.

He showed the police and federal investigators an identification card and was allowed to pass through the line keeping everyone else away from the site.

Official vehicles cluttered the runway like wagons circling against some exterior threat.

The man in the lab coat seemed unconcerned by any of it. His eyes fixed on the wrecked SUV—Wells' getaway car.

Except he hadn't gotten away. He'd died there on the tarmac, and now his body was gone—consumed by the mist, never to be found. Just like all the others.

The man in the lab coat wasn't distracted by all the people standing around, trying to figure out what exactly happened here. He paid no mind to all the vehicles littering the runway. His focus remained on an area close to the SUV sitting on its roof.

He stalked across the tarmac and stopped next to the vehicle. The man focused on something on the ground, but I couldn't tell what it was.

Then he retrieved a vial from his lab coat pocket and bent down to one knee. He crouched lower, putting his face to the ground as if inspecting something extremely small on the surface.

A warm breeze tossed his shaggy brown hair around, but he didn't seem to notice. His eyes were locked on something. I couldn't tell what.

He reached into his other jacket pocket and pulled out a little tool that looked like a hybrid between a flathead screwdriver and something a surgeon would use.

I watched the man scrape something into the vial, put a lid on the glass tube, and then drop it into his left pocket.

He stood up and walked unceremoniously back across the runway to his vehicle parked by the control tower.

When he stopped at his black sedan, he climbed in and pulled out a cell phone.

He dialed a number and put the device to his ear.

I wondered who the man was and how I was able to see him, but it reminded me of the incident with the cartel thug I'd seen in the interrogation room during that dream or vision.

This was similar, except I felt no power to control the mist as it glowed and pulsed around this man.

"Sir?" he said when someone answered the call. "I have it."

He listened for a few seconds, then added, "If it's his, we'll know soon enough. Then it will be up to your operators to bring him in."

The scene faded away, and I woke up in one of Mike's guest beds.

Through the bedroom window, the light of morning swelled on the horizon to the east. I heard a rooster announcing the coming daylight.

I shook off the strange vision and swung my feet over the bed, planting them on the floor.

Whatever I'd just seen, I had a bad feeling it was more than just a dream.

THANK YOU

I just wanted to say thank you for reading this story. You chose to spend your time and money on something I created, and that means more to me than you may know. But I appreciate it, and am truly honored.

Be sure to swing by ernestdempsey.net to grab free stories, and dive deeper into the universe I've created for you.

I hope you enjoyed the story, and will stick with this series as it continues through the years. Know that I'll be working hard to keep bringing you exciting new stories to help you escape from the real world.

Your friendly neighborhood author,

Ernest

OTHER BOOKS BY ERNEST DEMPSEY

Sean Wyatt Adventures:
The Secret of the Stones
The Cleric's Vault
The Last Chamber
The Grecian Manifesto
The Norse Directive
Game of Shadows
The Jerusalem Creed
The Samurai Cipher
The Cairo Vendetta
The Uluru Code
The Excalibur Key
The Denali Deception
The Sahara Legacy
The Fourth Prophecy
The Templar Curse
The Forbidden Temple
The Omega Project
The Napoleon Affair
The Second Sign

The Milestone Protocol
Where Horizons End
Adriana Villa Adventures:
War of Thieves Box Set
When Shadows Call
Shadows Rising
Shadow Hour
The Relic Runner - A Dak Harper Series:
The Relic Runner Origin Story
The Courier
Two Nights In Mumbai
Country Roads
Heavy Lies the Crown
Moscow Sky
The Adventure Guild (ALL AGES):
The Caesar Secret: Books 1-3
The Carolina Caper
Beta Force:
Operation Zulu
London Calling
Paranormal Archaeology Division:
Hell's Gate
Guardians of Earth:
Emergence: Gideon Wolf Book 1
Righteous Dawn: Gideon Wolf Book 2
Crimson Winter: Gideon Wolf Book 3

ACKNOWLEDGMENTS

As always, I would like to thank my terrific editors, Anne and Jason, for their hard work. What they do makes my stories so much better for readers all over the world. Anne Storer and Jason Whited are the best editorial team a writer could hope for and I appreciate everything they do.

I also want to thank Elena at Lı Graphics for her tremendous work on my book covers and for always overdelivering. Elena definitely rocks.

A big thank you has to go out to my friend James Slater for his proofing work. James has added another layer of quality control to these stories, and I can't thank him enough.

Last but not least, I need to thank all my wonderful fans and especially the advance reader team. Their feedback and reviews are always so helpful and I can't say enough good things about all of them.

Made in the USA
Monee, IL
19 May 2022

96698130R00173